Damon Quinn b...

At least legally.

It seemed impossible. This man, who made every nerve in her body tingle whenever he was in a one-mile radius, belonged to *her*—plain, practical Matty Stewart.

Her new "husband" smiled at her. And Matty's heart beat a little faster. Her palms began to sweat.

And suddenly, Matty believed in miracles.

It was a miracle that she was Damon's wife. It was a miracle that baby Heidi, cooing and gurgling on the sidelines, was now her very own daughter. Her wedding day was a miracle. Her entire life was turning into a miracle!

And Matty knew that, no matter what happened next, she would believe in miracles until the day she died....

Dear Reader,

As the long summer stretches before us, July sizzles with an enticing Special Edition lineup!

We begin with this month's THAT SPECIAL WOMAN! title brought to you by the wonderful Jennifer Greene. She concludes her STANFORD SISTERS series with *The 200% Wife*—an engaging story about one woman's quest to be the very best at everything, most especially love.

If you delight in marriage-of-convenience stories that evolve into unexpected love, be sure to check out *Mail-Order Matty* by Emilie Richards, book one in our FROM BUD TO BLOSSOM theme series. Written by four popular authors, this brand-new series contains magical love stories that bring change to the characters' lives when they least expect it.

Pull out your handkerchiefs, because we have a three-hankie Special Edition novel that will touch you unlike any of the stories you've experienced before. *Nothing Short of a Miracle* by Patricia Thayer is a poignant story about a resilient woman, a devoted father and a cherished son who yearn for a miracle— and learn to trust in the wondrous power of love.

If absorbing amnesia stories are your forte, be sure to check out *Forgotten Fiancée* by Lucy Gordon. Or perhaps you can't pass up an engrossing family drama with a seductive twist. Then don't miss out on *The Ready-Made Family* by Laurie Paige. Finally, we wrap up a month of irresistible romance when one love-smitten heroine impulsively poses as her twin sister and marries the man of her dreams in *Substitute Bride* by Trisha Alexander.

An entire summer of romance is just beginning to unfold at Special Edition! I hope you enjoy each and every story to come!

Sincerely,

Tara Gavin,
Senior Editor

Please address questions and book requests to:
Silhouette Reader Service
U.S.: 3010 Walden Ave., P.O. Box 1325, Buffalo, NY 14269
Canadian: P.O. Box 609, Fort Erie, Ont. L2A 5X3

EMILIE RICHARDS
MAIL-ORDER MATTY

Published by Silhouette Books
America's Publisher of Contemporary Romance

With thanks to Virginia Taylor,
who never thought twice about loaning
her computer to a total stranger.

 SILHOUETTE BOOKS

ISBN 0-373-24113-5

MAIL-ORDER MATTY

Copyright © 1997 by Emilie Richards McGee

All rights reserved. Except for use in any review, the reproduction or utilization of this work in whole or in part in any form by any electronic, mechanical or other means, now known or hereafter invented, including xerography, photocopying and recording, or in any information storage or retrieval system, is forbidden without the written permission of the editorial office, Silhouette Books, 300 East 42nd Street, New York, NY 10017 U.S.A.

All characters in this book have no existence outside the imagination of the author and have no relation whatsoever to anyone bearing the same name or names. They are not even distantly inspired by any individual known or unknown to the author, and all incidents are pure invention.

This edition published by arrangement with Harlequin Books S.A.

® and TM are trademarks of Harlequin Books S.A., used under license. Trademarks indicated with ® are registered in the United States Patent and Trademark Office, the Canadian Trade Marks Office and in other countries.

Printed in U.S.A.

Books by Emilie Richards

EMILIE RICHARDS

Award-winning author Emilie Richards believes that opposites attract, and her marriage is vivid proof. "When we met," the author says, "the only thing my husband and I could agree on was that we were very much in love. Fortunately, we haven't changed our minds about that in all the years we've been together." The couple has lived in eight states—as well as a brief, beloved sojourn in Australia—and now resides in Ohio.

Emilie loves writing about characters who make positive changes in their lives. And she's a sucker for happy endings.

Dear Reader,

Can love change the world? Well, I think it's possible. Can love change individuals? I'm absolutely convinced it can.

When love ignites, it's like a tiny fire smoldering inside us. As we're warmed by it, we're slowly strengthened. Of course, that doesn't mean everything is suddenly easy or we're suddenly without flaws, but it does mean that we can take chances, reach further, try harder. Because someone will be there if we fail, or even if we succeed. Someone who believes in us and knows who we really are deep inside.

I've written about the power of love many times. I believe in love and even in the real-life possibility of happy endings. My characters may not be people I've really spoken with, but at their core is my own conviction that love can transform lives. If love is a smoldering fire, its radiant heat and energy can heal wounds, open hearts, expand minds and spread through everyone it touches to the people they touch and the people they touch....

So in the long run, maybe love *can* change the world. Even if it starts with just two people.

Emilie Richards

Prologue

Matty Stewart was well educated, mature and unfailingly responsible. She was also a wide-eyed adolescent when it came to resisting the siren call of champagne, particularly when her best friends were in charge of the bottle.

"Come on, Matty. A swallow for every year of your life." Liza Fitzsimmons crooked a finger sporting a fire-engine-red nail that was longer than the brown hair that spiked her elegant head. "I've been counting. That was sixteen. Only sixteen."

"Sweet sixteen and never been..." Felicity Brown wrinkled her forehead in concentration. "Never been..."

"Never mind what I've never been." Matty giggled, and the sound alarmed her. Matty was not a giggler. Not a giggler, not a whiner, not a woman of extremes. She was just Matty, plain, intelligent, dependable Matty, who had turned twenty-seven that morning and been turned down for promotion that afternoon.

"Here goes..." Liza filled Matty's glass again. "Seventeen and counting."

Matty had never developed a tolerance for alcohol. In high school her small circle of friends had been "good girls," relentlessly dedicated to keeping their heads in the unlikely case any "good boys" lost theirs. By the time she was in college, she was too busy caring for her invalid father to frequent fraternity parties or to sit for hours over pizza and pitchers of beer. And afterward, his comfort and happiness during the final years of his life were far more important than sowing her wild oats. But tonight there was no longer any reason to be good.

Which was why she was fast getting tipsy.

"Drink up now," Liza insisted. "You're not nearly done."

The sensible part of Matty was off duty today or sleeping soundly. The champagne was cheap but effective. It had nearly silenced the memory of her supervisor's voice regretfully explaining that once again a choice administrative position at Carrollton Community Hospital had gone to someone with less seniority but more guts. "Everyone likes you, Matty," she had said, without quite meeting Matty's eyes, "and that's the problem. You get along too well. You compromise when you should confront. You give too much of yourself and don't ask enough in return."

Now Matty wrapped her fingers around the glass, sturdy, capable fingers with blunt trimmed nails and skin scrubbed so clean she sometimes wondered if her fingerprints would survive into middle age. She lifted the glass to swallow the contents, then thrust it out again. "More..."

"Thata girl..."

"You ever been sloshed, Matts?" Felicity, who worked in the hospital's public relations department, was two years younger than Matty and Liza, with a yard of golden blond hair and eyes as blue as an Oklahoma sky. Coming to Minnesota as a teenager had softened the edges of her Tulsa accent, but the champagne was honing them again.

"To firsts..." Matty shook her head and thrust out her glass at the same time. The simultaneous movements almost undid her.

"I like the sound of that. Firsts," Liza said.

"Your firsts are definitely over," Felicity told her. "S'nuthin' you haven't done."

Liza patted Matty's knee. "But Matty's a different story, aren't you, baby?"

"What first shall I try next?" Matty managed a smile by making sure she wasn't doing anything else at the same moment. Smiling seemed easier now than it had that afternoon. She could almost pretend away her failures and loneliness. She was with her best friends, in the living room of the brick house she had lived in since her birth, and the champagne seemed to be opening up a world of possibilities.

"Travel? Distant exotic places?" Felicity laid an index finger against her soft pink lips.

"Flashy clothes and fast cars?" Liza closed one eye as if to see her friend better. "Dye your hair?"

"Sex?" Felicity said.

Matty sputtered and set her glass on the coffee table. "With whom?"

Liza wiggled her eyebrows. "Funny you should ask."

"The question seems rev...rev...relevant." Matty made a stab at dignity.

Liza drew a scrap of paper from her pocket and reclined regally against a stack of cushions they had removed earlier from the sofa and armchairs. The tiny living room was beginning to resemble the site of an orgy instead of the neat, uncluttered quarters of three of Carrollton Community's most reliable staff members. White cartons of partially eaten Chinese takeout dotted the floor amidst birthday cake crumbs, discarded champagne bottles and wadded napkins. Soft rock rumbled softly from an outdated stereo system, and candles melted into wax pools on unmatched china saucers.

"I shall acquaint you with his attributes." Liza waved the sheet of paper.

"Singles ads." Felicity wrinkled her snub nose.

"Not quite..." Liza snapped her *t*'s with military precision. *"Carrollton Alumni News."*

Matty could feel her eyelids drooping. Sober and wide-eyed, she was nobody's ideal vision of American womanhood. She had a long, almost rectangular face ungraced by one outstanding feature. Had the beauty mavens of the world united to establish an average by which to judge young women, Matty would have set their standard. Nothing about her was too large or too small, too long or too short, too wide or too thin. Her hair was dark blond—dishwater blond, to be exact—her skin neither rosy nor sallow, her eyes neither clearly green nor brown. Her body was much the same, small-breasted and wider at the hips, with legs Lloyds of London would never have to insure and feet one size too large to look sexy in flirty little sandals.

"*Alumni News?*" Matty tried to discern a connection between eligible, beddable men and the newsletter of the college she and Liza had attended together.

"It came today. There's an interview with Damon Quinn."

Matty's eyes were wide-open now, and the sudden explosion of pink in her cheeks wasn't alcohol-induced. "Damon Quinn?"

"I believe you have eight good swallows to go." Liza gave a vague wave toward the last of the champagne.

Matty held up her glass and let Felicity fill it again. Neither of them was as steady as she should have been, but luckily they wavered in the same rhythm.

When Liza seemed satisfied with Matty's progress, she began to read. "'Where Have All the Alumni Gone?'"

Felicity groaned.

Liza looked up. "Your alumni newsletter is better, I suppose?"

When Felicity answered by sticking out her tongue, Liza looked down and began to read. "'The old newsletter caught up with Damon Quinn this week.'" She paused, obviously skimming before she continued. "'Quinn, Carrollton's science wunderkind, is still planning to cure cancer in between his other projects. And he has projects aplenty, including a brand-new daughter he is trying to raise by himself on a remote

Caribbean island. When asked what he yearned for more than anything else, Quinn replied, "A wife." It seems our wunderkind is up to his ears in dirty diapers and the cure for cancer is coming in a distant second. Any Carrollton ladies with fond memories of Damon, a penchant for Goombay smashes, and a deft hand with baby powder just might want to apply for the job. Send Damon a note care of the post office at George Town, the Bahamas. Who knows what might happen?"

Liza looked up. "You can't go wrong, Matty. Caribbean cocktails, Damon Quinn and tropical sunsets, with a baby thrown in for good measure. Beats staying around here and getting passed over for promotion again because you're so good at what you do that none of the pediatricians wants to lose you."

Matty worked in neonatal intensive care, and Liza and Felicity had been telling her all evening that the only reason she hadn't gotten the promotion was that the pediatricians who staffed the unit had demanded that Matty stay right where she was. With Matty on staff, they knew their smallest charges had at least a fighting chance for survival. Matty was renowned for her persistence, her compassion and her creative solutions to even the most difficult problems. But Matty wasn't thinking about that now or weighing the possibility that her friend might be right. She was thinking about Damon Quinn.

"You remember Damon, don't you?" Liza sat up again.

Matty considered a denial, but the champagne was behaving like truth serum. "Clearly."

"Who is this Damon person?" Felicity said.

"The dark prince of Carrollton College. The brightest of the bright, with a face for the Brontë sisters to write about and a body that..." Liza paused and shrugged, as if she'd run out of superlatives. "A grrr...eat body."

"Why does a guy like that have to advertise?"

"He's not," Matty said. "It sounds like something he tossed up—off—in conversation." The last word came out in four separated syllables, and she felt proud to have gotten them in the correct order.

"Damon Quinn wouldn't be anyone's vision of the perfect husband," Liza said. "He's so brilliant he probably can't concentrate on anything as mundane as earning a living or raising kids. Ask a guy like that to go to the store for a gallon of milk and he'll stop by the lab on the way home to reformulate its proteins."

"No. He's not...he wasn't that way." Matty shook her head and wished that she hadn't.

"What way was...is he?" Felicity asked.

"Kind. Access-ible."

"Did you really know him that well, Matty?" Liza turned the champagne bottle upside down, but not a drop remained. "He never gave me the time of day."

"I didn't really know him." But Matty had shared one experience with the great Damon Quinn that had convinced her of his integrity. And that day so many years before, she had fallen instantly in love with him, one hundred percent in love, as only a plain young woman with expansive romantic fantasies and a difficult reality could do. She had loved him desperately, completely, as well as from afar, until the day he had walked out of Carrollton and her life into a prestigious Ivy League fellowship.

Felicity's eyes were glazing over, and her words drifted into whispers. "Well, why is this guy off on some deserted island if he's so brilliant? I mean, why isn't he working for a big pharmaceutical company, or the government, or...something?"

"I don't know," Liza said. "'Sa mystery."

"Whatever the reason, it's a good one." Matty closed her eyes.

"Devoted," Liza said to Felicity. "She's obviously devoted to this guy."

"Write him." Felicity widened her eyes, as if to demand that they stay open. "You can be his wife, Matty."

Matty had been trying to picture Damon Quinn's face, and

for a moment she didn't notice the silence. Then her eyes flew open. "What?"

But Liza was already scrambling through the drawers of the old walnut secretary that stood in the nook by the entry hall. "You've got to do something. You're going to live your whole life in Carrollton if you don't. You're going to die in this house, Matty. You want adventure, don't you? A husband? A baby?"

Liza found a box of notecards and held them up victoriously. "Your ticket to a new life."

"I'm sure this Damon person will want you, Matty," Felicity said. "We'll just tell him the truth."

Liza plopped back into position on the floor. "I'll write it for you. He won't know. What'll I say?"

"'Dear Damon,' for starters," Felicity said, ignoring Matty's bursts of laughter.

"Got it. How about 'You don't remember me,'?" Liza looked to Matty for approval.

Matty managed a small nod. It would be true, of course. "Say I was two years behind him, but we were in Evolutionary Biology together. And Advanced Biochemistry."

"Matty was studying for medical school," Liza told Felicity, although the other woman already knew. "She graduated at the top of our class."

Felicity didn't ask what had happened to Matty's dreams. She and Liza had moved into Matty's house after Frank Stewart's death two years ago. Both women knew about Matty's sacrifices. "Be sure you tell him about Matty's work in neonatal. Tell him how good she is with babies. Nobody's better."

Liza scribbled frantically. "'I have always lived in Carrollton,'" she read as she wrote. "'I'm ready for new adventures and a warmer climate. I've always done the expected and the safe. Now I'm looking forward to taking risks.'"

Matty wondered if that part, at least, was true. The letter to Damon was just a joke, but even her alcohol-fogged brain cells could realize that at their root the things that Liza was writing were no laughing matter. She *could* spend her entire life in

Carrollton, living in this house, working at the hospital taking loving care of newborns someone else would have the joys of raising. She had respect and friendship here, an adequate income. But unless she took some drastic steps, she would never have anything else.

"Say, 'I'm slender and attractive, with a terrific smile.'" Felicity tapped her lips again. "And say, 'I'm bright enough to understand at least half of what you talk about.'"

"More than half." Liza scribbled some more. "Anything else?"

Matty spoke up. "Tell him I've never forgotten the way he came to my rescue one day, and now I'd like to return the favor."

Liza frowned. "What?"

"Just tell him."

"It's your proposal, not mine." Liza finished with a flourish. She reread the letter silently, then slipped it into its envelope, which she addressed with a bold scrawl. "Stamps?"

Matty was suddenly all too aware of how much champagne she had drunk. She watched Liza rise to rummage through the drawers again. "Liza, don't waste stamps. We've gone far enough."

"Of course we haven't." Liza gave a lopsided grin. "Damon Quinn's not nearly good enough for you. Nobody is. But he's a start."

"We're not mailing that letter...."

"Watch me." Liza glued a row of stamps in the proximity of the right-hand corner of the envelope, then wove her way to the mail slot in the entry hall and stuck it halfway through. "There!"

Matty began to giggle again, and by the time Liza had rejoined them on the floor, all three women were laughing so hard they were gasping. They fell asleep that way, heads pillowed on cushions, bodies covered by worn afghans they'd thrown over each other, cuddled together like teenagers at a birthday sleepover.

Matty didn't even bother retrieving the envelope before she

fell asleep. The mail always arrived in late afternoon, as it had every day since her childhood. Damon Quinn would never see the letter that had been nothing more than a birthday salute from her best friends. He would never know that Felicity and Liza had used him to try to open her eyes to the world of possibilities that existed beyond the safe, familiar confines of Carrollton, Minnesota.

She fell asleep trying to visualize Damon's face, and she was still sleeping soundly early the next morning when the mail carrier, following the map of his newly divided route, removed the letter addressed to Damon and stuck it in his pouch.

Chapter One

Miami International was every bit as crowded and harried as Damon had expected it to be. His flight in from George Town had been uneventful, but as he'd neared Miami, he had asked himself again and again exactly what on earth he was doing. He had made some huge mistakes in his life. He had trusted the wrong people. He had looked at the world through a distorted eye, refusing to see that the ordinary events of everyday life were as important, as earthshaking, as anything he could discover in the laboratory. But never, at any time in his life, had he set out to unfairly use another human being.

Not until now.

An airline official in quasimilitary garb began to announce the arrival of another flight at the nearest gate, and Damon watched idly as people who had been lounging in the chrome-and-imitation-leather chairs began to stand expectantly. He didn't join them. Matty Stewart's flight had been rerouted due to a freak blizzard in the Midwest, and nobody seemed to know which alternate flight she had been switched to, because computers had succumbed, as well. She'd had no way to reach him, of course, so he had been forced to meet every potential flight, hoping that she was on board and, more important, that they would recognize each other if she was.

He was about to marry a woman who might pass right by him and never know she'd done it.

A trio of casually dressed young women, one with a baby slung over her shoulder, passed just in front of him to line up outside the roped-off exit. He wondered whom they were meeting, and if the baby had been lugged through the busy airport for a tender reunion or simply because baby-sitters cost too much money.

The first passengers stepped through the jetway, and Damon watched without getting to his feet. He counted four men in business suits, a middle-aged couple with three carryons apiece, a mother and father dragging a screaming blond-haired toddler between them. The parade of passengers continued as he ticked them off mentally. By the time he began to lose interest, the three young women had disappeared with three equally young men.

Unlike the last flight he'd met, there hadn't even been any near misses on this one. The two unaccompanied women of the right age hadn't begun to match Matty's description or resemble the photo she'd sent him. One woman had been short and dark-haired, and the flurry of Spanish she'd uttered when she caught sight of a dark-haired young Romeo behind the rope had confirmed his opinion.

The other woman, a willowy blonde in a pale gold sweater and dark stretch pants, had seemed too self-possessed to match the voice he'd come to know so well. Matty had a sweet voice with an unmistakable flutelike waver that said everything about how unsure she was that she was doing the right thing by becoming his bride.

And how could he blame her? He was asking a total stranger to give up the next year of her life, perhaps much longer, to make his own life more convenient.

There was more to it than that, of course. Heidi's future was at stake, too, a reality that eclipsed anyone's convenience. And even though fatherhood was a relatively new experience for Damon, he had already learned that a father did anything for his child. Anything and everything and the entire spectrum in between. A father even begged a stranger to marry him if it meant that his daughter's future would be safe and secure. And that was exactly what Damon had done.

The flight attendants strolled through the exit, chatting and pulling their black flight bags behind them. Damon glanced at his watch, then back at the gate. But obviously the plane was empty now and Matty was on a different flight. He consulted the list he'd been given at the ticket counter to check what he already knew. The next possibility didn't arrive for two hours. He was stuck in the Miami airport waiting for a woman he was going to marry, a woman he didn't know. And when and if she ever arrived, he probably wouldn't even recognize her.

He was hit with such a wave of self-disgust that for a moment nothing else mattered. Then, as he leaned over to pick up the bouquet of pink and white carnations he had bought at an airport gift shop, he heard his name over the intercom.

"Would Mr. Damon Quinn please come to the airport information booth in front of..."

He listened intently to the entire message and wondered how many times it had been repeated before he had registered the words.

And what would he find when he arrived at the booth to get his message? That Matty had been seized with an attack of good sense and skipped the flight altogether? That something was wrong with Heidi back on Inspiration Cay and no one there knew what to do about it? That Gretchen's parents had arrived on the island, warrant in hand, to take his daughter to a new home in Ohio?

All disasters. All possible. For a moment he couldn't move; then, clutching the flowers in an iron grip, he went to find out which calamity had struck.

Matty tugged at her gold sweater and wished it were a few inches longer to completely hide her hips and rump. Liza had bought it as a going away gift, along with the black leggings, the butter-soft ankle boots and the long gold chain that hung between her breasts. Her suitcases were stuffed with clothes from her other friends, too. The Carrollton female staff had given her a shower unlike any she'd ever witnessed. Liza and Felicity had orchestrated it, first shepherding Matty to a salon to have her colors done, then to have her hair cut and streaked with subtle warm highlights. The shower had come one week later, and all the clothes had mysteriously matched the new colors she was supposed to wear. Soft golds and delicate greens, rust and camel, and a turquoise the color of the ocean that would surround her new home.

When she looked in the mirror now, the Matty peering back at her was altered. Short wisps of hair framed her face and tapered to her shoulders. Long light bangs brushed her eyebrows and emphasized the wide set of her eyes. The effect was pleasant and gave her a surge of confidence when she caught sight of herself. But she was still essentially the same, still the same plain Matty Stewart who was about to sell herself for the promise of adventure and warmth, and the presence of people in her life who might one day come to care about her.

"Miss Stewart?"

She turned to give the young man behind the information booth a wide smile. "He doesn't seem to be coming, does he?"

"Would you like me to try again?"

"That would be terrific."

She watched him lift the microphone and start his announcement again. She guessed he was no older than twenty-one, dark and tanned, with a salad bowl haircut she recognized from teenagers on the Carrollton pediatrics ward. Six other people had demanded his attention since she had asked for his help, but the young man still hadn't forgotten her.

She was always surprised when she heard complaints about how rude people were to each other. True, she had run across difficult people at the hospital, but most of the time they were in pain or immersed in the worst throes of grief. She was drawn to people like that, the healer to the sufferer, and she discounted their rudeness as temporary and in some perverse way therapeutic. But in her experience most people were kind and helpful, willing to go the extra mile on the flimsiest evidence. Despite her work, despite some of the horrors the hospital had dealt with, she had never lost faith in her fellow human beings.

Which might explain why she was willing to marry a man she hadn't seen in nearly a decade, a man who had probably never even *seen* her at all, not even when they had stood face-to-face.

"Matty?"

She had been gazing into the throngs hurrying toward gates or ticket counters, so the deep voice behind her left shoulder was a surprise. But she didn't spin around. She took a deep breath, then another for good measure, before she turned.

For the first time in eight years she was face-to-face with Damon Quinn. And this time he couldn't fail to see her.

"Damon." She created a smile from the turmoil within her. "I wondered if we'd ever find each other."

"I saw you get off the plane, but..." His voice trailed off.

She didn't want to finish his sentence, but she did. "You didn't recognize me. I'm not really surprised. There's no reason why you should have."

But she recognized him, both with her eyes and the distinctive fluttering inside her that had characterized every glimpse she'd ever had of him.

"You don't look like your photograph."

"The hair's different. I know." As she spoke, she did not have the self-control to resist examining him. Damon was older, but every bit as beautiful as she remembered. And *beautiful* was the right word, not because he was in the least bit feminine, but because *handsome* failed to drive right to the heart of the matter. He had the face of an angel, or at least a tormented poet, wide cheekbones, a rock-solid jaw and dark eyes that burned like smoldering coals, even when he was at his most casual. His black hair was too long, and it curled over his forehead, his nape and ears in a style that more than suited him. It defined him somehow, his perpetual distraction, his flouting of convention, his disdain for the inconsequential.

"More than your hair is different," he said after he had studied her, too. "You've grown up."

"Then you remember me?"

He smiled a little. "What's it to be, Matty? Bare-bones truth? Or something a little gentler?"

"I'm totally incapable of telling a lie. And eight years ago you never took the time to try."

Some internal scorecard seemed to register a point in her favor. "I remember you, but vaguely. And only now that you're here."

She was pleased somehow. She hadn't expected that much. "I did grow up, but I haven't changed a lot. Carrollton's pretty much the same as it was when you left, and I'm afraid I am, too."

"A woman who was too afraid of change wouldn't find herself in this situation."

She laughed lightly. "A woman who knew how to hold a few glasses of champagne wouldn't have, either."

His smile broadened, a flash of emotional lightning that transformed him into someone more approachable. "Right, the champagne. Soon to become my favorite drink, since it's brought you here."

Before she could respond, he took her elbow, as if to guide her through the crowd. "Did you get your luggage? You wouldn't have had time for that, would you?"

She had been fine—or nearly fine—until that moment, coasting along on excitement and curiosity. But now she was blindsided by an attack of nerves. "Damon, we're...uh...not heading right out, are we? I mean the plane—"

"No. I had the good sense to book the last flight of the afternoon to George Town. We can't take this any way that approaches normal, but I thought we could at least spend the afternoon getting to know each other before we go off to get married.''

"But we can't get married right away. There's the license."

"That's all a formality, but you're right. You'll still have a few days to decide once we're there."

"And so will you."

He looked down at her from his six feet of solid masculinity. "I'm not going to change my mind. I know everything I need to know about you."

His words weren't surprising. She knew he had checked her background with a thoroughness usually reserved for top-level security clearances. And she knew why.

As Damon silently guided her through the crowds and toward baggage claim, she thought about everything that had transpired since she had awakened in horror on the morning after her birthday party to find that the letter Liza had penned to Damon was gone.

She remembered how panic had seized her, and she had awakened her friends to demand that they tell her exactly what they had done with the letter. Felicity had been as horrified as she was, but Liza had been philosophical. "He'll see it was done in good fun," she'd said. "He'll have a good laugh and toss it right out."

But Matty hadn't been so easygoing about something that had, in its own excessive way, revealed too much of her heart. She had felt wounded and vulnerable, and she had sat down that night to write Damon a real letter apologizing and explaining. "It was my twenty-seventh birthday," she'd written, "a time to look backward and forward. My friends and I were talking about what I wanted from life by the time I was thirty, then we started in on the first of too many bottles of champagne. I almost never drink, Damon. I shouldn't have had so much that night. I'm afraid I acted like an idiot. Please forgive me, and if you remember me at all, please try not to include this with the rest of your memories."

She had wished him the best of luck, sealed the envelope and driven it right down to the post office. Writing the letter had helped a little. At least Damon would know the first one had been a prank and a mistake. She had hated the fact that he would probably think she was immature and featherbrained, with too much time on her hands, but she had realized there was nothing more she could do.

His birthday card had arrived two weeks later, and his first telephone call a week after that. "I wasn't advertising for a wife, and you weren't really applying to be one," he'd said, just minutes into the conversation. "But, Matty, I'm in a desperate situation here, and I don't know where else to turn."

And then he had proceeded to outline his dilemma.

"That looks like the right carousel up ahead." Damon gestured to a baggage carousel that was slowly circulating, although by now there were only a few pieces left on it. "Point out which are yours when they come around and I'll get them off."

Matty glanced at him from the corner of her eye. He was wearing dark slacks and an ivory dress shirt unbuttoned at the neck. His sports jacket was loose and casual, a natural open-weave fabric that seemed perfectly suited to tropical living.

"Your hands seem to be full, Damon."

He looked down at the bouquet of carnations he had been choking since she'd first turned around to face him. Then he looked up at her and grinned. "They're for you. I'd completely forgotten I had them." He held them out.

"They're lovely." Actually, they might have been lovely once, but the white paper stapled around them was crumpled now from fingers that had gripped it too tightly, and Matty suspected the stems were mangled.

"I'm sorry," he said. "Maybe I'm not as calm as I thought."

"I'm sure if there was a handbook on mail-order marriages that would be on the first page. I guess our palms are supposed to sweat and our hearts are supposed to beat double time."

"Is yours beating double time?"

"Triple." She heard her voice waver. She had talked herself into coming here with a bravado she hadn't even known she possessed. She had marched in to her supervisor at Carrollton Community Hospital to give her resignation, and she hadn't even considered the immediate promise of a pay raise if she would just rethink her decision. Without a backward glance she had rented her house to Liza and Felicity and said her goodbyes.

And somewhere along that path she had used up all her stores of courage.

Damon took her hand. The gesture so surprised her that she froze. She knew her eyes gave her away. She excelled at warm good cheer, at encouragement and empathy, but right now she needed someone to give all those things back to her.

"Matty..." His voice was kind, even kinder than she remembered. "I'm not going to pressure you. I know I'm asking too much. Let's just get to know each other today. One step at a time. Okay?"

"Damon, look at you. There have to be a dozen women who would have said yes to marrying you, women you know well, women you're attracted to. I'm nearly a stranger. Why me?"

He had answered that question before, but he seemed to sense her need to watch his face as he explained once again. He linked his fingers with hers, and her heart skipped erratically.

"Not a dozen. But I do know some women who might have said yes. None of them could offer what I really need. The only question is whether you need Heidi and me enough to take this step. Do you?"

The answer was yes, of course. Perhaps there had been a thousand possibilities for her future, but somehow, after Damon reentered her life, she had only glimpsed two. She could continue at Carrollton Community taking care of other people's beautiful babies, continue living in the house and town she had lived in all her life, continue wondering what the world was like outside that small frozen speck on the map. Or she could accept Damon's astounding offer of marriage and motherhood and a new life on a distant tropical island.

In the end the choice had been easy, because the second possibility had come attached to Damon Quinn, a man she had once loved with unrestrained passion. And this gift of Damon in her life once more, even under these strange and unromantic circumstances, had been too tempting to reject.

"I'm here," she said. She would not reveal more of her heart than that.

He seemed to think it was answer enough. "Let's get your suitcases, then we'll go somewhere for lunch." He squeezed her hand before he dropped it. She felt absolutely alone when he was no longer touching her, but she lifted her chin and managed a smile.

Matty Stewart was not what Damon had expected. He had done his research, probing, in-depth research that should have distilled the essence of the woman. He knew how she had sacrificed a normal youth to care for her father. He knew that Frank Stewart's illness had been long and difficult, an illness that had taken his strength and finally his mind, and that Matty had given him tender, unremitting care until his death two years ago.

And he knew that she was regarded by hospital supervisors and colleagues alike as one of the finest nurses ever to walk through Carrollton Community's doors. If she had faults they tended toward the most admirable. She was too accepting of others' faults, too giving, too undemanding. Everyone seemed to like and trust Matty, from the man-eating head nurse in maternity to the lowliest emergency-room clerk. They all went to Matty if something special needed to be done, and most of the time she was able to satisfy them.

Her personal life was just as flawless. To make ends meet she had shared her home with two of Carrollton's most eligible women, and the three seemed to be close and loyal friends. The other two were well liked, but everyone seemed to think it was Matty who glued their friendship together. There were no hints of competition for men or prestige. At home, as at the hospital, Matty seemed determined to believe the best and give her best.

Knowing all that and more, Damon had expected someone subtly different from the woman who had been waiting at the information booth. First, he had been surprised to feel such an instant tug of attraction toward her. She wasn't really pretty, not in any classical sense of the word, but she had a vibrant, natural smile and smoky hazel eyes that never looked away when she spoke. Her creamy skin was flawless, and her hair was fine and silky. Her best points were subtle but undeniable. She was not a woman a man might pick out in a crowd, but once exposed to her, she would nibble away at his concentration until she had his undivided attention.

Damon knew there was no man in Matty's life. Caring for her father had made that impossible, and then there had been months of readjustment and, naturally, grief after his death. By the time fate had allowed her to seek a relationship, the pool of eligible men in Carrollton had been small. But now that he'd seen her, no excuses seemed good enough. Why hadn't some man noticed her anyway? Had she been so busy taking care of everyone around her that no one had seen she could be more, much more, if she was just given the chance?

"All this sunlight!" Matty spread her hands as if to catch sunbeams to store away. "Damon, I've never seen light like this. It's like liquid gold."

"This will seem overcast compared to the island." Damon watched Matty examine the restaurant where he had brought her to have lunch. He hadn't chosen it carefully; in fact, he didn't even remember its name. But he had been here before with Arthur Sable, the man who owned Inspiration Cay, and he had remembered that the food was good and the location close enough to the airport to make it easy to get back that afternoon.

Now he was glad he had thought of it. Wide windows looked out on a narrow blue inlet adorned with the requisite seagulls and palm trees. Light wood and tropical prints completed the statement indoors, where Latin rhythms competed with rattan-trimmed ceiling fans for dominance of the warm spring air.

Matty loved it. He hadn't intended to impress her, but clearly he had. She seemed more relaxed here. She had even stopped toying with her iced-tea glass and the wedge of lime perched on its sugared rim. For the last few minutes she had even seemed to forget that the man sitting across from her was her husband-to-be.

"Are those hibiscus blooming against the wall?" Matty pointed to her left.

He nodded. "And the purple flowers behind them are bougainvillea."

"Paradise."

"The last man to own Inspiration Cay spent a fortune on landscaping. It's gone wild, but Arthur prefers to leave it that way."

"Jungle appeals to me. Things that grow and thrive without restraint, abundant good health..."

"You've seen little enough of that, haven't you?"

She seemed startled, whether at his insight or her own guileless revelations he didn't know. "Not enough, I guess," she admitted.

"Was that one of the reasons you said yes to this arrangement? Because you needed to be away from illness and suffering?"

"For a while, maybe." She folded her hands. "I'm good at what I do, but it's possible I need to do something else, something I might do even better."

"So you need some time to think? To reconsider your life?"

"Does that bother you?"

"Absolutely not. It reassures me. I'm not sure I could go through with this if I thought I was the only one of us who was going to benefit."

"Don't forget Heidi."

"I couldn't possibly. She absorbs every waking minute. You'll see, once we get to the island."

"Damon, tell me the whole story. You've told me bits and pieces on the telephone, enough to get me here. But I need to know it all. How you feel about Heidi's mother, why you didn't marry her. How she feels about you and Heidi, too. Where and how I'll fit in."

And that was the other way that Matty didn't fit with Damon's picture of her. He had expected a woman so eager to please, so accommodating, that she wouldn't ask pointed questions or show the wealth of insight that was a part of the real Matty Stewart. He found her perceptions unnerving at the same time that he found them refreshing. She did not suffer from self-absorption, but on the other hand, she was too intelligent not to recognize the problems that might affect her own happiness.

He tried to cull out the things in his past that didn't matter and cut right to the things that did. "I met Gretchen in Washington, D.C. She had just ended a relationship with another man, and she was looking for someone to take up the slack. She'd be the first to tell you that. She was very clear about it to me."

He paused as their server brought them steaming bowls of spicy black bean soup and garnished them with a splash of sherry and dollops of sour cream. He watched Matty lift her spoon and begin to eat. Her hands were unadorned, no rings, no polish on her short nails. Just broad strong hands that looked as if they could solve a multitude of problems, hands that probably rarely fluttered or trembled.

"And what was she to you, Damon?" she asked.

"She was a one-night stand that lengthened into weeks," he said bluntly. "She was in no hurry to move on, and I was in no hurry to get rid of her. We were both new to the city, and lonely. When she finally found an apartment in Arlington, I helped her move. We saw each other less and less as the weeks went by, and finally, when it was time for me to leave D.C., I couldn't even catch her at home to say goodbye."

"So you didn't know she was pregnant?"

"It's the nineties, Matty. When we had sex I was careful

to protect us both." He read her expression. "Technology is imperfect. It failed us one night. I didn't think too much about it, since Gretchen seemed to think it was the wrong time in her cycle to matter."

"Damon..." She returned to playing with the wedge of lime. "Could she be lying about who Heidi's father really is?"

"No. The timing's right, and Gretchen swears that Heidi's mine. I was there when the condom broke. I have to accept responsibility."

She nodded, and he knew that accepting responsibility was something she would understand completely.

"Gretchen never contacted me until after Heidi's birth. She says she intended to keep her, that she thought it might be a lark. Gretchen likes to be entertained, and she thought Heidi would be endlessly entertaining. Two weeks of staying up all night with a screaming infant cured her of that. Gretchen can act decisively when she needs to. She realized her maternal instincts were nonexistent, but she felt a responsibility to her daughter. So she sat down and listed the alternatives, and I was at the top."

"How did you feel when you discovered you were a father?"

"Furious."

Matty cocked her head, and her eyes searched his. "But you took Heidi anyway? Out of responsibility?"

"I had begun my research on Inspiration Cay." He drummed his fingers on the table and tried to decide how much of that story to tell her. He settled on only the most salient details. "This work is my whole life, or at least it was then. I was sure that having a baby on the island with me was impossible, unthinkable. So I flew to Arlington to help Gretchen make arrangements to place Heidi in a good adoptive home. You know the kind I mean. Two devoted, educated parents with love and time to give her, both things I was sure I couldn't manage. And then I saw her and held her." He looked away and shrugged. He was still embarrassed at the depth of his attachment to the squirming, screaming scrap of humanity who was his umbilical cord into the future.

"And so you brought her back to the island?"

"It seemed the right thing to do. Gretchen wanted it that way. Officially we'll share custody, but I doubt she'll ever be much of a presence in Heidi's life. She'll breeze in with gifts and kisses, whisk her off to Disney World and back again. But she can't meet Heidi's emotional needs, and she knows it."

"How do you feel about Gretchen, Damon? It sounds like she's going to be part of your life for a long time."

"Are you asking if we might take up where we left off?"

She didn't look away. "This whole situation is strange enough. If another woman is involved, it's impossible."

"Gretchen and I were briefly attracted to each other. The attraction was briefer than the relationship, and that was brief enough. I don't hate her. I have a grudging respect for her willingness to give birth to Heidi instead of the obvious alternative, and then for her willingness to find the best solution for Heidi's future. But Gretchen will be a part of Heidi's future, not mine. After I realized I was going to raise Heidi, I asked Gretchen to marry me, and she said no. We were both profoundly relieved that that was out of the way, because our marriage would have been an unqualified disaster."

He let that dangle a moment before he added the clincher. "But Heidi won't be a part of my future at all if Gretchen's parents have their way. And that's where you come in."

"I can't believe they have a prayer of getting custody. You're her father."

"I'm a father without a real job, at least the way the court sees it. A father living on a remote island in the Bahamas without a doctor, a grocery store, a church, a school. A father with no experience caring for a baby and no time to do it properly. I can't hire help. Most older women with good credentials would find life on the island too lonely and harsh. And a younger woman would look suspicious to the courts."

"Like a live-in lover?"

"Exactly. Not the kind of role model a child would need."

"Why did Gretchen choose you over her parents? She could have handed Heidi over to them and never even told you that you were a father."

"In Gretchen's words, the Otts are rigid and incapable of either love or understanding. They exist to do their duty, and they see Heidi as a duty and nothing more. Gretchen's childhood was miserable. She's not much of a mother, but she doesn't wish that kind of life on Heidi."

"Would the Otts be content if you just allowed them to visit when they wanted?"

"I've spoken to them once. They made it clear that they intend to control Heidi's upbringing. They see Gretchen as a failure and Heidi as their chance at redemption in the eyes of their church and community."

"So there's no compromise in sight?"

"They want all or nothing. If I retain custody, I don't think they'll even want to see her. And if *they* get custody, they'll throw up every possible roadblock to keep me from visiting."

Matty was silent as the server took away their soup and plunked down the sandwiches they had ordered. Damon had eaten half of his before she spoke. "You told me during our first phone call that your attorney thinks you'll have no problem keeping Heidi if you're married to me."

He understood that she needed to hear the reasons again. He obliged her. "You're not a stranger, Matty, or at least the court won't see it that way. We were friends in college—"

"We weren't."

He went on. "We knew each other. A case could easily be made for a friendship that continued through the years and turned into a romance. No one will ask for proof. We stayed in touch, fell in love..." His voice trailed off, and he sipped his tea. Everything tasted like ashes.

"You don't like this, do you?"

"I like losing my daughter less than I like lying."

Her eyes were grave. "And I have all the perfect qualifications to be Heidi's mother."

"Matty, you have nothing in your past that anyone could object to. And you're a pediatric nurse, one of the best. No one could question Heidi's safety or your loving care of her. If we marry, my attorney believes the custody hearing will be a formality and nothing more."

"How long?"

He wasn't sure what she was asking, but he was sure how important the answer was to her. She looked as if everything in both their futures depended on it.

"How long before I'll know if I retain custody?" he asked.

She shook her head slowly. "No. How long before you can safely divorce me?"

There were still half a dozen questions she could be asking, questions he might not even comprehend. The ashes in his throat seemed to sift deeper, layering his heart. "I don't know." He leaned forward, but he didn't touch her. "If you can only make a brief commitment to us, this can't work. I might be at Inspiration Cay a year, a month, a decade. And as long as I'm there, Heidi's vulnerable."

"A decade?" She voiced the question softly. "And then a divorce when you no longer need me?"

Now he understood exactly what the question was, and he was almost giddy with relief. "Matty, have I ever mentioned divorce? I'm not planning to divorce you the minute I don't need you anymore. Heidi needs a mother, not a baby-sitter. She needs the emotional ties that Gretchen can't give her. I don't know how long our marriage will last. Maybe we'll grow to hate each other despite every effort not to. Maybe you'll decide you need more than I can give you. I can't see the future. But I've never thought this was going to be less than a real marriage. Maybe we have to pretend about our past, but not about our future."

Her cheeks flushed a delicate rose. "A real marriage?"

"Were you really ready to settle for less?"

She bit her lip, small even teeth pressing hard enough against the soft tissues to be dangerous. He folded his arms over his chest to keep from covering her hand with his own.

"We're adults, and we're going to be almost alone in paradise. And we're going to be married. I don't work in the lab day and night...."

"Well, that puts things in perspective."

He smiled, dredging it up from some place deep inside that hadn't been touched by the cruelties and disappointments of the past years. "We'll take that part slowly. I'm not expecting you to jump into bed with me. I'm not making demands." The smile disappeared, and he tasted ashes again, because he knew he was not above using his most foolproof weapon. And he used it now.

"I need you. No one will ever need you more than Heidi and I do, Matty."

She nodded. If she was aware that he was playing on her greatest vulnerability, she gave no sign. "I'll go with you to Inspiration Cay."

"And I'll do everything in my power to be sure you're never sorry that you did."

He told himself it was true, but even as she smiled in answer, he wondered what he could ever give her in return that would be half as important as what she was giving him.

Chapter Two

Matty was used to exhaustion. She had worked graveyard shifts, double shifts and even, during the worst years of her father's illness, around-the-clock vigils, snatching sleep when she could as she hovered at his bedside. What she wasn't used to was the muscle-clenching, nerve-pinging meltdown of a body stressed to the limits of its endurance. She had survived the flight to Miami with its delays and rerouting, and the first sight of Damon with its emotional intensity. She had survived their lunch together with its revelations and evaluations. She had survived her own decision to accompany him to Inspiration Cay.

But she wasn't at all certain she was going to survive the trip there.

"Matty, you're as white as a ghost." Damon's voice vibrated against her ear.

She wanted to smile reassuringly, to explain in a cheery nurse voice that nothing was wrong except that her blood had drained to her feet. But she couldn't summon a smile or an explanation. She closed her eyes and promised her stomach that the flight to George Town was almost over.

"You've never flown in a small plane, have you?" Damon shifted subtly closer in his seat. The heat from his body felt like an electric blanket cranked up to nine.

"Tell me we're almost there."

"We promised to be honest with each other."

Something surprisingly close to a groan rumbled through her throat. His voice was kind. "This wouldn't be bad if it weren't stormy. But we're perfectly safe. We'll pass through this in no time."

She wanted to keep him talking. She needed to concentrate on something besides the jolting of the plane and the roiling of her stomach. "Tell me about the island."

He didn't answer immediately. "First, I'd better tell you about Kevin. And Nanny."

She knew that Kevin Garcia and Nanny Rolle were the other two adults who lived on Inspiration Cay. During one of their phone calls, Damon had mentioned that much in passing. He had left her with the impression that they were caretakers, and she had pictured them as a friendly older couple who trimmed hedges and swept verandas in exchange for a small cottage in paradise.

"Kevin first," he said.

Matty waited, but moments passed before Damon began.

"About six months ago I was in Miami on business, and I'd stayed out later than I'd expected at dinner. My colleagues grabbed cabs back to their hotels somewhere on the other side of town, but I decided to walk to mine because it was less than a mile away. About halfway there I met Kevin."

She frowned. This didn't jibe with her notions about who Kevin was. "You mean Kevin was visiting from the Cay?"

"No. He was living in Miami." He paused. "On the streets."

Her picture of a smiling old man who would show her shells on the beach and identify tropical shrubs dissolved. "Go on."

"Kevin ran away when he was fifteen. That was almost two years ago."

"He's only seventeen?"

"Not quite."

"How did you meet him?"

"He tried to rob me."

The plane lifted, and Matty's stomach dropped. She squeezed her eyelids shut and pictured herself on the beach with a maniacal teenager who was pelting her with deadly-looking seashells. She forced open her eyes. "I see."

"He was carrying a knife. A very sharp knife. And I wasn't carrying anything of interest except a few dollars. I thought I was..." He shrugged.

"Dead?"

"Or thereabouts. Then I noticed the knife was shaking, the kid was shaking. And while I stood there waiting for the right moment to jump him, he collapsed."

She made a noise low in her throat that was meant to be comforting, but it sounded more like a plea for help.

Damon continued. "He was half starved, crawling with lice, and well on his way to pneumonia. I ended up taking him to the nearest emergency room and telling them he was my nephew, so they would agree to treat him. They shot him full of antibiotics and cleaned him up, then I took him back to my hotel."

"Minus the knife?" Her voice was faint.

"Definitely. He slept for twenty-four hours straight, and when he finally woke up we had a good long talk. Actually, I did most of the talking, but I found out enough about him to make some decisions. He has no family worth discussion. His mother was an American who died just after he was born. His father's still living in Cuba. Kevin came to the U.S. with an aunt who moved to California when he was thirteen and didn't invite him along. His mother's brother teaches in Peoria, but he doesn't want a half-Cuban nephew with an attitude. The state stepped in and put him in a group home, which he ran away from three times. The next stop would have been a locked facility, but no one was in hot pursuit. The older a kid is, the less interest the system has in him. At Kevin's age they'd be only too happy to let him look after himself.''

"But he couldn't..."

"Of course not." Damon shifted in his seat so that he could watch her face. "Kevin's brilliant, Matty. One of the brightest kids I've ever met. He's tough and profane and unpolished, to say the least, but he's got so much potential. I had to do something to give him a chance to use it.''

As sick as she felt, Matty still noticed the way Damon stepped in through the back door of his own humanity. He hadn't admitted to compassion or affection for the teenager who had been dealt such a lousy hand by fate. He had rescued Kevin because of his potential. The rational scientist making a decision based solely on logic. Except that there was much more than objectivity in his voice.

"So you brought him to Inspiration Cay?" she said.

"He was too sick to argue. He's been with me ever since. He works in the lab, helps take care of the place. And he inhales whatever books I give him. He doesn't know it, but I'm tutoring him. I get books with the information he'll need for a GED, then we talk about them when we're working together. Once he gets his diploma and takes the SATs, he'll be a shoo-in for a good university.''

She digested the fact that in addition to marrying a near stranger, she seemed to be taking on a teenaged boy with a dark past. "And Nanny? She's not a runaway, too, is she?"

"Of course not." He paused. "Not exactly."

Her head was pounding now, in rhythm to the dips and shimmies of the nine-passenger Cessna. She felt for her air-sickness bag, just to be certain it was there.

"Nanny is seventy," Damon said. "She used to cook for a small guest house in George Town. Until everyone refused to work with her anymore. She's...cranky. And odd. Nanny wants things her way. Her children want her to stop working and enjoy her final years. Nanny won't have it. She still has moments of genius in the kitchen...."

"And the rest of the time?"

"Her eyesight's not good, and her sense of smell, or maybe taste, seems to be going. She's apt to use red pepper as paprika, mix up her herbs, french fry turnips instead of potatoes. Nanny's meals are an adventure. Her housekeeping is... interesting."

"Damon, where is Heidi now? She's not with—"

"Kevin and Nanny have her. But don't worry. They both adore her. Heidi'll be perfectly safe, although the things they'll do for her will be unconventional, to say the least."

She pictured a sixteen-year-old pirate and a crotchety old woman burying a squalling infant up to her neck in the sand.

"About now you're wondering what you got yourself into, aren't you?"

"About now?" She closed her eyes again. The plane seemed to flutter in the air, then it dropped suddenly.

The tone of Damon's voice changed. "Matty, are you going to be sick?"

She was, but not with Damon sitting beside her. She unsnapped her seat belt and leaped to her feet. The one advantage of a small plane was the short distance to the one and only lavatory. She found her way there with no trouble. And just in time.

George Town, with its Caribbean rhythms, its vigorous good cheer and unfailing fascination with its own goings-on, had lost its charm by the time Damon helped Matty off the plane. Her skin defined white. In fact, she was so pale she was nearly translucent. He expected to glance at her in a moment and see her bones etched in full display.

"Technically this is Moss Town," he told her. "But it's just a short cab ride to George Town and the boat that will take us to the cay." He paused. "If Samuel's waiting..."

"Boat?"

He had told her about the boat. He was sure he had. He suspected that she was firmly into denial, the only way to cope under the circumstances. "I wish we could just stay here tonight and go to the cay tomorrow, but I can't be away from Heidi overnight."

"I understand." Her voice seemed to grow fainter every time she used it.

He considered leaving her at a hotel in George Town, where she could rest and recover. He could return for her tomorrow, when she was feeling better. He could bring Heidi with him, dressed in her frilliest sunsuit so that Matty couldn't resist her. Then he could take Matty back to Inspiration Cay, where Kevin and Nanny, under his strongest threats, would be on their best behavior. There was only one problem.

He might return to find that Matty had flown the coop.

"It's still hours to sunset...." He couldn't make himself say that she would enjoy the boat ride. "We'll probably make good time."

"What's...good time?"

He guided her through the easygoing customs ritual and helped her gather her suitcases before he answered. "The trip takes several hours...in good weather."

"Oh..."

The weather wasn't going to be good. He knew that from the turbulence on the plane. "I brought something for sea-sickness, just in case. You probably should take it now, if you think you can manage."

She gave a brief heroic nod. He took her elbow. "We'll get you a drink to wash it down and wait a few minutes. Sometimes the taxi rides into town are enough to make *me* queasy."

Her breath caught. He was afraid that at this point it was the most forceful protest she could manage.

Matty took a double dose of motion sickness tablets. They had nearly worn off by the time Samuel arrived two hours late—Bahamian time, Damon called it—to ferry them to the cay. He was a large man, with smooth dark skin and hands as large as shovel blades. He ushered them on board with friendly chatter as the waves slapping at the jetty threatened to toss Matty to the deck. Damon seemed unaffected.

"The crossing, it'll be a rough one," Samuel said with a distinctive Caribbean lilt. "The boat go up and the sea go down, not always at the same time. But we'll make it, no problem. I'll be staying at the cay tonight for sure. Just don' want old Nanny makin' my supper. Bought food for us to eat." He lifted the lid on a gigantic plastic cooler. The pungent smell of fried seafood, of garlic and a nostril-tingling assortment of herbs and spices, rose to greet her. "Plenty for all."

Matty glanced wordlessly at Damon. He started forward to slam the lid, apparently all too aware of her reaction. She heard the click as the lid fell back into place, but it was already too late. She was fumbling blindly toward the side of the boat to hang her head over the rail.

At some point on the boat trip to Inspiration Cay the waves began to seem like allies. Matty knew that if she could just struggle to the side again and this time manage to throw herself overboard, the waves would swallow her and put her out of her misery. Dying that way seemed preferable to dying by inches. And she was sure she was dying. She would not live to see Inspiration Cay, not live to see the baby she was to raise or to marry the baby's father, a man she had loved silently and passionately so many years ago.

"We'll be there before the last rays of light fade away." Damon said. "Are you going to make it?"

"No."

Something much too close to a chuckle rumbled through his chest. He pulled her a little closer. Sometime during the last hour he had slung his arm over her shoulders to keep her warm. "I really am sorry about this. Do you always get seasick?"

She had never been on waters like these. She had canoed and rowed on placid Minnesota lakes without a qualm. "How often...?" She couldn't finish.

"How often do we have to make this trip?"

She nodded weakly.

"Only as often as you want. We'll have to go to Nassau to

get our wedding license in a few days. But after that you can stay put if you like. The water's not usually this rough, and you'll be rested and ready the next time you brave the waves.''

"Never..."

"It's been a big day, Matty."

She wanted to tell him to turn the boat around, that the day had been much too big to absorb, and she had made a terrible mistake. But if he did as she asked, the trip back to George Town would be longer than the trip to Inspiration Cay. And she was a slave to what was left of her stomach.

"There are 365 cays in the Exumas, did you know that?"

She had done her reading. She knew cay was pronounced "key" and that many of the Out Islands of the Bahamas, of which the Exumas were a part, were uninhabited. "One for each day," she whispered.

"I've been to a number of them. Some don't even exist at high tide. Some, like Inspiration Cay, are high enough above sea level to live on comfortably. The house at Inspiration is on a low rise. It makes for spectacular sunset views."

She tried to hold on to that thought. The sun was setting right now, and had she not been dying she might have termed it spectacular. As it was, she couldn't watch the heavenly light show, because every time she focused on the horizon the boat dipped and her head went spinning in protest.

"The house has stood on that rise for almost a hundred years." Damon seemed to know that she was soothed by the sound of his voice and the warm weight of his arm. Matty knew he was trying to offer his support in the only way he could. Both his voice and arm were impersonal, the comfort anyone might offer. In fact, every time he had touched her—and in their hours together he had touched her five times—he had scarcely seemed to notice what he was doing. She, on the other hand, had noticed every pressure, every movement, every texture.

"It's a wonderful house," he said. "Spacious and airy, with sun-filled rooms, and breezes sweeping through that keep it cool enough to bear on the warmest days. You'll recognize the architecture from pictures of Key West. Double verandas, hipped roof and French windows you can step through into the sunshine. My room—'' He broke off abruptly.

She sat very still and waited for him to continue.

"*My* room's facing east," he said, after a moment. "I can see the sunrise, and I'm usually awake to do it with Heidi over my shoulder or on my lap. I don't expect you to share my room right away. Heidi's room is beside mine in what was probably a dressing room at one time. And then there's another room that shares the same balcony. That will be yours until…" He didn't finish.

He was absolutely right, and she knew she should feel relieved. Instead she felt more dispirited, if that was possible. And what had she hoped? That Damon would be so attracted to a seasick mouse of a woman that he would demand that she crawl into his bed on this, their first night together, and make passionate love to him?

"I'm never going to make any demands on you," he said. "I'll never be able to thank you enough for marrying me, and I'm not going to ask you for anything else. When and if you're ready, you'll know where my room is."

"If I'm ever steady enough…on my legs again…to walk that far."

He laughed, a spontaneous eruption that almost convinced her that he hadn't given up on her completely. "You'll be fine after a good night's sleep. I promise."

"I'll hold you…to it."

"The cay just ahead," Samuel shouted. "Follow the wide purple streak to the sea, Matty, and look left."

Damon got to his feet. "Can you stand?"

She really didn't know. Theoretically it seemed possible. She wanted to see the island that was to be her new home, to get her first glimpse with Damon at her side, his arm around her waist. Surely she could summon up enough physical and emotional reserves to take her in to shore.

He held out his hand, and she took it, letting him pull her

to her feet. For a moment she felt fine, as if the mysterious concept of sea legs was a reality in which she shared.

"Rough water here," Samuel shouted. "Hold on tight. I be takin' her in to Inspiration slow, and the boat, she gonna shake."

Samuel's words were a prophecy. The powerboat began to dance over the water's surface like a hippo in an out-of-control conga line. Matty had already lost everything she'd eaten. Her stomach was beyond revolt, but her head was not. The world grew black, and just before she lost sight of it, it began to spin. She made one valiant attempt to take her seat again before the deck rushed up to meet her.

"Matty, this is Kevin," Damon said.

Matty peered into the near darkness, illuminated by a row of lamps strung along a winding path that rose toward a two-story house set behind palms. Kevin was about ten yards away, nothing more than a hazy man-size shape in the distance.

"Matty's not feeling well," Damon continued. "She's had a rough day. Would you mind helping Samuel with her suitcases, then take him up to the guest house? He's brought enough food to feed an army, if that's any incentive."

Kevin grunted in response, then started toward them, making sure to give Matty a wide berth. She wanted to say something, anything, that might signal good intentions, but she was still trying to cope with ground that didn't quake and a world that only revolved at its normal speed. "Hello, Kevin," was the best she could manage to say as he passed.

This time he didn't even grunt in answer.

"Kevin's not an easy nut to crack," Damon said when Kevin was out of earshot. "He liked things the way they were, and until he's sure you're not a threat of some kind, he won't welcome you."

She nodded, too ill to ask for any pointers on dealing with the teenager.

"Nanny won't welcome you with open arms, either," Damon said as they started back up the path. "I'd avoid getting in her way for a while. Don't make suggestions or changes until she's sure you're not trying to get rid of her."

Despite everything, she was touched that the feelings of two outcasts of such disparate generations mattered this much to Damon. "I'll be careful."

"I hope Heidi's asleep," he said as they drew closer to the house. "That would be a better introduction for you. She's tolerable when she's sleeping."

She disregarded his attempt at cynicism. She already knew that Damon was head over heels in love with his daughter. Why else would he have orchestrated this amazing situation?

By the time the house loomed just fifty yards in the distance, Matty got her first unimpeded view. It was both grander and shabbier than she had expected, a soft pink twenty-carat jewel trimmed with white latticework along first and second-story porches that wrapped around the house. The roof was metal, a surprisingly homey touch in a house as stately as this one, and the ever-present Bahamian sun had softened the paint into swirling patterns, as if a pricey decorator had hired a crew to sponge it with a dozen different shades of rose. The porch floors were a deep sapphire blue, and so was some of the window trim. The overall effect was of a doll's mansion, Caribbean-style.

"Like it?" Damon asked.

"Oh yes."

"It's called Inspiration. The cay was named for the house. The man who built it wanted this to be a place where artists and creative people of all kinds could come and spend time to gather their thoughts or start work on their next projects. Over the century some very important people spent time here, but no records have been kept. The owner didn't want people stopping by to ogle Inspiration's guests. The next owner carried on the tradition, and Arthur is trying to, as well."

"And that's why you're here…"

"Time will tell if Arthur's made a mistake or not."

She wanted to ask him more about that, and planned to later. She knew very little about what Damon was doing or why he was doing it on a remote Bahamian island. He had told her that he had needed a place and time to do his research, and Arthur had provided them. But everything else was foggy.

"Can you make it up the steps?" Damon asked.

"I promise...I won't throw myself at you again."

"Something tells me that was a new experience for you."

She apologized, as she had when she had regained consciousness in his arms. "I started out training as a surgical nurse. I never felt dizzy no matter what I had to do."

"I wasn't talking about fainting. I was talking about throwing yourself at a man."

She laughed, embarrassed. "I don't seem to have much talent for it, do I? I was unconscious during the best part."

"I don't know. You made sure I was right there to catch you. That shows some talent. Maybe you just need practice."

"Not if the aftermath is a pounding headache and total humiliation. I'll have new sympathy for my patients when I go back to nursing."

He had been walking beside her without touching her. Now he took her arm, his fingers just barely brushing her skin. "Let's get the introductions over, then we'll get you to bed. A couple of aspirin and a good night's sleep. I bet you won't even radio for help tomorrow."

"You're safe. Getting off the island would be worse than staying."

"You'll probably never have to endure another trip in by boat like that one. Normally we can fly in to Staniel Cay and be here by boat in twenty minutes. But I couldn't charter a flight to Staniel yesterday."

"Oh..."

"I'll make this up to you."

The thought of that sent heat skidding down her spine. She felt suddenly giddy, even without waves tossing the deck beneath her. "I'll hold you to that."

He looked down at her and smiled a little. Nothing as wonderful as a promise showed in his eyes, but neither did he seem disgusted with her for all her weaknesses. Their gazes caught and held, and for a moment she couldn't draw breath. She was standing in paradise with Damon Quinn at her side, a Damon who was set on marrying her. And Minnesota seemed very far away.

He lifted a hand, as if to smooth a lock of her hair back into place. Before she could even smile or breathe, the front door was flung open with a bang and a wizened old woman appeared, silhouetted against the light of a central hallway.

"Your li'l girl, she be crying for an hour, and not a thing Miss Nanny done for her turn the tide."

"Nanny..." Damon dropped Matty's arm and started forward. "Did you feed her?"

"What is it you t'ink I do, Damon Quinn?" She said his name as if it were one lyrical word. "You t'ink I stand there, bottle in hand, and tease her with it? You t'ink I wave it in her face? That what you t'ink?"

"I think you've taken excellent care of her, as usual. I'm just trying to find out exactly what you've done."

"This your woman?"

Damon turned, as if he'd forgotten Matty. "I'm sorry. Nanny, this is Matty." He reversed the introduction, clipping off his words. "Where is she?"

"She be in the screen porch, Damon Quinn. I rock her in the hammock. She cries I not rock, so I rock an hour. More." She lifted narrow bony shoulders almost to her earlobes.

"I'll get her."

"You do that. She stop you pick her up. She know I be tired of rocking."

Damon disappeared into the house and left the two women to confront each other. Nanny folded her arms. She wasn't much more than four and a half feet tall, although she might have been taller in her youth. She had a wiry body that seemed to have folded and compacted with age. Her dark face was furrowed with deep lines, as if life had plowed that field and harvested what it had sown again and again. She wore a faded cotton print dress and a red kerchief tied at the back of her thin gray curls. Right now the curls bounced as she shook her head.

"Somet'ing wrong with you?"

Matty managed a smile. "More than you'll ever want to hear about. Let's just say I'm a terrible sailor."

"No one in my family ever git sick on the water."

"No one in my family's ever even *been* on the water. At least, nobody who lived to tell about it." Matty started forward.

"You come here, you don't like the sea, maybe you don't like Inspiration, either, or people on Inspiration. Maybe you don't like coming at all."

Matty had never felt less like passing tests, but her smile only faltered a little. "Right now I don't. I'm glad you're so perceptive. It'll make getting along that much easier."

Nanny frowned, but she seemed momentarily at a loss for words.

"The thing is," Matty continued, "I don't like anything right now because I'm exhausted and my head feels like someone's inside it playing kettledrums. I wouldn't even like my own mother right now. So thanks for understanding."

"You got drums in your head, I got tea."

"I would kill for a cup of your tea."

"You sit in my kitchen." Nanny pivoted and started through the hallway. Matty climbed the stairs to follow her.

Inside, the screaming of an infant was easily audible. Either Damon hadn't yet rescued his daughter or Heidi hadn't succumbed to his charms. Either way, Matty wanted to follow the sounds and at least glimpse her new charge, but she knew she'd better do as Nanny had ordered. The old woman wasn't going to be won over easily.

She found the kitchen at the rear of the house by following the hall and cutting through lighted rooms. She was too tired to register much. The rooms were spacious, with high ceilings and tall windows. The furnishings were sparse but interesting, as if schooners from all over the world had docked here and traded ornately carved chests, cupboards and tables for whatever Inspiration's owners had offered them.

The kitchen was huge, crisscrossed by rafters hung with dried flowers and herbs. Nanny was dwarfed by an eight-burner range sporting one lonely teakettle. The room was painted the color of good French vanilla ice cream, and the cupboards, trim and counters were a range of soft sherbets. The effect was charming.

Nanny waved Matty to a long pine table. "Tell me 'bout your head."

"It's pounding. I still feel a little dizzy."

"It buzz?"

Matty wasn't sure where this was leading, but for the sake of harmony she was willing to play along. And besides, Nanny was right. "Yes, a little."

"And your insides moving?"

"Like they're training for the Olympics."

"I'll fix."

"I'd be grateful." Matty watched as Nanny eased her way around the room. She moved as if she were underwater, fluidly and in slow motion. She removed dried herbs from glass jars lining a counter, adding a pinch of this and a sprig of that to a brown pottery teapot. The water sizzled on the stove and grew louder until Nanny made her last decision and poured the water over the remedies she had selected.

Matty remembered what Damon had said about Nanny's eyesight and sense of smell. With a sinking heart she wondered how she could call a halt to this now. She had expected traditional black tea, perhaps Earl Grey, or even something as daring as chamomile or peppermint. She had not realized that Nanny would mix her own.

"Heidi don't like strangers," Nanny said, without turning to see how her words affected Matty. "Already she know who her family is...."

Matty refused to disagree, although she thought that kind of perception in an infant was unlikely. "Little babies are much more intelligent than we give them credit for."

"You pick her up, she probably cry."

"She might very well," Matty agreed.

"She probably cry a lot."

"She's certainly getting some practice right now." Matty could still hear Heidi screaming somewhere off in the distance.

"She be mad at Damon Quinn, he go off and leave her so long, go off to git you."

Matty still refused to take the bait. "It's amazing how good children are at making their feelings known." And little old Bahamian ladies, too. But Matty didn't add that.

Nanny selected a cup from one of the cupboards, one that had obviously seen better days, then she poured Matty's tea, squinting and lifting the cup so that she could survey its contents before she handed it over.

The cup was chipped along the rim in four different places. The handle had been broken off and glued. Matty hoped the glue held long enough for her to finish the tea. "It smells..." Words failed her. It smelled like an overripe compost pile.

"You drink it, it'll fix you quick."

Fix her to do what? Matty considered her options. She could refuse outright on the grounds that the tea might really end her suffering once and for all. Or she could say—quite truthfully—that her stomach was rebelling.

Or she could take up the challenge and show Nanny that she trusted and respected her. The first two wouldn't help Matty settle into life on Inspiration, but the third might—if it didn't kill her first.

"It smells a little like my favorite herbal blend at home," Matty said. "Thank you, Nanny." She lifted the cup to her lips and swallowed her first sip. The taste was vile, a cross between banana peels and some mutant relative of the cabbage family. She waited for her throat to close or her muscles to clench spasmodically. When nothing happened, she cautiously took another. "It's so...warm." She smiled at Nanny. "I guess it was cool out on the water."

The kitchen door flew open, and Kevin stepped through. She saw he had dark hair down to his shoulders and the faint tracing of a mustache, but a more detailed appraisal would have to wait, since he was obviously in a hurry. He carried one of Matty's suitcases in each hand. And as he strode past the table he left a trail of water behind.

"You be raining on my floor, Kevin Garcia," Nanny said.

"Suitcase fell in the water," he mumbled.

Matty closed her eyes and took another sip of the tea, but not before she had seen the glow of triumph on Kevin's face. She suspected that *fell* was not the appropriate word, and that when she opened the suitcase in question she might find anything from dead fish to exotic coral formations in among her new Victoria's Secret bras and panties.

"You leave it in bathtub, you be sure." Nanny followed behind him, mopping the water trail with a dishtowel. "You t'ink you can spill water my house, you gotta new t'ink coming."

"Yeah...yeah..." Kevin disappeared through the doorway.

"Kevin Garcia don't want new faces on cay," Nanny said.

"I've guessed that much," Matty said pleasantly. "Do you suppose all my suitcases will be properly baptized, or just that one?" She took another swallow of her tea and discovered it was the last. Somewhere between the first and the final she had developed something like a fondness for it. The taste was truly terrible, but it had spread a warm lethargy through her body, weighting her limbs and even her eyelids. Her stomach was no longer an angry tempest, and the steady beat behind her eyes was slowing to lullaby tempo.

Nanny brought the teapot back to the table and refilled Matty's cup. Matty didn't even protest.

"Kevin's not the onliest person on Inspiration likes t'ings the way they always be," Nanny said.

"Nothing ever stays the same, does it?" Matty sipped her tea and contemplated how the rhythm of her own words had slowed. "But I can tell you, Nanny, that if life does stay too much the same, it's not good either. In fact, it's terrible and lonely. New things aren't necessarily bad...they're... just...new."

Nanny was frowning. In fact, there were now *two* Nannys frowning at her, identical twin Nannys, who were matched wrinkle for wrinkle, curl for curl. Just as Matty was about to comment on this remarkable phenomenon the tranquility of the kitchen was shattered by a foghorn. Matty tried to remember if she had noticed a lighthouse as they had approached, wondering if even now it was signaling a ship about to enter dangerous waters. The possibility was so romantic, so thrilling, that she wanted to ask, but somehow her lips, curved into a wide smile, refused to move.

"This monster child is my daughter, Heidi," Damon shouted above the din. "And she refuses to stop screaming."

Matty heard Damon's voice, and she even made some sense of what he said. The foghorn was a baby, Damon's baby, in fact. She was supposed to turn around, acknowledge the child in his arms, perhaps even offer professional advice on calming her. Some part of Matty—a part growing steadily smaller—wanted to do just that. As for the rest...

Her eyelids gave up the fight and closed, screening out everything except Damon's next words.

"Nanny! What the hell did you put in that tea?"

Chapter Three

Sun poured over honey-colored walls and made feathery tracings of the palm fronds that were dancing in the Caribbean breeze just off Matty's balcony. Matty had been watching the shadows for longer than she cared to admit. She wasn't sure what she hoped for. That their hypnotic sway would put her back to sleep. That if she concentrated hard enough she would find she *was* asleep in her lonely bed in Minnesota and that yesterday was just a disturbing dream. That someone would come into her room and tell her that she had not disgraced herself again and again on the trip to Inspiration Cay, that she had not blacked out at the kitchen table at the trip's end.

That someone, and she was afraid to speculate who, hadn't carried her up to this room last night and undressed her as she'd slept the sleep of the dead.

She tried to remember the events of last evening. She had tried to make friends with Nanny. She had humbled herself to the point of neurosis, drinking a tea that could have done far more than put her to sleep. Damon had come into the room.

Thinking about it now, she suspected that he'd had Heidi in his arms. He had been angry at Nanny, then...nothing.

Except that at a deeper level of awareness she thought she remembered arms around her, arms that had laid her gently on this bed, and hands that had smoothed away her clothes. Warm, strong hands that had lingered against her skin. Had she really moved against those hands, arched her back and sighed as they stripped away her sweater?

She was never going to find the courage to leave this room again.

The light seemed to grow brighter and the shadows sharper. At home she could have judged the time easily, but here the light was bright enough to destroy her frame of reference. It might be morning or late afternoon. She could have slept for days or weeks. As the warm honey of the walls lightened to palest gold, she realized that however long she had slept, it was time to get up. She might wish that she could avoid facing the population of Inspiration Cay, but she was trapped here with that tiny and decidedly odd band, and with her own humiliation. If possible, it was time to start putting yesterday behind her.

A soft rapping sounded at her door, then a voice. "Matty?"

She sat up and pulled a sheet over her breasts just as the door swung open. Damon stood in the doorway, a Damon completely transformed since yesterday. Gone was the man in the tropic-weight sportscoat and neatly pressed slacks. This Damon was barefoot, his hair tousled as if he had just dried it with a towel, wearing ragged cutoffs and a faded green T-shirt. This Damon, too, was outrageously gorgeous. "Good," he said, with no ceremony. "You're still alive."

She hadn't decided what to say today or how to act. She said the first thing that came to mind. "Am I supposed to be?"

"Look, there are just a few rules here. Don't let Nanny play doctor, and don't let Kevin scare you."

She tucked the sheet under her arms. She was still wearing a bra and panties. That was one of the first things she had made sure of this morning before she set about wallowing in her memories and embarrassment. But she felt curiously naked facing Damon this way, her legs drawn up to her chest, her shoulders bare except for flimsy lace straps the color of her skin.

She was a master at sounding as if nothing bothered her. She was unflappable Matty, everyone's rock of Gibraltar. "Was Nanny trying to kill me?"

"They're both harmless. But if I were you, I'd watch my back for a while. And don't worry. I've spoken to Kevin about the suitcases."

With a sinking heart, she registered the plural. "Do I have anything left to wear?"

"Nothing inside them was damaged. Apparently Samuel retrieved them before they sank. Kevin was just making a point."

"Well, I'll have to tell Kevin it's all right to talk to me if he's upset. The suitcases are old. I don't know if they can stand much more."

"He won't talk about his feelings. He won't talk to anybody."

It was time to talk about her own, or at least some small part of them. "About yesterday…"

"I'm sorry, Matty. I should never have asked you to come."

Her eyes didn't flicker. She supposed she had anticipated this, that she hadn't gotten out of bed before this to avoid it. How could Damon possibly want her after everything that had happened? She was a complete failure. Even if Damon had still been willing to give her another chance, Nanny and Kevin weren't going to. And she had already seen how fiercely and surprisingly loyal he was to them. "It's all right, Damon. I understand." She continued to keep her voice light and struggled with a smile.

"I wouldn't blame you if you swam back to George Town. I've been so caught up in my own problems, I just didn't try hard enough to put myself in your shoes."

"You couldn't have."

"I should have made arrangements for us to stay in George Town last night. Heidi would have managed without me. And you could have rested. The trip here wouldn't have been so awful. You wouldn't have had to face Nanny and Kevin when you were sick and exhausted. I won't blame you if you tell us all to go to hell."

She managed a feeble joke. "That would be a long way from paradise, wouldn't it?"

"Will you give us another chance, then?"

Moments passed before she realized what he'd said. There was no particular warmth in his voice, and he wasn't looking at her directly. Despite his casual clothing, his posture was anything but. He looked like a man who was preparing himself for an assault.

"You mean you'll let me stay?"

"Let you?"

"I disgraced myself, didn't I? Why would you want me?"

"I still need you, Matty. The question is whether you're willing to live here under these circumstances. I doubt if you see any reason to after yesterday."

She was flooded with relief, swimming in it, surfing in it. She didn't know what to say. When she could speak, she continued to keep her voice light and make no emotional demands with her tone. "I can think of one very big reason."

"What?"

"I don't think I can swim as far as George Town."

"Thank you," he said gruffly.

"Just so you know. I almost never get sick. And I never faint. And I don't usually succumb to a cup of tea."

"You don't have to be superhuman. You just have to be here."

"A warm, maternal female body?"

This time his gaze met hers directly, nearly pinning her to the spot. "The maternal part remains to be seen."

Heat rose in her cheeks, but before she could say anything, he went on. "Have some breakfast, but I'd advise fixing your own. Then I'll introduce you to Heidi, and you can see just how maternal you feel."

He closed the door, and she was left alone to wonder exactly how warm and how female he had found her.

"All right. For some strange reason she's willing to give the two of you another chance, and me as well." Damon glowered at Nanny and Kevin, who was clasping Heidi like a football under one arm, crosswise against his chest. They were standing on the back veranda, screened from view by some wildly fragrant vine that was perfuming the air from its vantage point on the lattice-work. "She's more forgiving than I would be under the circumstances."

"Not'ing in that tea they arrest me for." Nanny was glowering, too, glowering and sucking on a pipe that one of her sons had carved for her. Damon and Arthur had forbidden her to smoke it inside, but she spent hours each day with it clamped unlit between her lips. He had no idea what she burned in it each evening when she went outside to sit on the beach and stare in the general direction of George Town, but she had assured him that whatever it was, *it* was nothing they could arrest her for, either.

"You knocked her out with that tea," Damon said. "And you knew you would. No more of that, Nanny. And, Kevin, there's no point in trying to chase Matty away. You might as well write yourself a ticket back to Miami if you do, because I'll be moving back there with Heidi to deliver pizza if this custody issue can't be resolved in my favor here on Inspiration."

"I can leave anytime." Kevin's posture was defiant, one hip thrust forward, his chest puffed out, the hand not holding Heidi thrust deep in the pocket of his jeans. He looked like a young Blackbeard, angry and violent and aching for trouble.

"No, you can't," Damon said shortly.

"You can't stop me."

Damon wasn't in the mood to argue. Kevin was partially right. If it ever came to it, Damon couldn't stop the boy from leaving. But Kevin owed Damon money for his medical care, for room and board, for clothing and incidentals, and Kevin, despite appearances and despite the way they had met, always paid his debts. For his part, Damon made sure that Kevin never came out even in any exchange. That way he knew Kevin would stay on Inspiration, and he could continue to keep an eye on him. He didn't know how much of this Kevin understood, and he didn't even care. So far it was working, and that was all that mattered.

"I'm putting Matty's suitcases on your bill," Damon said.

"Why? She's still got 'em, doesn't she?"

"We're going to have to have them cleaned professionally. And it won't be cheap."

"You ever heard of child labor laws?"

"You ever heard of juvenile detention centers?"

Kevin sank into a sullen silence.

Damon ran his fingers through his hair. "Look, Kevin, you're very good at making your point. You don't want her here. We all know that. But give her a chance. Please? She'd like to be friends."

Kevin made a noise that was every bit as descriptive as the profanity that Damon insisted he eliminate from his vocabulary.

"All right. You don't have to be friends," Damon said. "Just don't make her life miserable. Got it?"

"I've got work to do." Kevin swung Heidi forward, and Damon was left with no choice but to take her. Kevin ambled off, both hands deep in his pockets and his back hunched defiantly.

"He don't stay, I don't stay," Nanny said.

"He'll stay. And this is not a contest. It's not you and Kevin versus Matty. For Pete's sake, Nanny. Give her a chance."

"Don't know no Pete. Don't want to." She went back into the house and slammed the door behind her.

Heidi wiggled in Damon's arms, and he noticed for the first time that she was wearing a diaper and nothing else. "You cold, sweetheart?'' He lifted her so that she was hanging in front of him. "Is Daddy's little sweetheart cold?"

She gave a toothless grin, and his heart kicked into overdrive. The day she had learned to smile had been the best day of his life. He clasped her close and wrapped his arms around her, noisily kissing the soft top of her head. She was going to have dark hair like his, despite the fact that Gretchen's hair was nearly—and naturally—white. Her eyes looked as if they were going to stay blue, but he didn't know enough about babies to tell anything about the final decision on her coloring. Whatever the details, he knew for certain that she was going to be the most beautiful little girl, teenager and, finally, woman in the entire world. He could tell that much, and the rest didn't matter one bit.

"Let's put some more clothes on you," he said with that peculiar timbre in his voice that he'd developed since their first meeting. He couldn't seem to talk to Heidi as if she were an adult. She wasn't, after all. She was so tiny, so fragile, so unbelievably...cuddly. He was certain there was a biological reason why babies evoked baby talk. Something about pitch and decibels and the fragile auditory system of infants. He was certain that he was just playing along with Mother Nature, who couldn't always be understood, but who always seemed to know exactly what she was doing.

Inside the house he started upstairs to find Heidi more clothes. It wasn't really cold outside. She was probably perfectly comfortable just as she was, but he had an ulterior motive. She was charming in diapers, charming any way, for that matter. But dressed in one of those ridiculous outfits that grandmothers the world over seemed to favor she was absolutely...perfect. And he wanted Matty to see just how perfect she was.

In Heidi's room he settled her on the change table and set her mobile of fuzzy yellow ducks spinning so that she could bat her fists in their direction as he chose something else for her to wear. The room was tiny, just large enough for a crib, the table and a rocking chair. The house had eight bedrooms, and he was welcome to make a nursery in any of them that weren't in use, but he had chosen the old dressing room because he could enter it directly from his bedroom.

He had never allowed Heidi to cry at night and never intended to. Until she was old enough to need more space, he wanted her nearby, where he could hear her when she wriggled or sighed or laughed. He had never realized just how short childhood was, but he was all too aware at the end of each day how swiftly it had passed and how much his daughter had changed.

He was a hopeless sap.

In the bottom drawer of the change table he sorted through sunsuits and dresses, T-shirts and overalls. Gretchen hadn't wanted custody, but she sent their daughter clothes as if that would somehow make up for her lack of maternal instinct. Arthur Sable, the man who owned Inspiration Cay, seemed to have bought stock in a baby boutique and was taking his dividends in merchandise, and even Nanny and Kevin had pooled their funds to buy Heidi whatever caught their eye among George Town's meager baby supplies. Damon wondered what Matty would think when she saw how packed these drawers were.

He wondered what Matty would think, period.

The subject of Matty stilled his hands, and for a moment he stared at the heap of baby clothes and tried to imagine what she must be feeling. He couldn't imagine a worse beginning for them all. He had dragged Matty through hell yesterday. Even he had felt queasy after the boat trip in from George Town, and he was an experienced sailor. He could so easily have made the day easier for her, but he hadn't thought it through well enough. He wasn't good at putting himself in anyone else's shoes. He had always found it easier to concentrate on ideas, on theories, on statistics, rather than on people and what they were feeling. Feelings confounded him, his own included. He suspected that was why he'd never had any serious thoughts about marriage or parenthood.

Until he'd been presented with Heidi.

He supposed something valuable must have come from yesterday's experiences. He had observed Matty under the worst of conditions, and he had seen that she was a trouper. She had taken Nanny and Kevin in stride, and struggled gamely with her own physical discomfort. She hadn't uttered a word of complaint, not even this morning, when she'd had plenty to complain about. Everything had to feel strange to her, insecure and overwhelming. Yet she had managed to stay cheerful. She hadn't blamed anyone else; she hadn't insisted he apologize.

In every way Matty was a surprise. He had believed that he knew everything important about her. The retired police detective who had investigated her had been thorough. But no one could have prepared Damon for how guileless she was, how completely feminine, how trusting. She had sat at the kitchen table last night drinking Nanny's outrageous tea as if it were something rare and delectable from the choicest fields of Sri Lanka. She must have suspected that Nanny was up to no good. But she hadn't been willing to hurt the old woman's feelings. She was tactful and funny and...

She was more than the sum of her good qualities.

Despite himself, Damon remembered the way Matty had felt in his arms as he'd carried her upstairs to her bedroom. He had tried to wake her. He'd had no desire to play Rhett Butler after all they'd been through getting to the cay. But Nanny had done her work well, and there had been no hope of Matty waking before morning. So he had lifted her in his arms, which had been easier than he'd expected, and carried her through the hallway with a satisfied Nanny trailing behind.

At the top of the steps he'd shooed Nanny away and taken Matty to her room. The room hadn't been readied, as he'd requested. The windows had been closed all day, and the stale air was smothering. The linen was clean enough, but not fresh, and the bed was heaped with blankets. He'd been forced to prop Matty in a chaise longue while he opened the windows to allow the fresh sea breezes to chase away the heat and at least rattle the cobwebs that Nanny and Kevin had left in place like ghoulish welcome streamers.

He had folded the blankets, leaving just one at the foot of the bed, then pulled down the spread and the sheets. And at that moment, as he'd realized that he was ready to move her to the bed, he'd realized something else.

There was no one else on the island who could undress her. Either she was going to sleep in a bulky cotton sweater and thigh-hugging pants, or he was going to have to strip off her clothes.

She was about to become his wife, but he had stood there helplessly staring at her cuddled against the terry cloth of the chaise. And that was when he'd no longer been able to deny what he'd tried to ignore since spotting her at the gate.

Matty Stewart was an attractive woman, and he was not immune to her attractions. And he certainly hadn't been immune last night when he undressed her.

Someone made a sound in the hallway outside Heidi's room. He knew who that someone was. Matty hadn't yet come downstairs, and he knew she was finally ready to risk seeing them all again. For a moment he considered calling to her and introducing her to his daughter here in Heidi's room. But just as he opened his mouth, Heidi began to whimper. The baby's patience was amazingly short, and she had already reached her limit. He grabbed the next item of clothing he touched before he straightened. He had done everything wrong yesterday, but today was going to be different. He would wait until Matty had eaten something and wait until Heidi was smiling again. He would introduce them to each other when they were both at their best. And then he would pray.

Matty couldn't really blame Damon for not calling to her when she passed Heidi's room. She had made enough noise to let him know she was there, but he hadn't responded as she'd hoped. And how could he be faulted? He had brought Heidi to meet her last night, and she had fallen sound asleep without even looking at the baby. Despite everything he'd said to her this morning, she knew she was on trial. How could she not be? He was giving her time this morning to adjust, or so he said. But she suspected that he was giving himself time to reconsider, too.

At the bottom of the steps she looked around to see who might be lurking to make her feel even less sure of herself. Blessedly—if the silence was to be believed—both Nanny and Kevin seemed to be somewhere else. The island didn't present a lot of possibilities, but she hoped they were outside taking advantage of the white sand beaches or the waves frothing happily at the shoreline. Anywhere except where they could aim their hostility at her before she had her first cup of coffee.

She started toward the kitchen, admiring the highly polished wood floors, the pastel walls and the exotic furnishings in every room in between. The house was exquisite, each room a little museum of fascinating antiques, of paintings and sculpture and fine porcelain. Light rushed in from every window, and the air sweeping through was heavy with the salt spray of the sea and the perfume of exotic flowers.

"Toto, we're not in Minnesota anymore," she whispered. For a moment everything she had suffered yesterday faded away, along with her insecurities. How could things not go well here? She pushed open the kitchen door with new resolve, only to find Nanny waiting for her.

"I made breakfast. You didn't come, so I t'row it in the garbage."

Matty considered a dozen rejoinders, some surprisingly un-Mattylike. "That's too bad. I'm sure you went to a lot of trouble."

"You always sleep so late?"

"No. I wonder why I slept so late this morning?" Matty let that hang between them for just a moment before she continued. "Do you suppose it's the air?"

Nanny lifted her chin. "I never sleep so late. Same air."

"Since I seem to be on a different schedule from everyone else, I'll fix my own breakfast. Please don't worry about me again."

"I'm the cook."

"And I'll bet it keeps you busy. This will be one less job

you'll have to worry about." Matty turned her back before the old woman could argue and went to the pantry. As she'd hoped, there was an assortment of cereal, all repackaged in glass jars. She chose what looked like cornflakes and brought the jar with her as she backed out. When she turned, she saw that Nanny had gone.

She sighed, half in relief, half in sympathy. She wished she knew exactly what to say to convince Nanny that she was no threat, but she supposed that time would make it clear.

Either Nanny would realize that she meant no harm or Damon would tell Matty he didn't want to marry her after all. Either way, the relationship with Nanny would improve.

She found a coffeepot on the counter, and a good sniff indicated that it really was coffee, warmed too long and much too strong to start with, but coffee nevertheless. The smell made her homesick for the coffee in the nurses' lounge at Carrollton, and she poured a mugful. She pulled down a bowl from a cupboard, found silverware and a carton of milk, and took them all to the table.

Alone, over coffee that made the hospital's worst sludge taste like a sidewalk café specialty, she contemplated how to prove to Damon that she was still the dependable, sensible woman he needed to marry. She wasn't ready to give up on this arrangement. She had days to decide if she could really say "I do" when the moment came, but for now she wasn't ready to turn tail and run. Still, yesterday had stripped her of all artifice. She had told herself again and again that if she didn't accept this amazing offer, another might never come along. Now she knew how absurd and self-deluding that had been. Experienced nurses were needed all over the world. She could have chosen almost any sun-drenched country and made her application, and after some paperwork and soul-searching, she could have been on her way to foreign shores. She could have joined the Peace Corps or the Army. She could have adopted a child.

But none of those options would have included Damon Quinn.

The kitchen door slammed, and she glanced up over her cup. Kevin stood with his back to the door, looking as if he was about to flash a gun. She didn't smile; she wasn't about to give him a chance to deepen his sneer. She just waited for him to say his piece.

"What'd you do with Nanny?"

Matty lifted her cup higher and finished the grounds-laced remnants of her coffee before she spoke. "Kevin, I don't know Nanny very well, but I doubt seriously that there's anything I *could* do with her. She'll win every battle. Just like you."

"What's that supposed to mean?"

"Well, it means that I know when I'm out of my league. You and Nanny just need to get together and decide what you want from me. Short of leaving, I'm probably at your disposal."

"You talk too much."

"You don't talk enough. That probably means we'll get along perfectly if you'll just give it a try."

He made a noise low in his throat. "Heidi doesn't need you."

"Obviously she has a fan club, even without me."

"We can take care of her."

"You know, you can't be all bad if you're that crazy about a baby."

"Don't bet on it!"

"Look, please don't go out of your way to prove your point. I'll take you at your word." She sighed. "But don't you think it would be better for everybody if we tried to get along?"

His expression was all the answer she needed. He had an amazingly communicative face. She could almost see a lifetime of rejection and pain written across it. He turned and went back out the door, slamming it behind him.

"Kevin never closes a door quietly."

Matty turned to see Damon lounging in the doorway. And this time, unlike last night, she saw Heidi, too.

"Oh..." She stood and set her mug on the table, skirting it quickly to go to him. "Well, look who's here."

He propped Heidi against his chest with an arm across her middle protectively. ''Matty, this is my daughter.''

Matty had probably held a thousand infants in her lifetime. She was a connoisseur of infants of all races, nationalities, sizes and shapes. She had seen some so marvelously beautiful that the most jaded nurses had gathered around them in the nursery to exclaim and extol. She had seen others who even the most generous of nurses couldn't praise. She knew from experience that some of the least lovely infants grew into the most attractive and interesting adults.

She hoped to heaven that Heidi was going to be one of them.

''Damon, she's a little doll.'' Heidi was little; there was no lie there. Her father was six foot, but Heidi at three months wasn't even twenty-four inches. She was tiny and delicate in form, but her face had the scrunched-up features of a sad-eyed circus clown.

Damon's voice was gruff. ''She might not want you to hold her. She doesn't take to strangers.''

''At three months? Obviously she's brilliant.'' Heidi was dressed in the most absurd sunsuit Matty had ever seen. It was white with huge turquoise polka dots and yellow ruffles. Damon had stretched a red band with a green-and-red bow around her fuzzy dark head in decoration. Matty was immensely touched that he had struggled so valiantly to present his daughter in her best light.

''She was just six pounds when she was born. She's gaining nicely.'' He rubbed his thumb against Heidi's cheek as he spoke. She turned toward it, as if looking for something to suck.

''How does she sleep at night?''

He shook his head ruefully.

''How do *you* sleep?''

''No better than any other new father, I guess. And she has colic. She screams from about five every evening until seven or so. It's not our favorite time of day. And she has a rash—'' He stopped. ''But she's a wonderful baby. The best.''

"I can see that." She was sure that any moment the mushy space inside her was going to firm up. Damon couldn't keep this up. Eventually she would have to stop being touched by everything he said or did. Eventually she would have to develop some distance, some objectivity.

She forced her gaze back to Heidi's face and away from his. "Blue eyes," she said decisively. "And dark hair. A wonderful combination."

"My mother has blue eyes."

Heidi's ears were more like Prince Charles's than Damon's. In years to come she would probably always cover them with the hair that was nearly nonexistent now. Her bunny rabbit nose made "snub" seem patrician in contrast. Her cheeks were flushed and unforgivably chubby compared to the rest of her face.

Matty wondered if she would have fallen so swiftly in love with Heidi if she had been the perfect infant, the beautiful child of beautiful parents, that she had expected.

She held out her arms. Damon looked skeptical. She shook her head when he started to protest. "Don't worry," she promised. "She'll be all right."

He still looked hesitant, but he seemed to know there was nothing else he could do. He presented his daughter to her as if Matty were planning to serve her with potatoes and green beans for dinner.

Matty had held a thousand babies, but never one who might be hers to raise. "Hello, sweetheart," she cooed. She lifted Heidi higher, tucking her into the soft curve of her arm and raised her head so that Heidi could gaze at her face. "Would you like to go for a walk?"

Heidi puckered up to cry, but Matty began to rock her slowly back and forth and hum. The baby hiccuped, then grew silent. She listened quietly, and at last she smiled.

"What did you do to her?" Damon said.

"Nothing much." Matty's eyes felt suspiciously moist. She hoped he couldn't tell. She looked up at him and tried to smile.

"Well, you have to be doing something. This is nothing short of a miracle."

"It's nothing, Really." She looked back down at the baby who had begun to gurgle happily. "Nothing at all. Just a mother's secrets."

Chapter Four

Heidi had been tucked in snugly for a morning nap before Matty began to wonder where Damon had gone. She'd had trouble persuading him that she wanted to spend the morning alone with Heidi. She supposed he no longer feared that she was going to sacrifice his daughter to the local shark gods, but even though he no longer seemed worried about Heidi's welfare, he was still worried about something.

It was that anxiety, almost smothered under masculine nonchalance—but still obvious to her—that had made her beg to have Heidi to herself. If she was really going to get to know the baby, she was going to have to do it away from the baby's father. With Damon hovering, apologizing, explaining, both she and Heidi would have been tense and worried. And that wasn't the way to start a relationship.

She and Heidi had spent the morning in exploration. Damon had promised her a guided tour later in the day, but Matty and Heidi had sneaked a preview. With the baby well protected from the sun by sunblock and the soft folds of a cotton shirt, and Matty under the shelter of a wide-brimmed straw hat that she'd found on a peg by the back door, they had strolled—or at least Matty had strolled—Inspiration's grounds and gazed out at the turquoise water, which was as calm as glass and nearly as clear.

Heidi hadn't so much as fussed as they'd walked along fondling the fernlike fronds of poinciana trees, the waxy leaves of gardenias, the rough brown bark of coconut palms. They had talked—or she had—about Matty's reasons for coming to stay on Inspiration, about Heidi's desire for a live-in mother, about Damon and the man he had been eight years before. They hadn't ventured as far as the beach or the other end of the small island. They had stayed where Matty could easily take Heidi back to the house if she tired. But she didn't tire. She kept her blue eyes fixed on Matty's face, and she smiled often enough to let Matty know she was contented. When she finally began to grow restless, they went into the kitchen for a bottle, and Matty fed it to her on a rocking chair looking over the side garden, a tangle of shrubbery and vines that seemed to grow wilder with every passing moment.

When Heidi's eyes began to droop, Matty carried her upstairs to change her diaper, then she tucked her in and watched her fall asleep.

It was a morning unlike any she'd ever spent.

Downstairs she searched for Nanny, finding her at last in a room at the back of the house, where she was polishing furniture.

She waited until Nanny finally looked up before she spoke. "Heidi's asleep. Would you mind listening for her? The baby monitor is on."

"Don't be needing you to tell me to listen out for my baby."

"I'm going to look for Damon. I just wanted you to know I won't be inside the house for a while."

"You be bothering him while he works, he won't like it."

"I'll remember that."

"Onliest thing he do is work. Onliest thing he ever care about. Work and that little girl."

Matty wasn't sure she had the local vernacular or accent down well enough to be sure of Nanny's meaning. But she was afraid she did. Nanny was going right for her Achilles' heel. Matty's greatest fear about this situation was that Damon was never going to see her as anything more than a glorified baby-sitter. He might call her his wife; he might even sleep with her. But she was afraid that he was never going to care about her. Not really.

She tried not to let Nanny see that she'd scored a hit. "Heidi's a wonderful little girl. You've all done such a good job with her. If you hadn't, she wouldn't have felt safe with me this morning. She's lucky so many people love her, isn't she?"

Nanny glared at her. "You never get tired being nice?"

Matty managed a careful smile. "I don't know, Nanny. Wait and see. Maybe we'll discover my breaking point together." She turned before any number of other responses crossed her lips and went to find Damon.

Damon had mentioned something that morning about his laboratory, something about it being in an old boathouse on the other side of the island. She hadn't seen any sign of it on her walk with Heidi, but now she set out to find it.

It was early spring, but the tropical sun felt gloriously warm against her arms and legs. She wore a floral print summer dress of peach and green that had seemed wickedly luxurious when Felicity had presented it to her. Now she realized how practical it would be for this new life. Minnesota with its cold spring rains and unseasonal snows seemed as if it were on another planet.

Emotionally she felt much the same. In the same way that the warm sun had made her strip away the layers she had always worn against the cold, the circumstances of her life here seemed to be stripping away the layers she'd worn as protection around her heart. At home, surrounded by the familiar, she had been able to pretend that her life, if not complete, was still satisfying. Now, without that protection, she was filled with such longing for the things she'd never really known that she hardly recognized herself.

She hadn't really expected to fall in love with Heidi. Certainly not so quickly. Her life had been filled with babies. She had loved them all, but she had learned early in her career to keep a certain emotional distance. Not all of them had lived to leave the hospital and begin normal lives. She had known every day when she went in to work that there might be a new infant where one of the sickest had struggled the day before. She had trained herself to accept this, even to leave work and thrust it from her mind, or nearly so, at the end of each day.

But something told her that Heidi would not be so easily dispensed with.

No one had offered her motherhood before. Not the joys. Not the sorrows. And never the terror that came from losing a child that once had belonged to her.

She walked carefully along a path through waving grasses and unfamiliar groundcover. If she had realized how quickly her heart would be at risk, she might not have come here. Already today she had begun to wither inside when she had believed that Damon was about to ask her to leave. And now she had two people she might lose. These new fears were so un-Mattylike that she was at a loss for how to deal with them.

The path turned, and the line of trees and low scrub that had blocked her view of the beach ended. She turned with the path and saw what had to be the boathouse.

She wasn't sure what she had expected. She had seen some stylish renovations in the Twin Cities and beyond. Barns and churches turned into restaurants, factories into shopping complexes. She had expected something similar, a boathouse in name only, a structure that had been modernized and changed so that only its most essential characteristics remained the same. Instead she saw a building of slab boards weathered gray by sun and wind, a tin roof and sagging side porch. A short wing extended along a rotting dock, and wide doors that didn't quite meet faced the shore, as if watching patiently for sailboats that would never sail there again.

Last night Samuel had anchored in front of the house, and Matty had walked along a solid structure with new handrails and sturdy boards. She wondered why this dock, and the boat-house, too, had never been torn down. She was sure she must have the wrong place. This was no laboratory, certainly not for someone of Damon's abilities. Then a light went on inside, and she saw a man pass by the window.

She ventured closer, and when the man passed the window again she knew she had found the right place after all.

A door led into the boathouse from the side porch, and she hesitantly took the steps, half expecting the wood to splinter under her feet. She rapped softly on the door and waited, hat in hand. A minute passed, and just as she was about to raise her fist to knock again, the door opened.

Damon, his eyes unfocused and preoccupied and his brows furrowed, didn't say a word.

"I can come back some other time," she said.

He stared right through her. She wasn't sure if he didn't see her or only wished that he didn't. She felt increasingly uneasy.

"Acetic acid," he said at last.

"No, Matty Stewart." She gave him her brightest smile.

"I wonder if I specified the wrong solution."

"Well, if you have the wrong solution, you'd better have the wrong problem, too."

He stared, and slowly he focused on her until she thought he probably realized she was there. "Matty..."

"Hello, Damon."

"I've got to write something down." He turned and left her standing there. The contrast between the noonday sun and the dark interior nearly blinded her. She couldn't see anything inside except hazy shapes, but she was afraid to go farther in until she was invited. She leaned against the doorframe and waited for Damon to return.

Minutes passed. The sun beat against her back, and air-conditioning stroked her cheeks. Her vision sharpened, and she watched Damon at a tall table, scribbling like a preschooler with his first set of crayons. She was certain that he had forgotten she was there until he raised his head and seemed to look in her direction.

"Would you please shut that door?"

She was afraid to ask which side of it she was supposed to be standing on once it was shut. She made her decision and stepped inside, closing it behind her.

"Better..." He went back to his scribbling.

Her father had been a journalist. In the years before her birth, he had traveled the world, and in the years afterward, when he had been tied down to a daughter and a job at a small-town newspaper, he had often gotten that same expression on his face while he worked on the novel that was supposed to take them both to other, more exciting places. The novel had never found a publisher, but the experience of writing it had transported him.

Damon was transported now.

Matty watched the man who was soon to be her husband, completely understanding the creative process. She had no desire to hurry him along. Watching him was pleasure enough.

He dropped his pencil and stared at his work. His brow was still furrowed, but as she watched, it smoothed slowly. Then he looked up.

"Damn, I left you standing there, didn't I?"

"I don't mind."

He frowned again. "Well, you should."

She smiled, happy to have his attention at last. "If you'd left me standing there because you wanted to call an old girl-friend or have a drink with the boys, I might feel differently."

He looked at her as if he had never seen her before. He wasn't lost in thought now. He was examining her as if one or both of them was on trial and he was about to render a verdict.

"You've been out in the sun today."

"Guilty," she said. "But let's face it, there's nowhere else to go."

"You're going to have to be careful for a while. Your cheeks are pink."

She was a nurse, and she knew the effects of too much sun. Her cheeks were only pink because he was staring at her. She wished suddenly that she'd taken more time to primp. Before setting off to find him, she had combed her hair and freshened what little makeup she used, but there must have been something else she could have done, something that would spark a reaction other than analysis in his eyes.

"It's a beautiful walk over here." She didn't step any farther into the room, still not certain he wanted her there. "Do you ever grow tired of it?"

"Not tired. But I'm used to it."

"Damon, if I'm bothering you—"

"Of course you aren't." He moved closer until he was right in front of her. "I'm glad you're here." He paused, then, as if he couldn't live with a lie he added, "I guess."

"Oh."

"Matty, it's not you. I guess I was hoping we could put this off a little while."

"I'm sorry. Obviously my timing's bad. We'll wait." She turned toward the door and reached for the knob.

He rested his hand on her shoulder. "There is no good time. Come on inside. I'll show you around. I imagine you're going to have some questions."

She was thoroughly at a loss by now. He was glad to see her, but he wasn't. There was no good time to show her around, but he was going to do it anyway. She was surprisingly hurt, a sure sign that her emotions were already too involved to allow her to make any intelligent decisions in the next few days. She faced him and found him just a foot away. "I'll come back." It was her firmest tone, a marshmallow-soft squeak that wouldn't have convinced an ant.

His hand had fallen to his side when she'd turned. Now she gazed down and saw that it was clenched. "You're about to see what a failure I am," he said quietly. "I'd been hoping to hold that off for a while."

"You could never fail at anything you tried. How can you say that about yourself?"

"Look around a little, then tell me I'm a success."

"I think you'd better start at the beginning, don't you?"

"The beginning was some time ago. It's a long story."

She had an overwhelming urge to smooth the wrinkles in his forehead. She had been so caught up in her own distress that she'd completely missed seeing his. "If you're going to marry me, you're going to have to tell me your stories. You can't keep secrets. Look what happened to Jane Eyre and Mr. Rochester."

"There are no maniac wives locked in Inspiration's attic. Just a few skeletons."

"I have time to hear about them."

"Come with me first. I'll give you a tour. Then I'll tell you why all of this is necessary."

She put her hand on his arm. Just the lightest of reassuring touches. "Good."

He looked down at her hand for a moment, then he stepped back, as if to create some distance between them. "The boathouse is larger than it seems," he began.

Although she'd claimed that they'd been in some classes together at Carrollton College, Damon hadn't really remembered Matty at first. Not exactly, anyway. But when he'd studied her at the airport, vague memories had nibbled at the exteriors of his mind, memories of a shy, quiet girl who had a smile for everyone but never persisted beyond that. His impressions were of a girl who had been perpetually poised on the brink of womanhood, but never during the years that she had existed at the periphery of his life had she stepped over it.

Other memories had intruded since then. He thought he remembered a subtle challenge to his status as Carrollton's resident genius. He had never liked the title, not even when it was used as a joke, and he had never felt it was something to defend. But now he remembered comments from others more interested in competition than he was, comments about Matty and how she might overtake him someday.

Halfway through the tour of the boathouse laboratory he suspected that those memories were accurate.

"You understand all this, don't you?"

Matty looked up from a table cluttered with computer printouts and volumes of carefully recorded notes. "Of course not."

"But you understand a lot of it?"

"Well, yes. Except exactly where you're leading. You've been very careful not to tell me that, haven't you?"

There was no censure in her tone. He wondered if she was capable of it. Unless she was putting on the most convincing act he had ever seen, Matty Stewart was completely nonjudgmental. She took people at face value and accepted them for who and what they were. Even a man who wanted desperately to fool her.

He altered the subject a little. "You were a good student at Carrollton."

"Yes, I was."

"Good enough to do anything you wanted afterward."

She shrugged. "What I wanted to do was stay with my father and take care of him. And that's what I did."

"You must have had other plans before he got sick."

"I was going to go to medical school. He had saved for years so I could. In the end, his illness took every penny."

"And that's why you didn't go on to school after he died?"

"No, I didn't go because by then I'd lost my confidence." Her eyes widened, as if she was surprised she had revealed so much. Or perhaps she was just surprised she had admitted something she had kept a secret from herself.

"Your confidence?"

"I've been out of school for years, Damon. And I'm not sure I have what it takes, or even if I ever did. I'm a very good nurse. I decided to leave it at that."

The subject was closed. He heard the finality in her voice. "Let me finish the tour, and then I'll tell you a story."

"Fair enough."

He had already showed her the least interesting parts of his work. The detailed records he made of every experiment, the computer programs he'd designed, the library he'd collected over the years, and even some basic and to this point successful research that he'd begun involving plant proteins. He had presented it all in hopelessly dry scientific jargon. Most people would have been lost immediately. He'd even hoped on some level that Matty might be one of them. But she wasn't. Her questions had been probing and intelligent, even insightful. And her interest hadn't waned.

Now he led her into the next room, opening a heavy steel door that looked completely out of place in the dilapidated boathouse. "This is what it's all about." He ushered her inside and closed the door behind them. He watched her eyes widen. "I wouldn't have guessed," she said. "It's incredible."

The room was wonderful, a tiny gem of a laboratory. Arthur had spared nothing when equipping it. Damon had only had to ask, and Arthur had provided. The room was climate-controlled. The temperature and humidity never varied within any cubic foot of space inside these walls. The walls themselves were so well constructed and insulated that a hurricane could take down the boathouse and the laboratory might continue to stand alone, although Damon hoped never to put that to a test.

"Go ahead. Look around," he said.

"I won't disturb anything?"

"Not if you're just looking."

He watched her move up and down the three narrow aisles. He had experiments in every stage from beginning to end. He had terminated one just before she arrived, another agonizing failure. He had a hopeless feeling that every experiment in process here was going to end up the same way. Every one he had done for two years had. Only at the beginning had he succeeded, and sometimes he doubted that, too.

She stopped and read the notes at each station, skimming them as if she were gathering data for her own set of hypotheses. There wasn't much to see. No cages of tortured laboratory animals, no bubbling vats or organs in glass jars. This was not a science fiction movie; in fact, to the untrained eye the laboratory probably looked like something that belonged in a well-endowed high school. There were two soapstone tables, one with a ventilating hood and one without. Microscopes stood in a row along the wall, and the common tools of a chemist, test tubes, tripods, pipettes, beakers and centrifuges, decorated the tables and a set of cabinets with glass doors. An analytical balance and a high tech burner occupied opposite corners. An incubator took up another.

Matty came back to stand beside Damon. "What exactly are you trying to do here?"

"Have you seen enough for now?"

She nodded.

"Let's talk outside."

He locked the door behind them, since he probably wouldn't visit the laboratory again until evening. After they exited the boathouse he locked that, too, although he planned to come back and work out some more probability charts on the computer after Heidi's morning nap. He had almost forgotten what it felt like to sit at the computer without Heidi on his lap. She was certainly the most demanding lab assistant he'd ever had.

"There's a nice view up there." He pointed toward the top of a small rise near the center of the island. "There's a bench. It's a good place to sit."

She climbed the hill at his side, not making any demands. He wasn't used to being with someone who seemed to have so few needs of her own. Her very presence was comforting. Not that "comforting" was the first adjective that came to mind when he thought of her.

He hadn't gotten nearly enough sleep last night. He was more aware of that now than he had been then. After putting Matty to bed, after smoothing off her clothes and unavoidably stroking his fingers over her warm satin skin and the subtly enticing curves of her body in the process, he had lain awake for hours thinking hard about this whole preposterous situation.

What kind of man asked a woman to marry him solely to

make his life simpler? He could pretend his motivations were purer than that, of course, that Heidi needed a mother and the world needed a cure for cancer, but at the very bottom of this situation were *his* needs. Not Heidi's. Not Matty's.

He had faced another fact that was every bit as disturbing, too. He had chosen Matty because he had believed her to be so retiring, so unassuming, that she would not penetrate very far into his life, no matter how long they were married. He had chosen a wife the way most men might have chosen a housekeeper. He had wanted someone to take care of him and of Heidi, but not to intrude emotionally. And after just a few hours in Matty's company, after talking with her, sitting beside her, slinging his arm over her shoulders in comfort, he had become sadly aware that life had thrown him another emotional curve. He liked Matty Stewart. He admired her. And, far more dangerous and surprising, he wanted her, as well.

"Damon, whatever this story is about, you must know it wouldn't make me think less of you." Matty seated herself on the bench and turned so that one hip and shoulder rested against it and her eyes could search his.

And that was another thing. He didn't want her to think less of him. Not just because he was afraid she would turn tail and run, leaving him in the same dilemma he'd been in since Heidi's appearance. He realized that Matty's opinion of him mattered. It already mattered more than it should. The situation was growing more complicated with each passing hour.

"How did you and Heidi get along this morning?" He turned so that he was staring out to sea.

If she realized he was stalling, she didn't point it out. "She's wonderful. She was sleeping soundly when I left. Nanny's listening for her."

"Nanny will check on her every fifteen minutes. Like a clock. She doesn't trust the baby monitor."

"I'm glad she cares so much about Heidi."

"Nanny misses her grandchildren. She doesn't see them often enough. She's angry at her daughter and sons, so she refuses to visit their homes. She only sees her grandchildren when I make arrangements and run interference with her children.''

"I'm sorry. Are her children...?'' She was obviously searching for a word.

"No. Jake, Ralph and Kitty are wonderful. Kitty was a supermodel when she was younger. She's still gorgeous enough to be on the cover of *Vogue,* but now she runs a flourishing travel agency on Grand Bahama. Jake is an engineer with a weekend house outside of George Town, and Ralph is a carpenter there. They all want Nanny to live with them, but that's the problem. They want to do things for her. They want her to take life easy and enjoy her final years. They can't see how crucial it is for her to be independent. Nanny can't admit she's growing older, even that her eyesight is failing and she needs glasses. She won't see a doctor about anything. They nag, and she gets more stubborn. That's why I brought her here. She needs to be away from them. But she misses them all the same.''

"Outcasts.''

"What?'' He had to turn to read her expression.

"Kevin and Nanny. Outcasts, both of them. And Heidi, too, in a way. You wanted all of them when no one else did.''

"Don't make me out to be some kind of a hero.'' He paused, then knew that the time had come. "I'm an outcast, too. The very worst kind.''

She frowned, but she didn't try to argue. She waited.

"I promised you a story. Well, here it is. I was kicked out of graduate school when I was only three weeks from defending my dissertation. Along the way I had won top honors in my field. I'd been offered three postgraduate fellowships for the following fall, which I'd turned down because I already had a job waiting for me at the National Institutes of Health. I was going to head up my own project, with half a dozen assistants to start with and more promised if things turned out the way they were supposed to. I was scheduled to speak at some of the major conferences of the year. I was the new kid on the block, the golden boy of biochemistry.''

She nodded, and her eyes betrayed no dismay. "What happened?"

"I was caught in a lie. Except that it wasn't a lie." The waves were lapping at the shoreline below them. He watched them again. "I never lied to anyone. But I may have made a terrible mistake."

"Why don't you start a little further back."

"You've probably figured out from what you saw inside that my major interest is in using plant materials to inhibit the growth of tumors. Hardly revolutionary. Scientists all over the world are interested in the same thing. There have been some moderate successes, but not enough major breakthroughs. For my dissertation, I researched the folk medicines of different island groups, including the Bahamas. I wasn't the first to be interested in this, and I won't be the last. But I decided to focus on one plant, something no one else, to my knowledge, had taken a serious look at. A weed that flourishes on some of the local cays but in few other places in the world." He intoned the dry scientific name, then managed a wry smile. "Nanny calls it 'plant-for-all,' which I like better."

"Why that one?"

He tried to make a complex subject simple, not because she wouldn't understand, but because he wanted to end this quickly. "The incidence of certain types of cancer is lower in the Exumas than in other parts of the world. There's also a reliance on natural remedies for minor illnesses here. I found that plant-for-all was often given as a kind of a tonic in the spring and fall, and in between whenever anyone wasn't feeling up to par. I decided to see if there was any relation between the ingestion of plant-for-all and the low incidence of cancer. I was skeptical. I didn't expect anything to materialize, but it was a good subject for research. I got a small grant from the Bahamas government, and spent six months down here interviewing people. That's how I met Nanny. Once she decided I was harmless, she helped by introducing me to local families and asking them to cooperate with the questions I asked. My study was limited, but there was a surprisingly high correlation between people who drank a tea made from plant-for-all on a regular basis and their continued good health.''

"That must have been intriguing.''

The tide was going out, and seagulls were circling the shallow water as if looking for a quick lunch. Damon stared at them as if he had never seen seagulls before. "I decided to see what I could find out about the plant itself. I spent months in the laboratory examining it in a thousand different ways and writing up what I'd found. I'm probably the world's expert on plant-for-all. And at the end, I just couldn't keep myself from taking it to the next step. I didn't have the kind of sophisticated equipment I needed or the best kind of laboratory, but I decided to spend the next months determining whether I could find any evidence that plant-for-all really might inhibit the growth of cancerous cells. And so I conducted a series of experiments, primitive experiments, to see if anything turned up. My adviser, a world-renowned biochemist, discouraged me, since there was so little chance I'd get any results under those circumstances, but I was too stubborn to listen.''

He fell silent.

"You found something, didn't you?'' Matty asked at last.

"I was almost at the end of my trials, and nothing interesting had shown up. I was about to terminate the entire thing and begin to write up what I had, which was more than enough for an acceptable dissertation. The day after I made that decision I went into the laboratory and discovered that one of the experiments I'd conducted...'' He didn't even know how to phrase this anymore.

"It was a success?''

"It seemed like it at the time. I was beside myself. Stunned. I decided not to tell anyone yet. I repeated the experiment exactly using my notes, which were meticulous and extensive. The same thing happened all over again. So I went to my professor, and he and a committee of faculty came to examine what I'd done. I did it a third time, and it was successful. No one could believe it, but the proof was right there for them to see. It was such a major breakthrough. Not a cure for anything, certainly, but a step forward. Word got out. Offers began to pour in. I locked myself away to write up everything I'd done.'' He shook his head, his lips compressed in a tight line.

"What happened?"

"My adviser and the faculty committee tried to replicate the experiment using my notes. Everyone thought it was a good idea, additional proof that my research was sound. I thought so, too, although I wasn't happy about relinquishing control like that. I was afraid mistakes might be made and my results might be questioned. But it seemed necessary, and I agreed. They followed my notes to the letter and found...nothing."

"Nothing?"

"I couldn't understand it. I was given the benefit of the doubt, of course. So it was agreed that I would run the experiment again, from beginning to end, with my adviser present for every detail. The laboratory was locked in between. He had the only set of keys to one lock, I had the only set to the other. We had to enter and leave together. We had to keep records of everything we did. I was sure that together we'd succeed where he'd failed. And instead we failed together."

"You must have been devastated."

"We tried it again. We had the same failure. By then the consensus was that I'd lied, that I'd done some laboratory magic tricks to gain prestige, even though nothing could be proved. Not everyone in the department liked me. I was known for challenging prevailing wisdom whenever it seemed appropriate, and that worked against me in the end. I was asked to leave the university. There was no formal dismissal, because nothing could be proved. I was given a graceful way out. I was to tell anyone who asked that I'd decided to pursue the research on my own, that I wasn't ready to share it with faculty or anyone else. I was supposed to fade away so that nobody would look bad. But, of course, everyone who mattered could guess what had happened. The job offer was withdrawn, the fellowships disappeared. And suddenly I was a pariah."

"Oh, Damon." She covered her hand with his. "I'm so sorry. I can't understand why they couldn't trust you."

"They couldn't trust me because I proved I couldn't be trusted! The experiment failed. Don't you see? It failed for them, and it's failed for me every single time I've tried to replicate it since then. Sometimes now I wonder if it was ever a success, if I just wanted it to be and fooled myself."

"That's ridiculous!" She squeezed his hand hard enough to send pain shooting up his arm. "Don't tell me you actually believe that!"

He looked at her and saw nothing in her eyes except indignation. No doubt. No pity.

Something inside him eased by slow degrees. Something that had been clenched since he'd first considered asking her to marry him. "How can you be so sure?" he said. "You don't know me."

"Yes, I do. Old friends are the best kind, Damon. Even old friends you hardly remember. Because I know who you were, and after just a day together again, I know who you are. And you're incapable of deceit. You're incapable of faking research for any purpose. You were successful. More than once. And now you have to find out why you haven't been successful again. Something changed between the successes and the failures, and you have to find out what it is."

He could feel her faith in him, as warm as the sunshine beating down on his bare head. Her face was shadowed by the brim of her hat, but her eyes shone with conviction. "That's why I'm here," he said. "Six months ago Arthur Sable found me working in a two-bit hospital lab. He knew about my research. Until then I'd been trying unsuccessfully to find someone to sponsor this project. He's giving me a chance to prove myself. It's far more than I deserve."

"It's much less than you deserve. But I'm so glad he came along."

She smiled encouragement at him. Her lips were soft, and they trembled slightly, as if she was afraid he might push her away. For the first time in a long time he felt encouragement lighting the darkness that seemed to rule his professional life. "I'm so glad *you* came along," he said.

She drew a breath, as if she was completely surprised at the sentiment.

"Matty…" He leaned toward her and bent his head to hers. It was a kiss of gratitude. He told himself it was nothing more. He was overwhelmingly thankful that she had listened and believed him, that she hadn't rejected him for the sins so many other people were convinced he had committed.

Her lips were softer than he'd imagined, and they trembled against his. The sweetness of that, of her faith in him and of her reaction to his kiss, shot through him and warmed him more. He rested his hands on her shoulders, and somehow, he couldn't seem to break away as he'd expected to. She was warm against him, and she smelled of lemons and baby powder. Her hair, silky and fine, tickled the backs of his hands as his fingertips pressed harder on the warm flesh of her shoulders.

Her hands came to rest at his waist, but not to push him away. She splayed her fingers over his hips and brushed them lightly back and forth. It was the most provocative thing she could have done, a featherweight touch that aroused him more quickly than a more substantial caress.

He had been one man when he kissed her. He was another by the time he reluctantly pulled away. This man couldn't pretend that marrying Matty was all about Heidi and a sensible life anymore. This man was all too aware that it might not be Heidi who needed Matty the most.

And with the realization came a surge of caution.

Her eyes were wide and unshadowed. He could hurt her. He saw that as clearly as he'd seen her belief in him. His need was one thing, but hers might be another. And just as he no longer had faith in his own abilities as a biochemist, he also had little faith in his abilities to give Matty more than casual affection and satisfying nights in his bed.

"I believe in you," she said. "You'll find out what went wrong. And in the meantime, I'll be here to help."

The better part of him wanted to tell her to run as far and fast as she could. Another part of him spoke. "Shall we get the wedding license tomorrow?"

She nodded.

He stood, but he didn't hold out his hand to help her up. He wanted distance. He needed control. "I'll show you the island. We'll go back to the house the long way."

"I'd like that."

He hoped there was more that she'd like in the weeks to come. He just wished he could be certain of it. Because no matter what she thought about his integrity, he didn't have enough of it to let Matty Stewart go.

Chapter Five

The turquoise water was as unruffled as a backyard goldfish pond, and Inspiration's small skiff, the *Mink,* made the trip to Staniel Cay seem like nothing more than a Sunday drive in the old family station wagon.

Matty stared at the horizon as the boat neared the island and let the wind toss her hair without an attempt at restraint.

"Still feeling all right?"

She had sensed Damon's presence behind her before he spoke. In their short time together she had developed a strong instinct that seemed to track and chart his every move. She almost always knew where he was. She was as aware of him as of the ever-present sun and the fresh ocean breeze.

"Absolutely fine." She turned to look up at him. "Maybe it helps that I'm not exhausted this time."

"And that the weather's cooperating. No storms on the horizon. We'll make it to Nassau without problems, too."

"Are you worried about Heidi?"

"No. She'll be fine with Nanny. And we'll be back by dark."

Matty wasn't as calm about leaving Heidi as Damon seemed to be. But at least Kevin wouldn't be on Inspiration to demonstrate his dubious talent as baby-sitter. He was coming to Nassau with them, and even now was piloting the boat to shore.

"Someday I'd like to spend some time there." She stopped herself, afraid it might sound as if she were complaining. "I mean, it sounds like it might be fun to explore Nassau a little, but later, when Heidi's older and can come along."

"I wish we could spend the whole day today." Damon looked out to sea. "I'm cheating you again. I know it."

"No. Please, don't worry. I'll get a good glimpse, and I'll know what I have to look forward to."

"You are truly amazing." She didn't know what to say, and he continued. "You can make anything sound like it's happening for the best."

"Pollyanna at her worst, huh?" She turned around to watch the water again. She was hurt by his words and didn't want him to know.

Warm hands weighted her shoulders. "At her best. There's nothing forced about your optimism. Nothing sugary. I think you just decided somewhere along the way that your survival depended on making the best of things."

She wanted to lean back against him, to take full advantage of this rare personal moment. Since yesterday morning, when Damon had kissed her, he hadn't said more than a passing sentence to her. And he certainly hadn't touched her.

She would have remembered.

She didn't lean back, afraid he might step away if she did. "My father was the same way. He even made the best of his illness. Until, well…until he just couldn't anymore."

"A brave man."

"The best."

"The next man in your life has a lot to live up to."

He was the next man in her life, but she couldn't tell from his words if he remembered it or not. Or if he was happy about it.

"Is Kevin going to…ummm…dock the boat?" she asked.

"Are you asking if he can be trusted?"

"Something very close."

His hands lifted. "Then you've noticed that since he took control we've been zigzagging a little?"

"I noticed."

"He's doing it for your benefit."

"Not to impress me with his prowess, I suspect."

"If it makes you woozy, let me know."

"He'd love that. Maybe I should complain just to make him happy."

"Kevin thinks he hates everybody, but he thinks he hates women most of all. When his aunt left him in the lurch, it was probably the worst moment of his life. Nanny's the only woman he doesn't snarl at."

"There's no telling what she'd put in his food if he did."

His laughter rumbled in the space between them. "Even Kevin is incapable of sustaining this much anger for too long. He'll soften up. You'll see."

"Will I be able to tell? The difference between hostile and belligerent could be pretty subtle."

"He's a good kid."

"I believe you. I'm just looking forward to being able to tell for myself."

She felt him move away, probably to make Kevin stop swinging the boat. She'd had another full day of Kevin and Nanny's antagonism, and although she was far from giving up, she had become more realistic. Neither of them was going to relax into acceptance of her without a fight. Yesterday had been filled with slights, dozens of them. Then Nanny had served rice and beans for supper as if she was now in charge of a prison cafeteria, and Kevin had slopped and crunched his portion with such noisy abandon that all attempts at dinner conversation had ground to a halt. She had been delighted to go to bed at last, only to find that her queen-size mattress had been remade with double sheets so that no matter how carefully she turned over, the sheets turned over, too.

Damon took over the wheel, and they docked without incident. The short flight to Nassau progressed without incident, too. It was only after the taxi ride in, when they were standing on a sidewalk in the center of town, that Kevin finally spoke.

"I've got stuff to do."

"I figured you did," Damon said. "It shouldn't take us too long to get the license. Shall we meet you somewhere for a late lunch before we head back to the airport?"

Kevin shot Damon a look that would have withered a lesser man. "I'll see you at the plane."

Damon reached in his wallet for a twenty-dollar bill. "Here's cab fare and lunch. Let's say about three. Don't be late. And don't get into trouble."

Matty had noticed that Kevin and Damon never spoke to each other with anything approaching affection in their voices. Yet she could swear that they thought the world of each other. She wondered if that was the key to dealing with Kevin, or if Damon just didn't know how to express his feelings.

"What do you care?" Kevin said. "I won't tell anybody I work for you."

"I'd rather not have to bail you out of jail."

"Then leave me there to rot." Kevin punctuated his words by starting off down the sidewalk.

"That's exactly what I'll do if you get in trouble again," Damon called after him.

"Will he be back?" Matty had to keep herself from running after the boy, but Damon just shrugged.

"He'll be back. He doesn't have anyplace else to go."

"Apparently that never stopped him before."

"He'll be back. Cruise ships are in town, I'm afraid. This place is a zoo. Let's get our business done as fast as we can."

They started their quest with the U.S. Consul at the American Embassy, where they both had to swear that they had never been married before. Then they progressed to the Registrar General, where, after producing a folder of documents and waiting in more lines, they finally received their marriage license.

Matty was feeling giddy with terror by the time they stepped from the building onto one of Nassau's main streets.

"At least we didn't have to have blood tests," Damon said.

She risked a glance at him. He seemed to have taken the whole experience in his stride. They were going to be married, and he was as calm as if he'd just spent forty dollars on a fishing license.

"Let's have lunch. Your choice." Damon checked his watch.

"Lunch?"

"It's past time. You must be starving."

She was hungry, there was absolutely no doubt about that. But food was not uppermost in her mind. She stood under the tin roof that sheltered the Bay Street sidewalk, and although she'd gawked at Nassau's picturesque lanes and pastel Colonial architecture on their way to get the license, now her surroundings were forgotten. She debated what to say next.

"Matty?" Damon frowned. "Is something wrong? Aren't you feeling well?"

She looked just past him, where several small boys were playing tag among a group of cruise boat refugees in wide-brimmed straw hats. "I think we've forgotten something," she said at last.

"Like?"

She sighed. She really wished she didn't have to bring this up. Her request seemed overly romantic, almost as if a real marriage was going to take place and not a legal convenience for Damon.

She tried to come at her wish from another angle. "Damon, have you made any plans for the wedding?"

He looked contrite. "I should have talked to you about that before. I made tentative arrangements with someone at the Tourist Information Center last week. We can get a marriage officer to fly to the island and perform the ceremony this weekend. I'll call and confirm it while we're here. The service will just be a formality, some papers to sign, et cetera. I thought we could do it early afternoon. Is that all right?''

So just like that it would be finished. She would be Mrs. Damon Quinn, and he would have a good shot at keeping Heidi. She managed a nod. ''Okay.''

He didn't take his eyes off her face. ''I've forgotten something.''

''I think it's customary for me to have a wedding ring.'' She said the words as if they didn't matter, as if it was part of the deal they'd made. They had to get married. They had to look married. A ring was part of that. The end.

But something else crept into her voice, and at the same time something crept into his eyes. He had looked contrite. Now he looked stricken.

''Matty...'' He shook his head. ''Of course you do. What was I thinking?''

''You were probably thinking that a ring didn't matter because this isn't a real marriage.'' She waved away his attempt to break in. ''It's *not* a real marriage, Damon, no matter what you want to call it. You're not marrying me because you love me and want to be with me forever. And that's okay. We both understand the difference.''

''Do people really marry for love? It seems to me that most of the time marriage is a convenience for one reason or another.''

''I always planned to. I would like a wedding ring,'' she said, when he didn't venture anything more. ''Maybe it's silly. Maybe it's a sacrilege, I don't know. But I would like one.''

''Then how about a quick lunch and a shopping trip afterwards?''

She lifted her chin, ashamed of her own sentimentality and yet proud that she'd asserted herself. ''Okay.''

''There's a place around the corner that makes terrific conch chowder.''

She slung her purse over her shoulder and straightened her spine. ''Lead the way.''

* * *

He had forgotten a wedding ring. It was as simple as that. He had forgotten. In the rush to get Matty to Inspiration, in the chaos of being a new father, in the search for a reason why his experiment was still failing again and again, he had forgotten about a wedding ring.

Damon watched Matty finish her chowder. She'd had very little to say during lunch. She'd smiled appropriately, made fast friends with their waiter and answered all Damon's comments as if nothing momentous had just happened between them, but Damon wasn't fooled. Matty had been hurt by his oversight. No matter what she said, this wedding was more to her than a formality. It was a wedding, something little girls practiced for with dressed-up Barbie dolls or their mothers' bridal veils. Matty was going to be a bride. And afterward she was going to be a wife.

His wife.

"I know there's a jewelry store not too far away. They cater to the duty-free crowd." Damon leaned back in his chair and watched as Matty dabbed her lips with a napkin. "What kind of ring would you like?"

"Just a ring. We should look married."

Even if we're not. He heard the unspoken addendum and felt a pang of remorse.

"Gold," he said, after he'd stared at her a moment. "Like your hair."

"All right. That's traditional."

"You don't wear much jewelry."

"I'll wear this."

"Do you want a plain gold band? Or something more exotic?"

"Simple will do." She dropped her napkin on the table and got to her feet. "This shouldn't take long. We'll have time to get back to the plane."

"I'm not worried, Matty." He stood, too, and followed her outside after he'd paid the bill.

He led her several blocks, but the shop he'd planned to visit was crowded with tourists. And even though it was packed with hairy-legged men in knee-length shorts and women in colorful cotton sundresses, the shop seemed sterile and cold. He realized he didn't want to select a ring from the pristine glass cases with their icy diamonds and elegant pearls. He didn't want Matty wearing a ring that looked as if it had come off an expensive assembly line.

"This looks promising," she said, peering inside.

"I have another idea." He took her arm and started down a side lane. Once, on a shopping trip to Nassau, he had found another shop that had intrigued him. The shop had been filled with beautiful handcrafted items, and he had bought Nanny a handblown glass vase for her birthday. As he had shopped, he had noticed a host of interesting items, including a case of rings. He just hoped he could find his way back.

"Didn't we just come this way?" Matty said.

Damon realized they'd made a circle. He turned her in a different direction. He was committed now, and he was bound and determined to find the shop in question.

"Maybe this wasn't such a good idea," she said, after several more fruitless blocks.

"I'll get us there eventually."

"I'm beginning to worry about Kevin."

"Relax. We might even see him in some shop along the way with a stocking mask and water pistol."

"You have a very odd sense of humor."

"Just wait until you really get to know me." He turned her down another side lane. He was about out of possibilities. They had already skirted the straw market, and he knew for certain the shop wasn't there.

"Damon, really, any one of the jewelry stores we've seen would be—"

"Here. I knew I could find it." Damon stopped in front of the shop he'd remembered. It was on a corner, set back from the sidewalk and dwarfed by a striped canvas awning. The windows were smudged, and the front display needed to be refurbished, but inside he knew there were treasures to be had. "Come on." He gestured for her to precede him.

She frowned, but she allowed him to open the door and usher her inside. The shop was dimly lit and musty, and the woman behind the counter was too busy filing her nails to glance up as they entered.

Damon told Matty about Nanny's vase. "I know it doesn't look like much in here, but they really do have beautiful things. And last time there was an entire shelf of rings in the display case."

"Wedding rings?"

"Let's look and see."

The woman finished her manicure and got to her feet. "You want to see our jewelry?" She favored them with a blinding toothy grin and was instantly forgiven.

Damon told her what they were looking for, then waited impatiently as she unlocked a case at the back of the shop and fiddled with another lock on a small wooden chest. Finally she opened the chest and pulled out the lowest shelf. "We're changing displays," she explained. "We won't be putting these out again until next week. But here you go."

Matty breathed a deep sigh. If Damon hadn't been standing beside her, he wouldn't have heard it. But it was a sound of perfect pleasure.

Something inside him stirred restlessly. Since he had kissed Matty yesterday he'd made a conscious effort not to think of her as a woman. He had tried to think of Matty as Heidi's mother, as someone who was helping him out of a jam, as an exceptionally intelligent person who believed in him.

But other, more disturbing, thoughts had crept in anyway. His fingertips remembered the satin warmth of her skin. His lips remembered the moist softness of hers. He remembered the feel of her breasts sinking against his chest, the way that her hands had stroked his hips as she'd kissed him in return.

He wished that she would sigh again, and at the same time he prayed that she wouldn't.

"Damon, these are perfectly beautiful."

He stepped closer to her, and his hip grazed hers. He told

himself it was an accident and knew he was lying. "I hoped you'd like them."

"Look at this one." She looked to the sales clerk for permission, and the woman nodded. Matty picked up one of the rings, a twisted chain of yellow gold.

"Try it on."

She frowned. "I don't know…"

"Matty, try it on and see how it looks."

"It's so…" She looked up. "It's not simple at all, Damon. It's a very…" She shrugged. "It's a very complex ring."

He tried not to smile his delight. "And you're not nearly as simple as you think. In fact, you're a very complex woman in a complex situation. And I think it's perfect."

"There's a larger one, too." The sales clerk pulled out another drawer in the chest. "A man's ring that's identical."

"Oh, no," Matty said, before Damon could respond. "We only need one. But thanks."

Damon touched the woman's hand before she could push the drawer closed. "I'd like to see it, please."

The woman grinned again and dug for the ring. She lifted it from the back of the shelf and held it against the palm of her hand. "Pretty, isn't it?"

Damon picked it up and slipped it on the ring finger of his left hand. He supposed he should have been surprised that the fit was perfect. But he wasn't.

He looked up at Matty. "Your turn," he said.

She wasn't smiling. "Damon, no one is asking you to wear a wedding ring. The wedding might be your idea, but the ring was mine. And I don't expect—"

"No, you don't. You don't expect anything, and it's the only fault I've noticed so far. *We* are getting married, Matty. Not you. And if you're going to wear a ring, so am I."

"Oh…"

He was supremely glad he'd realized how much this would matter to her. He'd slipped up on the ring in the first place, but maybe, just maybe, he had redeemed himself a little now.

For a moment she looked as if she was going to cry. Then she smiled instead. "It looks pretty spectacular on your finger."

He slid off the ring and held it in his palm. "Your turn."

He supposed he should have been surprised that Matty's ring fitted perfectly, too. Statistically, one or both of the rings should have needed resizing. But he wasn't surprised. Because somehow, even though he didn't believe in such things, the rings just seemed meant to be.

They strolled through the straw market, where Matty bought a woven baby carrier so that Heidi could nap outside in the shade. She refused half a dozen offers to have her hair braided but struck up so many conversations as a result that it was getting close to three before Damon led her out to the street to find a taxi.

She thought he had been amazingly patient. Everything was new to her and old to him, but he had seemed to enjoy the day as much as she did. He had promised her that they would come back and spend a whole weekend here just as soon as they could, and she believed he meant it.

He was going to wear a wedding ring.

Damon's ring burned a hole in the pocket of Matty's skirt as they headed toward a nearby hotel with a taxi stand. She had insisted on buying his. It only seemed right. And she had taken it to give him at the ceremony. She had no illusions that the ring was symbolic of happily-ever-after. Damon was wearing it to please her, as well as to emphasize the fact that he was a married man and therefore a better candidate to retain custody of his daughter.

But the fact that he wanted to please her that badly was comforting, so much more than she'd dreamed that she had been filled with warmth all afternoon.

Settled in a taxi, Matty viewed Nassau from the window as the cab pulled away from the curb.

"Had a good day?" Damon asked.

"Absolutely."

He settled his arm across the back of their seat. He wasn't

touching her, not quite, but he was close enough that all he would have to do to kiss her again was turn his head...lean closer....

She turned to look at him, and just as her eyes left the passing sidewalk, she registered one Kevin Garcia.

"Stop!"

The taxi driver, obviously shaken by her command, slammed his foot down on the brake, and the cab screeched to a halt.

"Matty, what on earth?"

She was afraid to turn around and look for Kevin. She was even more afraid to tell Damon what she had seen.

"Damon, you must think I'm crazy, but I've...forgotten something."

"And it can't wait?"

"No. It can't. It absolutely can't." She moved away from the shelter of his arm. "I'll be at the airport by three. I promise. You go ahead."

"Don't be silly. I'll come with you. I don't want you—"

"Nope. This is personal. Girl stuff. You go on." She flung open the taxi door, narrowly missing a car coming from the opposite direction. "I'll see you at the plane."

"Matty, you're sure?"

"See you there." She slammed the door and waved the driver on. Damon was frowning as they drove away, as if he thought he was about to marry a crazy woman.

The cab was out of sight before she started back the way they'd just come. Kevin was not where he'd been, but then, that was exactly what she'd expected. Now that stretch of sidewalk was only peopled by a laughing, camera-toting group of tourists wearing souvenir T-shirts from previous vacations.

Some of them weren't going to be laughing when they tried to buy T-shirts from *this* vacation and found that their wallets were missing.

Matty stood, hands on hips, and tried to imagine where Kevin had gone. Working on her best guess, she entered a small mall that ran perpendicular to the sidewalk. Three shops sat on each side of a narrow courtyard. A quick glance proved that Kevin wasn't inside any of them, but a more concentrated search turned up a narrow alleyway that led to the next street.

She emerged to find Kevin immersed in another cruise ship crowd, lifting wallets as if he'd been born for it. She admired his finesse while she plotted how to thwart him, and she was still plotting as she waded into the fray.

"Hi," she said to the first woman who looked at her. "I saw you in the dining room last night." Matty figured that was safe, since eating seemed to be a big part of cruise ship entertainment. "I thought you should know there's been some trouble on the ship, and they're asking passengers to board."

The word swept through the group, and as one, they moved away toward the dock together.

And Kevin was left alone on the sidewalk with Matty.

"Not as smart as you think, are you?" she said. "You didn't even see me coming. What if I'd been a cop?" She allowed that to sink in for a moment, then added the clincher. "Or Damon?"

"Like I care." He almost spat out the words.

"This is what we're going to do," she said calmly. "I'm going to turn over your haul to one of those nice bobbies in the white uniforms. How many do you have?"

"How many what?"

"Wallets, tough guy. I saw you lift two right here and one over on the other street."

"I don't know what you're talking about."

"Wallets. I'm talking about theft, about spending time in foreign jails, about deportation, about a good-looking young man who won't last long in prison before he makes the kind of friends nobody needs. Get my point?"

"I don't know what you think you saw, but you're nuts."

"I can let a bobby be the judge of that. Shall I call one?"

He sneered at her. "You'd like nothing better, would you? You can get rid of me easy that way. Well, don't bother yourself. I'm making it easier. I've got money now, and I'm getting out of here. You don't have to do a thing!"

"You're going to give me those wallets. We're going to wipe them clean of fingerprints, and I'm going to take them to the police station and stick them through a mail slot." She was improvising, but the idea seemed sound. "Then you and I are going to go back to Inspiration together."

"You think Damon will let me stay after you tell him what I've done? You heard what he said. He said he'd let me rot if I got in trouble again. Well, I'm in trouble." The sneer deepened into something straight off Miami's meanest streets. His hands tightened into fists.

"I'm not going to tell Damon. Not if you come with me."

"Sure."

"Look, Kevin." She stepped closer, straight into the range of his fists. She didn't care, because there was a lot more at stake here. "I mean what I say. And here's why. I'm crazy about Damon Quinn. I have been since the first day I met him. And I will not, under any circumstances, see him hurt. And if you leave, he *will* be hurt. Make no mistake about it. Heidi will be hurt, too. She knows you, and she'll know when you're gone. And if you go, Nanny will go. She's already said as much. Everything will fall apart. And I'm not going to let that happen."

"What's in it for you? Nobody cares what you think. He's just marrying you because he has to marry somebody!"

"I know that." Matty looked down at her shoe. The warm feelings of the day evaporated. Suddenly Damon's ring seemed like nothing more than a weight in her pocket, something else tying her to an extraordinary situation.

She lifted her head with a sigh. "I hate it, Kevin, but I know it. You're absolutely right. I feel useless and foolish, like a second-hand dress somebody's trying to fix up for the senior prom. But even so, I still care about Damon, about Heidi...about you."

"Do-gooder!"

She wasn't sure, but she thought he'd said the words with a degree less hostility. "Certified," she agreed. "Unrepentant. And this is why. Because I know what it's like to suffer. I've done my share, and I don't wish it on anyone else. So now I'd like something better for you and Damon. You've both suffered enough already. I'd like to see that change. And along the way I'd like to be happy, too.''

He stared at her. She wished she could read his thoughts. People were passing on the sidewalk; she was all too aware that very soon someone in Nassau was going to notice that a wallet was missing. She and Kevin had to disappear and soon.

He stepped away from her, back toward the alley that led into the mall. She followed him, not sure exactly what was in store for her there. She only knew what Damon believed about this boy. And if Damon was wrong...

No one was around when they stopped. Kevin looked both ways and her heart beat faster. Then he reached in his pockets and pulled out a wallet, then another.... There were six in total.

She whistled softly and held out her hands. ''Amazing.''

''I don't care what you do with them. I don't care one bit.''

''Thank you, Kevin.''

He sneered again. But it was offset by something warmer in his eyes. Something that looked almost human.

Chapter Six

Damon had given little thought to a wedding ceremony, but the incident with the rings had opened his eyes. Matty might be a superior nurse, calm in a crisis and eternally levelheaded, but when it came to marriage, she was a dewy-eyed romantic.

A dewy-eyed romantic who in just four days was marrying a cynical opportunist.

"You could eat off this floor."

Damon looked up at Kevin, who had been mopping the laboratory for the last half hour with the concentration of an Olympic gymnast. "Thanks. Looks good."

"You finished yet?"

Damon dropped his pen on the table and rested his head in his hands. Finished? In what way? Finished with another failed experiment? Finished with the project? Finished pretending he was a scientist?

The room was as silent as a tomb, and the comparison didn't seem too far off. Damon knew that if he didn't come up with something promising soon, his career was going to be dead in the water. He had tried every subtle variation of the original experiment that he and his computers could concoct. Nothing had paid off. Today he was dumping yet another failure.

Damon lifted his head and laced his fingers behind his neck. "Saturday we start all over again. Round one."

"Yeah?" Kevin shoved his hands in his pockets. "I thought Saturday you were getting married."

"Sunday, then."

"So you're taking a whole day off? Oh, boy."

"So are you." Damon had sensed just the subtlest change in the way Kevin seemed to view Matty. He no longer flaunted his antagonism. In fact, he seemed to have backed off from trying to provoke her to mayhem.

Damon swiveled his chair so that he was facing Kevin. "I want you there, Kevin. Please do this for me."

"I'm not going to some stupid wedding."

"Look, Matty deserves a lot more than she's getting. She's doing me the most extravagant favor imaginable. And I want this wedding to go well."

Kevin did a hoodlum version of rolling his eyes.

"Please?" Damon said. "Can I count on you to cooperate?"

"I don't know why you're marrying her. Nanny and you and me, we can take care of Heidi."

"Look, Heidi adores you, Kev. She always will, whether Matty's here or not. You're the closest thing to a big brother she's ever going to have."

Surprisingly, Kevin didn't push aside Damon's words. He clamped his lips shut, but he didn't deny that Damon had homed right in on his feelings.

Damon felt encouraged. "I've never been married before. And I've avoided weddings like they were funerals. So I don't even know what to do to make this one special. But I owe Matty, big-time, and I'm going to do my damnedest. Do you have any ideas?"

Kevin's lips unclamped a millimeter at a time. Then he shrugged. "They like flowers."

They, Damon guessed, meant women in general. "Now that you mention it, Matty does likes flowers. She and Heidi are always hanging out in the hibiscus." He'd already intended to order a bouquet for Matty, to be brought from Nassau with the marriage officer. He did know that much, but now he wondered if that was enough.

"Where are you going to do it?"

Damon pretended that the question hadn't been asked as if they were discussing a potential site for human sacrifice. "Do you have any suggestions?"

"She likes the beach. She's always down there by that thing."

"The gazebo?"

"I guess. When the sun's setting and stuff."

"Is she?" Damon hadn't really noticed. Usually when the sun was going down he was back here in the laboratory, checking everything for the night. But the old latticework gazebo on the western side of the island was the best place to see the sunset.

"She talks about sunsets a lot. She talks a lot, doesn't she?"

"No, she doesn't. You just talk very little, and so do I."

"She's always talking about how good things are...."

Damon wondered if he and Kevin had ever had so long a conversation. Apparently Damon had Matty to thank for this, as well. "Her life hasn't been easy. She just makes the best of whatever she has."

"Yeah. She's suffered." Kevin's tone was heavy with sarcasm.

Damon wondered where on earth Kevin had picked up that bit of information. "Well, I don't intend to let her suffer while she's here on Inspiration. And that means we've got to plan a decent wedding."

Kevin didn't protest the "we." He scrunched up his face until he resembled a young Marlon Brando. "You won't ever catch me getting married."

"You'd be surprised what a man will do for love." Damon

meant for love of Heidi, of course. But the words stayed with him for the rest of the afternoon.

"No, of course you can't come. I didn't expect you to come." Matty closed her eyes and listened to the dearly familiar voices of both Felicity and Liza coming to her by way of two separate extensions in the little house in Carrollton. It was Friday night, and of course her friends had called to wish her well tomorrow. "I know how far it is. Believe me, I know."

The two women took turns bemoaning the fact that they'd tried everything under the sun to reserve seats on a plane from Miami to the Bahamas in time for the wedding. But everything, and most particularly a convention on Paradise Island, had made flight arrangements impossible.

"Listen," Matty said when there was a lull again. "This is no big deal. Okay? Damon and I are going to say 'I do' and sign a few papers. That's all. It's not worth coming this far to see me sign my name. Save your money and come later when you both have some vacation time, so you can stay a while."

There was another flurry of regrets, but at last the call wound down and Matty hung up. She was still staring at the upstairs hallway telephone when Damon spoke from behind her.

"It would have been nice if someone could have made it here to help you celebrate."

She turned and gave him her warmest smile. "It's all right. I explained it's just a formality, but Liza and Felicity are both hopelessly romantic."

"I suspect it's more than that. They recognize how special you are."

Her heart beat a little faster. "They're the best kind of friends."

"Are you ready for tomorrow, Matty?"

Matty was in her bathrobe, a long cotton affair that covered every spare inch of her body. But something about the wa

Damon asked the question made her feel decidedly near-naked.

Actually, he was decidedly more naked than she was. His short-sleeved shirt was unbuttoned, as if he was already thinking about getting undressed for bed. Swim trunks hung low on his hips, and his feet were bare. She wondered if he had just gone for a swim. There was a lovely round pool set back from the house, but they had never used it together. When one of them had free time, the other usually had Heidi in tow.

"Ready?" The word emerged in a hundred syllables. "Umm...I suppose."

He moved a little closer. "No second thoughts?"

"Thirds and fourths and a whole set of fifths. But I'm going through with it."

"We haven't had much time to talk. I'm sorry. Kevin and I are starting a whole new set of experiments, and we've had to prepare."

"We've probably said everything we need to say."

He seemed to have more to say. In fact, he looked like a man poised on the brink of something. She waited, forgetting to breathe.

"I'm about to go for a swim. Join me?"

She had been planning to go to bed. She'd been in the process of getting ready when the telephone rang. Now she realized she wasn't going to sleep a wink tonight anyway. "What about Heidi?"

"I'll ask Nanny to listen for her. She's still puttering around the kitchen."

"She's been puttering all day. It doesn't bode well."

He smiled. "Come with me?"

"All right. I'll meet you there."

"No, I'll wait for you."

For some reason she was all thumbs by the time she got to her room and fumbled for her bathing suit. Having Damon waiting on the other side of the door as she stripped down to bare skin was an odd experience. The two-piece suit—not quite a bikini—had been one of Felicity's wedding shower presents. It was pale aqua, with preposterous splashes of tropical flowers, a suit intended for a much more flamboyant woman.

But Matty loved the suit. She loved it, and she loved the flirty sarong that tied just under her belly button. She felt like someone else when she wore it, someone coolly self-possessed and hotly sensuous. Someone a man like Damon just might take a second look at, even if he hadn't been forced to find a wife.

She combed her hair, but denied herself a glance in the mirror. The temptation to change into something less revealing was already too great.

He was waiting right where he'd said he would be. His gaze traveled over her as if it had a mind of its own. He was not a man who ogled women.

She felt ogled. Deliciously so.

"Well." He cleared his throat. "That's... You look..." He grinned. "I'll bet you know how you look."

She was glad the light in the hallway was dim. "Like someone who needs a swim. I'd race you to the pool, but I bet you'd win."

"Oh, I don't know. I'd probably like the view from behind too much."

She couldn't do anything but smile.

She was still smiling—grinning, in fact—when they reached the pool. The night was warm velvet, lush and damp against her skin, and stirred by a tropical breeze scented with jasmine.

"I love the sounds here at night. The wind rustling in the trees, the insect nocturnes, the slap of waves against the shore." She untied her sarong and let it drop to the grass. "I didn't know any place could be this peaceful." She turned toward Damon. "I feel like I'm in another world."

He was standing absolutely still, watching her. She stopped and watched him, too. They were in paradise, alone, and for once there seemed to be very little separating them.

"Maybe I need to be reminded how perfect it is," Damon

said. "I get so involved in other things, sometimes I forget what really matters."

"I can understand that."

"Before tomorrow..." He paused, as if he were trying to find the right words. "Well, I just want to say thanks, Matty. Not just for coming here... Thanks for making this easy...." He shook his head. "That's definitely not the right word. It's better than easy. You've made it better than that."

She laughed, but she was shaken by the look in his eyes. "I haven't done much, Damon. I'm just trying to fit in."

Before she could move away, he rested his hands on her shoulders. His fingertips nestled together just under her hair. He pressed them lightly against her nape, and his thumbs rose to stroke feather-light caresses along her jaw. "You fit in so well that sometimes I forget you're here. Then I catch a glimpse of you. Sometimes when you're with Heidi, sometimes when you're alone." He smiled. "And suddenly I wonder how I could ever have forgotten something so important. So...exceptional."

She sighed, and he lifted a eyebrow. "I really wish you wouldn't do that," he said.

"Do what?"

"Sigh like that..."

"Oh, I'm sorry. I didn't even realize."

"I realize enough for us both." He pulled her closer with a sigh of his own, and his hands slid slowly down her back to rest at her waist. "I think I realize more than you do about a lot of things."

She felt as if he'd swallowed her in his arms, as if the careful distance they'd kept from each other until now had been nothing more than a tantalizing preliminary. His body felt natural against hers, natural and right and so perfectly, utterly arousing that fire shot through all her limbs.

"I said I wasn't going to rush you into anything except marriage." His voice was low and sexy. "I meant every word of it. But will it be rushing you if I kiss you?"

"You've already kissed me." She sounded out of breath, as if she'd been swimming laps for hours.

"I was thinking of something more...intense."

His lips took hers with surprising hunger. His arms tightened around her, and he nearly lifted her off her feet. His hips were rock-solid against hers, leaving her in no doubt at all that Damon wanted her.

She was swept by a pleasure so vast that she was out of her league immediately. Her arms circled his neck, and she pressed her hips harder against his. Their lips parted, as if by mutual agreement. His tongue danced with hers, taking the kiss somewhere new and even better. She made a soft sound of delight, of breathless discovery as his fingers spread wide against her bottom and nudged her even closer. Their bodies clung, bare skin to bare skin, and their hearts seemed to synchronize and pound in the same rhythm.

"Matty..." He drew away just for a moment and whispered her name before he kissed her again, nibbling at her lips, coaxing even more passion from them. Through the swirling depths of desire she felt herself sinking slowly into a place she'd never been before, a place where she couldn't hide, couldn't pretend, couldn't be anything except what she was.

A woman who loved Damon Quinn. A woman who had always loved him, even years ago, when he hardly remembered her name.

That was the realization that finally made her pull away. Because before she gave in to the feelings suffusing her, she had to find a way to keep Damon from knowing exactly how she felt. She could agree to marry him, even agree to share his bed. But she could never take the last and most important step. She couldn't let Damon know that she loved him. The moment that she did, he would feel an obligation to remain by her side forever. And even though that was what she wanted most in the world, she could never live with that humiliation.

"Definitely more intense," she said, when she once ag
had the presence of mind to speak.

"You are a very tempting woman."

She wanted him to explain how that could be. She was just sensible, capable Matty, everyone's friend. Yet for that moment in Damon's arms, she had felt like the most desired woman imaginable. She understood human physiology, and some things couldn't be faked.

"It's only a matter of time before we share a bedroom," Damon said. "You say when, and you say whose, but it's only a matter of time."

"Yes." She didn't blink; she didn't look away.

In the moonlight his eyes were too dark to read, but his lips twisted into something resembling a grin. "Just for the record, can you give me a timetable?"

And how long would it take her to be sure she could make love to Damon Quinn without giving herself away? A day? A month? A lifetime? Would she ever be able to lie in his arms and keep him from knowing how completely she adored him?

"The other side of tomorrow," she said. She couldn't help herself. She reached up to cup his cheek. His skin was warm against her palm, a day's growth of whiskers rough against her fingertips.

He covered her hand and held it in place for a moment. Then he turned away. "Let's take that swim. I need it more than ever."

She let him slip into the water. And when he was already swimming laps, she slipped into the water, too.

The morning of the wedding dawned with a sizzle. Rain fell softly in the earliest hours, then the sun came out with enough force to steam Inspiration's windows. By noon the inhabitants were steaming, but by three a breeze from the north had cooled the air, and the rest of the afternoon was nearly perfect.

Matty spent the morning taking care of Heidi. Normally a bride spent the day preparing both physically and mentally for the day and night to come, but Matty gave little thought to it. What exactly did one need to prepare just to say a quick "o" and sign the requisite documents? She and Damon would exchange rings. She supposed that could be worked into whatever ceremony the marriage officer performed, but she wasn't sure they would bother with repeating vows. She envisioned the ceremony as swifter than that.

She put Heidi down for a nap after lunch and wandered upstairs to think about what she would wear for the wedding. Last night by the pool Damon had mentioned casually that he was going to be busy with other things for most of today and would prefer a late-afternoon ceremony. The marriage officer would be coming in some time before then, and since he was spending the night on Inspiration, they could have the wedding whenever the spirit moved them.

She wasn't a completely atypical bride. She had thought about what to wear, although not for the usual reasons. Her own mother, who had died when Matty was a toddler, had been delicate and petite, and her wedding dress, even if Matty had chosen to wear something so formal, was three sizes too small. Her friends back home had expounded at length about what would be appropriate for the occasion. Liza had thought that Matty should buy a dressy white suit, while Felicity had preferred a more daring pearl-studded cocktail dress.

Matty had used her own good judgment. On a solo shopping trip she had seen a full-skirted dress of cream-colored Mexican cotton with a scooped neckline embroidered in pastel flowers. She had bought a wide striped sash in the same pastels to tie at her waist and strappy sandals that tied around her ankles. At the time she had thought the dress was festive but casual, the perfect garb for a wedding in the tropics. Now she wondered if it was too festive. She could almost imagine Damon attending the ceremony in his shorts. She supposed he wouldn't, that he would be more thoughtful than that and at least wear his sportscoat, but the image stayed with her as she gazed at the dress.

She didn't want to appear silly and sentimental. But neither did she want to pretend this was a day like any other.

The decision was interrupted by shouts somewhere outside her window. She stepped out to her balcony and leaned over the railing to see if she could find out what was going on. In the distance she saw a boat heading straight for the cay. Actually, *boat* was an understatement. *Yacht* was the appropriate term. *Big yacht* would not be a redundancy.

"Holy cow."

She knew that the Exumas were a yachtsman's paradise. On her walks with Heidi she had seen some fabulous boats in the distance, but until today she hadn't seen one this close.

Minutes later she emerged from the house and headed for the beach. She could see a barefoot Kevin in torn cutoffs and no shirt watching the yacht draw closer, and she joined him.

"Now that's a boat," she said.

"The *Crown Sable*."

She mulled that over. "It's been here before?" Even Superman might have trouble reading the yacht's name from this distance.

"It's Arthur's."

"Ohh…" She gazed at the yacht in appreciation. The *Crown Sable* had the characteristic pointed prow and graceful lines of other boats of her type, but she looked as if every inch of her extravagant exterior had been constructed of the finest woods by the finest craftsmen. She rose from the water like a sailor's finest dream, proud and haughty and eminently worthy of a prince or sultan.

"Sometimes he flies. Sometimes he sails." Kevin shrugged.

Matty was pleased that Kevin hadn't moved away the moment he saw her. They were even having a conversation. "I wonder if Damon knew Arthur was coming? Maybe he'll want to postpone the ceremony and spend his time entertaining Arthur."

"That would be pretty stupid. Arthur's here for the wedding."

"You mean, Damon told him?"

"No, Arthur's got telepathy!" Kevin shot Matty a disgusted look.

"Ouch. Sorry. That was pretty dumb, wasn't it?"

"It'll be a while before they get here. They'll anchor out there in deep water and take the dinghy in."

"They?" Matty was afraid she was asking another stupid question, but since she was hopeless in Kevin's eyes anyway, one question more or less hardly mattered.

"Yeah. They." Kevin turned his back on her and started down the beach.

"Who are 'they'?" she called after him.

"The people Arthur's got with him." He shook his head in disgust. "Jeez…"

Matty wondered who else was around to fill her in on the information she was missing. Damon hadn't even joined them for lunch, which was a lucky break for him, since Nanny had served a fish stew that had pickled Matty's insides. Despite what seemed to be an excess of energy on the other side of the kitchen door, Nanny's cooking had gotten worse in the past two days.

Nanny's cooking had gotten worse, but her manners had gotten better. Since their last conversation about Heidi's care she had stopped speaking to Matty almost entirely, which was a definite step in the right direction. Despite that, Matty headed for the kitchen to see if she could find out what was going on.

"Nanny?" She opened the kitchen door and poked her head through the doorway. "Nanny?"

Nanny was gone, probably in her room sticking pins into Nurse Nancy dolls. The kitchen sparkled, and not a smidgen of food was in sight. Dinner looked like a long shot. Matty gave up trying to find out who else, besides Arthur, might be coming, and went back upstairs to take a shower and wash her hair. At least there were going to be guests, whoever they were. She just hoped they planned to eat on the yacht.

A half hour later she was drying her hair in the bathroom when somebody knocked. Since Nanny and Kevin used the bathroom downstairs, and Damon had one attached to his room, she couldn't imagine who might be on the other side of the door. Pulling her bathrobe tighter around her, she opened the door a crack and stared.

"Felicity?"

"Surprise!" Felicity pushed the door wide, and Matty saw that Liza was standing just behind her.

"Liza? What are you doing here? You said you couldn't come! You said—"

"We lied," they said together as the three of them fell into one another's arms.

"But how?" Matty asked at last, when they were back in her room and the door was closed behind them. "How on earth did you get here so fast?"

Liza circled the room touching everything in sight. "We were already in Nassau last night when we called you. We flew in yesterday afternoon. Arthur made the arrangements. He has a couple of friends of Damon's with him, too. It's going to be a par-ty!"

"This place is unbelievable," Felicity said. "Can we come live here, too? Pretty please?"

"This is just too good to be true." Matty stared at her friends. Only a week had passed since she had said goodbye to them, but enough had happened to fill months of conversation.

"Your Damon is quite a mover and shaker," Liza said, picking up a silver box on Matty's dresser. "When he plans a wedding, he plans a wedding."

"Damon? But I thought you said Arthur—"

"Arthur did the legwork," Felicity said. "Damon told him what he wanted. Arthur has more money than the queen of England, by the way. I checked. The price of this island was just pocket change. And he treats the *Crown Sable* like it's an old junk Chevy."

"Damon arranged this?" Matty tried to absorb that. Damon, who had seemed as blasé about marriage as a man could possibly be, had asked Arthur Sable, one of the richest men in the world, to bring her friends to Inspiration Cay. Just to please her.

"Matty, you're crying...." Liza thumped down on the bed beside her. "Why are you crying?"

"Damon did this. For me."

"And why wouldn't he? By now he knows what a lucky man he is. He's just making sure you're happy. And well he should."

"There's really going to be a wedding."

"There had better be," Felicity said. "I spent forty bucks on a new manicure. If you don't marry him, I'll have to marry somebody just to get my money's worth." Her eyes lit up, and she smiled slyly. "Maybe even Arthur."

"Matty?" Damon held out his arm, and Matty moved down Inspiration's front steps to tuck her arm through his. The sun was sinking toward the horizon. Enough wispy clouds adorned the sky to guarantee that the sunset was going to be a beautiful one.

Matty could feel Liza and Felicity walking behind her. The two women were naturally beautiful, but they had carefully, thoughtfully, chosen not to upstage the bride. Liza wore a conservative taupe suit and Felicity a simple blue dress.

Matty wasn't dressed simply at all. The Mexican cotton dress was offset perfectly by a bridal wreath of orange blossoms, sprays of baby's breath and pale yellow rosebuds. Shimmering ribbons trailed down her back, as well as from the matching bouquet that Damon had sent up to her room just before she came downstairs. Felicity had done her hair; Liza had done her makeup. She wasn't sure how she looked, but she felt beautiful.

She had never felt this beautiful before.

"Where are we going?" As she and Damon strolled down the path, she smiled tentatively at the small group of people, three men and a woman, whom she hadn't yet met. Nanny in a flowered dress and Kevin in a white shirt and tie were standing with them, watching.

"You'll see."

"Thank you."

He squeezed her hand. "Those are my words to say."

"Heidi looks adorable." Someone, Matty wasn't certain

who, had dressed the baby in enough white ruffles to make her look like a wedding cake. Nanny had the baby over her shoulder.

"She's not screaming. That's particularly adorable."

Matty fell silent, the immensity of what they were about to do seeping through the excitement of the day. Just as she began to question this decision for the last time, she heard music. "Oh, listen. Where's that coming from?"

Damon turned her toward a path that led to the western portion of the island. "I'd say this way. Shall we see?"

The rest of the walk seemed as if it passed in seconds. They crested the small hill that was the only barrier to the ocean and looked down on the beach below. The old latticework gazebo had been freshly painted white and entwined with flowers. To the right of the gazebo a four-piece reggae band in Caribbean-bright clothing was playing a raucous steel drum prelude. To the left, chairs garlanded with more flowers awaited the guests.

"Damon." She turned toward him, her eyes sparkling. "It's beautiful."

"Not bad, huh?"

"But you didn't have to do all this. You really didn't."

"I think I did."

She could hear the others following a short distance behind them. She wasn't married to this man yet. No one had told her she could kiss the groom. But she rose on her tiptoes and kissed him anyway.

Behind her, the others burst into applause.

"Let's do it," Damon said.

"I'm right beside you."

He guided her toward the gazebo where an older man in a dark suit waited to marry them.

Chapter Seven

Matty looked down at the new wedding ring gracing the third finger of her left hand. She was married. She was a stepmother.

She was married to Damon Quinn.

"Looks great, doesn't it?" Liza gave Matty a huge hug, one of many they'd exchanged that day. "You know, Damon's a lot more gorgeous than I remembered. I should never have showed you that article. I should have written him myself."

"What on earth have I done?"

Liza grinned. "You've married yourself a genius who looks like he ought to be starring in a 007 movie. I don't know, Matty, it could be worse."

The band was playing a particularly energetic version of "Hot, Hot, Hot," and Felicity and Arthur were doing something that looked like the bunny hop down on the beach. The crew from Arthur's yacht were helping Nanny and Kevin set up a feast on tables not far away. Now Matty knew exactly what Nanny had been doing for the past two days. The thought gave her cold chills.

"Be happy," Liza said, giving Matty's shoulders a squeeze. "Now, go find your husband."

Husband. The word sounded as if it didn't belong in Matty's vocabulary. No matter what their reasons, she and Damon were now legally husband and wife. And her husband was off somewhere with their daughter, searching for a clean diaper.

More of the crew were setting up torches along the perimeter of the party site. The pleasant tang of smoke and citronella filled the air, and Matty complimented them as she wound her way up the hillside to find Damon. She found him on the grass with his back to a palm tree, a sweeter-smelling Heidi balanced on his knees.

Her heart beat a little faster. Damon belonged to her now, at least legally. It seemed impossible. This man, who made every nerve in her body tingle whenever he was within a one-mile radius, belonged to her.

He looked up and smiled at her, and her palms began to sweat.

"Caught you," she said. "I just wanted to see if there was something I should be doing."

"Not a thing." He pushed himself upright, swinging Heidi in the air as he did. She crowed loudly, as if to ask him to do it all over again.

"She's still not screaming," Matty said. "Maybe that's a good omen."

"I'll take what I can get for whatever reason." He turned from his daughter to his new wife. "Are you having fun, Matty?"

"It seems so odd...."

"To what? Be the center of attention for once?"

"Something like that."

"Enjoy it. You deserve it."

"Actually it's 'we.' We're the center of attention."

"I'm glad Arthur was able to arrange getting Liza and Felicity here. They obviously think the world of you."

"Mutual. And your friends are wonderful."

Matty wasn't just being polite. Damon's friends really did seem wonderful. Arthur Sable, lanky, tanned and in his late sixties, seemed to have the energy of a younger man and the wisdom of an older one. He had a pirate's twinkle in his blue eyes and the easy manners of someone who owned a fair portion of Mother Earth. He had brushed off Matty's thank-yous with a good-natured wave of his hand, claiming that he'd done what he'd done because it was fun and for no other reason.

Shelton and Clara Ames were friends of Damon's from the hospital where he'd worked before Arthur had helped him move his research to Inspiration. Shelton was an oncologist who was fascinated by Damon's research, and Clara was a professional fundraiser.

"Shelton and Clara were the ones to put Arthur in touch with me in the first place," Damon said, swinging Heidi in his arms. "I wouldn't be here if it weren't for them."

"They believe in you for good reasons."

"Arthur's wife died about three years ago. Ovarian cancer. Now he's dedicated his life to finding a cure. He thinks I'm a step in the right direction."

As he explained, Damon's eyes had gone from warm to bleak. She and Damon had hardly talked in the last few days, but Matty knew he was unhappy with the way his experiments were progressing.

"You *are* a step in the right direction." She held out her arms for Heidi. "But it's a long, grim battle, and it doesn't always go well. All you can do is keep on plugging."

"Well, that'll be easier now."

"I'll be around to take care of Heidi. That should give you some concentrated time to work."

"That's not what I meant...."

She looked into his eyes as he swung Heidi into her arms. "No?"

"I meant that having you here, having you believe in me..." He shrugged.

Nothing that had happened that day had been better than this. "Really?" she asked softly.

"You're making a difference here, Matty. I doubt that you can see it yet, but you are."

"If it's true, I'm glad."

She wasn't sure what was going to happen next. She almost thought that Damon was going to kiss her. Then someone shouted from behind them.

"Hey! You two come and dance. They've promised to play something slow."

Matty turned to find Felicity grinning at them and gesturing. She faced Damon again. "I'm sorry. They insist on making this seem like a real—" She stopped herself just in time. "Like a wild and crazy party. Do you mind too much?"

"I think I can handle a dance. And in case you haven't noticed yet, it *is* a real wedding. That's a ring on your finger." He held up his own. "There's one on mine. And now, if you decide you want out of this arrangement, it's going to take a real divorce to make it happen." He smiled to soften his words. "So let's have a *real* good time, shall we?"

"I'm sorry."

"No more apologies."

"Watch it. You're asking me to cut out a large chunk of who I am."

When Matty and Damon appeared over the rise the band struck up Bob Marley's "No Woman No Cry." The musicians kept the reggae beat, but slowed it a little, and Matty fell into rhythm with Damon the moment he pulled her into his arms.

She stayed there for the next song, too, an old Harry Belafonte ballad, "Scarlet Ribbons," that her father had sung to her as a little girl.

"You have to learn this one, Damon," she said. "You have to sing it to Heidi. It's a family tradition."

"Oh?" He leaned back to look at her. "Your father?"

She nodded. Her throat felt strangely clogged. "It's odd they would choose this song when there are so many. It was Daddy's favorite."

"Maybe it's not so odd. Maybe he's watching over you today."

"That doesn't sound like something a scientist would say."

"I consider everything I don't understand to be a miracle. And that means I believe in a lot of miracles."

She believed in miracles, too. It was a miracle that she was standing in Damon's arms, swaying to the song her father had loved best. It was a miracle that Heidi was cooing and gurgling on the sidelines. The day was a miracle. Her life was quickly turning into a miracle.

No matter what happened next, no matter what happened in the future, she would believe in miracles until the day she died.

The wedding banquet was spectacular. Damon had told Matty that when Nanny's cooking was good, no one's was better. As if she had set out to prove that she still had what it took, Nanny had planned and carried out a meal that any gourmet chef would have been proud to claim.

Matty sampled grouper steamed in a spicy tomato sauce, peppery conch salad tangy with lime, Bahamian fried chicken with the perfect flash of volatile bird peppers, crawfish thermidor and tiny black pigeon peas cooked with white rice and a variety of herbs. For dessert there was guava duff with a thick, sweet rum-and-butter sauce. And that was only to hold them until they could all board Arthur's yacht, where his chef had spent the day putting the final touches on a traditional wedding cake.

Before they'd sat down to eat, someone had thrust a Goombay smash into one of Matty's hands and a Bahama Mama into the other. Damon had gently pried them loose after she'd had a few sips of each. "I don't want you sending any more letters," he'd said.

She'd looked down her nose at him, confidence fueled by those tiny sips of rum. "And I was just beginning to develop my writing style...."

"I think it's my husbandly duty to make sure you don't develop a splitting headache."

"Darn. This time I was going after a millionaire."

"The way Arthur's been watching you, you wouldn't have to go too far."

She frowned, and Damon laughed. "He likes you. He told me so. He said you remind him of Karen."

"His wife?"

"It's quite a compliment, Matty."

After the meal, the band struck up again, and someone, Felicity, Matty suspected, demanded that they try the limbo. One makeshift pole, more loud music and much louder laughter later, a scowling Kevin was declared the indisputable limbo champion of Inspiration Cay.

As everyone settled into a mellower mood and champagne was served, Arthur held up his glass in toast. The band had finished their final set and gone off for a swim, and the only sounds were waves and the chirping of crickets.

"Here's to Matty and Damon," Arthur said.

Everyone held up their glasses, and Damon took Matty's hand as if they had been lovers forever.

"To the happiness that comes from knowing you've chosen well," Arthur finished.

Matty thought about all the things Arthur could have said that wouldn't have been appropriate. But this toast was perfect. Because she and Damon *had* chosen well. Under the circumstances, they had done what was right for each of them, and for Heidi.

"Now, to the *Crown Sable*," Arthur said when they'd all drained their glasses.

"What about Heidi?" Matty asked as everyone got to their feet. The baby had been blithely sleeping against the limbo champion's shoulder for the better part of twenty minutes.

"Nanny's going to take her back to the house. She and Kevin don't want to go for a sail."

"Are you sure you want to go?"

"Absolutely."

Matty was excited about seeing the yacht and too keyed up to give in to the exhaustion of a long day. She was also glad that she could postpone the moment when she went into her bedroom and Damon went into his. She knew that was silly. She and Damon had an agreement. When and if she was ready to sleep in his bed, she was welcome. Until then, he wouldn't push her.

But part of her wished she could talk about this arrangement with Liza and Felicity, who would listen carefully before they told her she was just plain nuts. She wished someone she trusted would convince her she was making a mistake. As the evening progressed, she had found herself yearning more and more to throw caution to the jasmine-scented winds and climb into bed with her husband tonight. No one could fault her if she did. She was a married woman, and sex was usually part of the bargain.

"Why so pensive, Mattolina?"

She lifted her head and gazed into Damon's eyes. "What did you call me?"

"Mattolina. That's your name, isn't it?"

She blushed a little. "Well, yes." There had been no way of keeping that particular secret. She'd had to sign all the wedding papers with her official name, and Damon had promised to love and honor Mattolina Stewart, not Matty.

"It's a beautiful name. Why don't you use it?"

She didn't use it because it had always seemed too effusively fanciful. It was a dreamer's name, a passionate, opera-heroine name that had always seemed too lush and provocative for a woman who was seldom noticed.

"Matty was easier," she said, after too many moments.

"Did your father call you Mattolina?"

"Yes. It means woodlark, in Italian. He loved Italy. He always said he would take me there."

"But he didn't?"

"He spent years working on a novel that was going to take us around the world." She smiled. "It's a wonderful, memorable book."

"He never sold it?"

"No. He hoped to. Right up until the moment he couldn't

hope anymore. But it was our entertainment, planning that trip. He taught me French and Italian. We went to art museums and lectures to prepare. In the end, it didn't matter that we never made the trip. I have those memories, and they're better.''

"You know what it's liked to be loved, don't you?"

"Yes." Her voice sounded breathy to her own ears. "And to love. I know that nothing else matters very much if you have love in your life."

He didn't respond, and she wondered if he thought that she was already regretting their marriage. Then he brushed a knuckle against her cheek. "Love comes in a variety of forms, Mattolina. You might just find it again."

She wondered what he would do if she told him that love was standing right in front of her.

The *Crown Sable*'s captain knew the waters around Inspiration Cay as if he'd personally charted each reef and sand bar. The yacht glided gracefully through the moon-silvered water as if its mission was to slip between waves without disturbing a molecule of sea foam.

The masterpiece of a wedding cake was nothing more than crumbs on a linen tablecloth, and half-filled champagne glasses sat unattended on teak and rosewood furniture. The party had settled down to a murmur and a sigh.

Someone had filled the stereo system with old recordings by Lena Horne and Billie Holiday. Matty stood against the railing listening to Lena sing "Stormy Weather." People had drifted to different parts of the boat, and she had been alone just long enough to relive the day.

"The bride's by herself?"

Matty made room at the railing for Arthur. "I'm just enjoying the air. This is so wonderful. I can't thank you enough."

"I understand not all your voyages have been this pleasant."

She smiled. "Damon's been telling tales. I hope he didn't relay every gory detail."

"He simply said that sailing didn't always agree with you and we should stay close to shore."

"I'm fine as long as the water's calm." She turned back to stare over the ocean. "Do you spend much time on the *Crown Sable?*"

"Short trips, mostly. As long as a week sometimes. Seldom more."

"Too little to do?"

"Too lonely." He stared at a splash of moonlight on the water. "I bought the boat for my wife. Karen didn't need a house. She would have been happy living on the *Sable* year round, or on something less pretentious. She was a very unpretentious lady."

"Damon told me that she died three years ago."

"He tells me that you lost your father about the same time."

"I'm a nurse. I've watched dozens of people slip in and out of life. But it's very different when it happens to someone you love, isn't it?"

"I have a thousand friends." He laughed, not cynically, but wearily. "Anyone with as much money as I have always has a thousand friends. But since Karen died, I feel like I'm the only person left in the world."

"You're not, you know. You're loved for more than your money. You make a difference in people's lives."

"The first time I met Damon, I recognized a kindred spirit. He hasn't suffered loss. We're not the same in that way. But he feels alone, too. He's always been separated from others by his intellect, his devotion to learning. Of course, now that Heidi's in the picture, that's changed. And, of course, he really doesn't know what to do with what he's feeling because it's so new."

"He adores her. It's a powerful thing to see."

"And you adore him."

She remained silent. Finally she sighed. "So it's that obvious."

"You could have denied it."

"I'm not a convincing liar. I'd just rather that Damon not know."

"Why?"

She faced him, watching the wind toss his gray hair back from his forehead. "Damon married me as a business arrangement. I think he genuinely likes me, which is wonderful. But I think if he knew that my emotions are already involved, he'd be torn with guilt about what he's done."

"What are you hoping for, Matty?"

She considered the question, as she'd considered it before. "A good life together as long as it lasts. I guess I hope that we'll be so compatible he won't feel a need for more. That even when Heidi's unequivocally his, he won't grow restless and ask me to free him."

"That's the most you want?"

"That's the most I'll let myself hope for."

"You so badly underestimate your own charm. And you underestimate Damon. He's a bit slow when it comes to his emotions, but he's not hopeless."

"Damon, slow?" She laughed. "Well, I guess he can't be a genius at everything."

"Karen and I fell in love an inch at a time. She knew me before I had money. She was in love with someone else, and so was I. We were friends. We would seek each other out to talk about how fortunate we were that we'd found our true loves. One day we realized we were seeking each other out more than we were seeking out the so-called great loves of our lives. Until that day, neither of us had realized what was happening. Love doesn't always hit a man and a woman over the head. Sometimes it's like a sledgehammer, but more often it's like a tide rising around you."

"I like that."

"See that you remember it." He patted her hand awkwardly. "I like you, Matty. And I like your friends. But please tell Felicity I'm too old for her."

"Don't worry. She's not serious. She's just a terrible flirt. I'll bet she winked at the doctor when he delivered her."

He chuckled as he disappeared into the shadows.

Matty wasn't alone long. Just as the yacht began to slow to a stop, Damon joined her. "There you are. I've been looking for you."

"You could search all day and never find me. This is a glorious yacht. I explored for most of an hour, and I'm not sure I've seen every bit of it."

"Then you enjoyed the sail?"

"It was the best." She hooked her elbow over the railing so she was facing him. "How about you?"

"Amazingly peaceful. A happy ending to a happy day."

"Now back to the real world." She shook her head mournfully. "Back to a mansion in paradise and white sand beaches. Palm trees and flowers. Spectacular sunsets. A baby with the cutest smile in the Exumas. Life's tough."

"Just the Exumas?"

"The Northern Hemisphere?"

"Closer." He moved a little closer. "Have I told you how lovely you look today?"

The compliment rippled along her skin like a warm caress. "Thank you. You look wonderful in that suit."

"Do you suppose we look married now?"

"What does married look like?"

"I don't know. Contented? Distraught?" He grinned. "Take your choice."

She felt the grin deep inside her. Everything about Damon seemed to be connected to some network of nerves and reactions. "I suppose I'd have to go with satisfied," she said. "Certainly not distraught. And we haven't been married long enough to be contented. I suspect that takes a while."

"I'm not sure satisfied is the right word at all."

Too late she realized what he meant. She elaborated. "Satisfied that we've done the best thing under the circumstances."

"Other kinds of satisfaction come with marriage. If a couple is lucky…and compatible."

She refused to dance around the subject any longer. "I have trouble believing physical satisfaction is going to be a problem between us."

"I'm glad to hear it."

Before she could think of some way of changing the subject, she heard the roar of the dinghy's motor somewhere to the port side of the yacht. "It sounds like the party's ending. Time to go ashore."

Damon frowned. "That's odd. Everyone else is staying on board for the night. You and I are the only ones who are supposed to head back to Inspiration. Arthur asked me to tell him when we were ready to go."

"Maybe he's tired and wants to go to bed."

"Arthur? I doubt it. He sleeps about three hours a night."

"Maybe we should go and see?"

But that turned out to be unnecessary. A cloud of white foam ruffled the waves, and Matty turned to stare into the darkness at the blur of a dinghy heading for shore.

"Goodbye..." A chorus of voices shouted. "See you in the morning..."

Matty watched the boat disappearing toward shore. Her eyes widened as it grew smaller and smaller. Damon was absolutely silent behind her. Then he began to laugh.

"What's the opposite of shanghaied?" she asked in a small voice.

"Abandoned? Cast to the winds?"

"They've left us here for the night. We're alone."

"Probably not completely. There must be a skeleton crew on board. But I bet we won't see hide nor hair of them."

"You knew, didn't you?" She tried to look angry. She even managed to slap her hands on her hips. But her lips turned up to give her away.

"I swear I had no idea." He held up his hand. "Scout's honor."

"All this talk about physical satisfaction? You're sure you didn't plan it as a prelude to the sound of the dinghy disappearing?"

Play "Lucky Hearts" and you get...

YOURS FREE!

This lovely necklace will add glamour to your most elegant outfit!
Its cobra-link chain is a generous 18" long, and its lustrous
simulated cultured pearl is mounted in an attractive pendant! Best
of all, it's ABSOLUTELY FREE, just for accepting our NO-RISK offer.

...then continue your lucky streak with a sweetheart of a deal!

1. Play Lucky Hearts as instructed on the opposite page.

2. Send back this card and you'll receive brand-new Silhouette Special Edition® novels. These books have a cover price of $3.99 each, but they are yours to keep absolutely free.

3. There's no catch. You're under no obligation to buy anything. We charge nothing—ZERO—for your first shipment. And you don't have to make any minimum number of purchases—not even one!

4. The fact is thousands of readers enjoy receiving books by mail from the Silhouette Reader Service™. They like the convenience of home delivery...they like getting the best new novels BEFORE they're available in stores...and they love our discount prices!

5. We hope that after receiving your free books you'll want to remain a subscriber. But the choice is yours—to continue or cancel, any time at all! So why not take us up on our invitation, with no risk of any kind. You'll be glad you did!

The Silhouette Reader Service™—Here's how it works:

Accepting free books places you under no obligation to buy anything. You may keep the books and gift and return the shipping statement marked "cancel." If you do not cancel, about a month later we'll send you 6 additional novels and bill you just $3.34 each plus 25¢ delivery per book and applicable sales tax, if any.* That's the complete price—and compared to cover prices of $3.99 each—quite a bargain! You may cancel at any time, but if you choose to continue, every month we'll send you 6 more books, which you may either purchase at the discount price...or return to us and cancel your subscription.
*Terms and prices subject to change without notice. Sales tax applicable in N.Y.

If offer card is missing write to: Silhouette Reader Service, 3010 Walden Ave., P.O. Box 1867, Buffalo, NY 14240-1867

BUSINESS REPLY MAIL
FIRST-CLASS MAIL   PERMIT NO. 717   BUFFALO, NY

POSTAGE WILL BE PAID BY ADDRESSEE

SILHOUETTE READER SERVICE
3010 WALDEN AVE
PO BOX 1867
BUFFALO NY 14240-9952

NO POSTAGE
NECESSARY
IF MAILED
IN THE
UNITED STATES

"I promise. I had no idea. Of course I would have discouraged them."

"Of course."

"Alone." Damon obviously struggled not to smile. He shook his head. "What kind of friends do we have, Mattolina?"

"Outrageously romantic ones. How did you and I, practical to the bone, end up with friends like that?"

"Just luck." He stepped a little closer. "Come here."

"What about Heidi?"

"Oh, I think they can manage Heidi. Liza's a nurse, isn't she? And Nanny and Kevin know what to do. Even Arthur could give her a bottle if he had to."

"But she'll miss you."

"Heidi will be just fine. Come here...." He put his arms around her and pulled her against him. "You know, I've wanted to ask you something ever since I got your first letter."

"Please don't ever mention that letter again."

"You said that you had never forgotten the way I came to your rescue one day, and you wanted to return the favor. Do you remember that?"

"Damon, I was smashed. Nothing I said in that letter should be taken seriously."

"You said you wanted to marry me. You married me today."

"Except that."

"Mattolina..."

In the future Damon would get his way any time he called her Mattolina. Whenever he wanted anything from her, all he had to do was say her name in that sexy rumble. The handwriting was on the wall; she just hoped he hadn't realized it yet.

"You really don't remember, do you?" she said with a sigh.

"I really don't. I'm sorry, but I don't."

"It was my sophomore year. You were a senior." She looked down, but all she could see was his collarbone, and it didn't make a terrific audience. She looked back up at his face.

"I was heading home from school. It was late at night. I'd been working on a project in the biology building. I'd stayed later than I'd planned, and I wanted to get home to my father."

"Go on."

"It's silly, really."

"That's okay."

"Well, the quickest way home was down Fraternity Row. It was a Saturday night, and late enough for half the residents of the street to have gone through a keg or two. And they had. Believe me. There were bodies draped over every lilac and forsythia, bodies hanging over porch railings."

Damon rested his hands on her shoulders and began a slow massage. "Does that feel good?"

"Ummmm...."

"So then what happened?"

She tried to remember. His touch was wiping out her memory banks. "Well... I almost made it to the end of the street. Then a group of fraternity brothers, I don't even remember which fraternity now, blocked the sidewalk. And they told me that if I wanted to get by, I'd have to—" She frowned. "Does this sound familiar?"

"I'm sorry. No."

"They were drunk enough to forget they were really nice guys. They wanted me to unbutton my blouse. They started to get a little rough. Someone with more experience and confidence probably could have joked her way out of it. But I was tired and humiliated and near tears. And then you showed up, Damon."

His hands stilled. "I hope I kicked butt."

"You had me out of there in about two seconds flat. And you made the worst guy, the one who'd been manhandling me, apologize."

"They had no right to touch you."

He was angry. Something as warm as the tropical air bloomed inside her. "I don't think they really would have hurt me, they—"

"They had no right to touch you. No right at all. Don't

excuse them. You remembered it all these years. It was that important to you.''

"It was important to me because you came along and helped me. Back then, I was carrying a lot of weight by myself. And having someone help me when I needed it, well, it was new and wonderful. And I never forgot that you cared about someone you hardly knew, cared enough to risk getting in a fight. Just for me.''

"And you married me because of something I did all those years ago? Something I don't even remember?''

"No, I wrote you that silly letter because of it. I married you because you're Damon Quinn, and I believe in you. The man you are now and the man you were then.''

"Don't make me into some kind of hero.''

She saw the wariness in Damon's eyes, and too late she saw where it had come from. Last night beside the pool she had realized how dangerous it would be to let Damon know that she loved him. He had entered into this arrangement because he needed a wife. He had not asked for love. He wanted her in his life, and he wanted her in his bed. But he did not want her in his heart. That was something that he didn't understand or trust. Not now, perhaps not ever.

She had nearly given herself away.

"All right," she said lightly. "I won't. Exit one hero. But I'm still grateful you were there that night.''

"I'm here tonight, too. And we're alone.''

Damon did nothing else to woo her. He didn't pull her closer; he didn't bend his head to kiss her. He waited. Matty could feel his tension everywhere that his body rested against hers. His hands were like iron weights, and his breathing was carefully controlled.

She knew that she couldn't share a bed with Damon tonight. If she'd had any doubts, they'd been resolved by his reaction to her story. They were alone; they were married, but the day stood between them. She was Mrs. Damon Quinn. They had shared a nearly perfect wedding, despite circumstances that might have dictated otherwise. He had been kind, considerate, affectionate. And he wanted her. Miraculously, he wanted her. It would have been so easy to go to bed with him.

But not easy to pretend it meant less than it did.

"I need more time, Damon." She forced herself to stare into his eyes as she said the words. "I'm sorry. But as wonderful as this day has been, this is too soon for me. I have to have more time to put everything together. Can you understand?"

"Apparently our friends didn't."

"I know. I'm sure they would all think I'm crazy."

"No, careful." His hands dropped to his sides, and he took one step backwards so that they were no longer touching. "You have every right to wait until you're ready. I keep telling you that, and at the same time I keep pushing you. I'm sorry."

"Please, don't be."

"Maybe it's the moonlight."

"Maybe."

He turned as if to walk away; then he turned back. "It's not the moonlight, Mattolina."

"No?"

"No."

He turned away again and started toward the stairs to the guest cabins.

She watched him go with a heavy heart, but somewhere inside her, hope sparked and caught fire. It was all she had to warm her that night, but it was almost enough.

Chapter Eight

Nanny chewed on her pipe and glared at Matty, her bony arms folded across her chest. Matty had the grace to look guilty. She had been warned.

Nanny's foot began to tap, and the pipe disappeared into her pocket. "What'd I tell you about taking that baby with you this afternoon, Matty Quinn?"

Matty dug her toe into the scatter rug outside Heidi's room. "I'm not sure...."

"You know. You know, no question about it."

"Nanny, I just can't help myself."

Nanny's eyes narrowed into slits. "That's the problem, you know. You don't help yourself. That's the problem."

Matty folded Heidi closer in her arms. Nanny was perfectly capable of snatching the baby from her. "Look, please don't be mad. It's just such a beautiful afternoon. And she loves to be outside."

"Not'ing you love?"

"Well, sure. I love being here. I love Heidi." Matty offered her warmest smile. "I love your red snapper with peppers and mushrooms."

"You trying to git out of this. You t'ink I don't know."

"Nanny, I'll be fine, really."

Nanny looked as if she wasn't completely convinced, but her pursed lips unfroze one bit at a time until she was no longer frowning. "Just don't come to me, you git so tired you don't know what's what...."

"I promise."

Nanny marched off. Matty hoped that no one and nothing got in her way.

"I think she's beginning to like me," Matty whispered to Heidi. Heidi lit up the hallway with one of her ear-to-ear grins.

As impossible as it seemed, in the weeks since the wedding, Nanny *had* begun to warm up to Matty. The signs were subtle. The food had gotten better, and at times it was absolutely inspired. Morning coffee had improved, too, and no offers of medicinal teas had been forthcoming.

Best of all, Nanny no longer huffed and puffed around the house, looking for excuses to tell Matty she wasn't wanted there. She never missed an opportunity to give her opinion, but more and more often the opinion was not something calculated to set Matty on her ear.

"She thinks I'm doing too much," Matty told the beaming Heidi. "She wanted me to take the afternoon off. She doesn't know what my life used to be like, does she?"

Heidi wiggled her whole body in answer. Apparently she didn't think Matty was doing too much. In fact, she had thrived under Matty's care. And as each day passed, Matty fell more in love with her new stepdaughter. In fact the word "step" had disappeared from her vocabulary.

"Let's go, pumpkin. I know a perfect spot for a little girl's nap. Sea breezes. The sound of waves. If you ever move to the mainland, you won't be able to fall sleep."

"Matty, have you seen—" Damon stopped at the head of the stairs and peered at the two females as if they had materialized from the very air. "What was I looking for?"

"Now that I can't help you with." Matty took stock of her husband. He was wearing khaki shorts and a T-shirt advertising a George Town hotel. The right pocket of his shorts was turned inside out, as if he'd been searching for the elusive something that was missing.

"I know for a fact—" He stared just past her, frowning.

By now Matty had grown used to Damon's fits and starts. Judging by how rumpled his hair was, he was obviously thinking about his work. In fact, she was surprised to see him in the house at this time of day.

She started toward him. "Heidi and I are going for a walk. It's almost her nap time. If you remember what you're looking for, I'll be somewhere between the beach and the tennis courts."

"Tennis?" His frown deepened.

"Earth to Damon." She waved her hand in his face. "Your daughter and I are going for a walk. Look for us near the tennis courts if you remember what you wanted to ask me."

"Nanny told me you were taking the afternoon off."

She wasn't surprised he had finally snapped to attention. Nothing about Damon's thought processes surprised her anymore. "Nanny's idea. She thinks I work too hard. I think I don't work hard enough."

He shifted his weight so that he was blocking the hallway. She would have to make a point of moving around him. His gaze casually swept her, as if he was trying to decide who he should believe.

"Refurbishing the flower beds wasn't part of any agreement we made," he said, when his examination was finished. "Neither was trimming shrubs, painting sheds or fixing the plumbing in the downstairs powder room."

Matty realized her cheeks were growing warm. "What can I say? I'm amazingly handy."

"Nanny's right."

"No." She shifted Heidi into a more comfortable position. "Look, I've never lived a leisurely life. Before I moved here...married you, I had a very involving job and an old house that needed constant maintenance. Old habits die hard. I like staying busy. Heidi's a breeze to take care of, and there are only so many novels I can read in a week's time. I don't sew or paint." She favored him with a grin. "I guess my hobby's taking care of people. So let me."

"You miss your job."

She did, although she tried not to dwell on it. "I knew I would. I still chose to leave it and come here. And I'm fine. I'm finding lots to do to keep me busy."

"What happens when there are no more sheds to paint? And no more weeds?"

"There will always be weeds. And gradually Heidi will become more demanding."

"Please don't tell me that."

"You'll love every minute of it."

He didn't seem convinced, but his eyes began to fog again, and she could see him drifting back to wherever he'd been before the beginning of their conversation.

"We'll see you at dinner," Matty said. "We'll be the well-rested ones with the tans." She skirted him and made for the stairs, and in a few minutes she and Heidi were outside heading for what had once been gardens behind the tennis courts.

Heidi was the sole owner of two strollers and a pram, but Matty preferred to carry the baby in a soft carrier that rested against her breasts and midriff. Heidi loved to cuddle before she went to sleep. In fact, by the time they made it to the gardens, her chubby little legs had stopped kicking, and her cooing and gurgling had diminished to occasional snuffles.

Under a trio of crepe myrtles, Matty set up the woven baby bed she'd bought in Nassau and tucked Heidi in for the afternoon. The day was warm, but the breeze cooled the dappled shade to perfection.

Matty was getting used to perfection in everything except her personal life.

Half an hour later she was busily pruning a thicket of poinsettias when she heard a noise behind her. She turned, expecting to see Nanny or Kevin, only to find Arthur smiling at her.

"Arthur!" She dropped her shears and went into his arms for a hug.

"Matty Quinn, are you ever going to stop pretending you're my gardener?"

She still felt shock when someone called her Matty Quinn. Under the circumstances it had been sensible to take Damon's name, but since she still didn't feel as if she were married to him, the name always seemed like it should belong to someone else.

She rallied quickly. "You know I love this. I hope you really don't mind."

"Mind? How could I? You're turning a jungle into gardens again."

"Damon told me that you liked the jungle theme. I promise I'm just taming everything a little. Just enough so we can get in here and enjoy it."

"You can do anything you want. I don't really like jungle, I just didn't want to hire a gardener. I didn't want to put more burdens on Damon. A gardener would be one more person to supervise, and he's not here to run a household. He's here to continue his research."

"You're such a thoughtful man."

"Don't be silly. I'm thoroughly selfish. I'd like to have the cure for cancer attributed to my foresight in sponsoring Damon's research."

"Of course. I keep forgetting that's the only reason why you're so wonderfully kind."

He strolled over to peek at Heidi, whose sleeping face was scrunched into a frown. "I think she's grown in the last week. And she hardly looks like the same baby. Do you think she's going to look like her father?"

"Sometimes I think she looks like Damon. Something about the way her face is shaped. But it's so hard to tell."

"Karen and I wanted children. It just never happened. She wanted to adopt...." He shook his head. "I wish we had."

This wasn't the first time Matty had suspected that Arthur, despite all his money, was a lonely man. In the weeks since the wedding, he had come to visit half a dozen times. On her wedding night he had told her that he seldom took long voyages on the *Crown Sable* because the yacht was too lonely. But now she thought that most places were probably too lonely for Arthur.

Most places except Inspiration Cay.

"Until Heidi, I wasn't sure I would ever have a child of my own," Matty said. "She's wonderfully shareable. I think she'll need a grandfather from time to time. My father and Damon's are both gone, and Damon doesn't think that either of Gretchen's parents will want anything to do with Heidi unless they can have sole custody."

"Foolish, foolish people."

"Well, if it weren't for their foolishness, I wouldn't be here."

"Silver linings, Matty?"

"Something like that. Damon says I'm like Pollyanna on her best days."

"You're a breath of fresh air."

"Thank you."

"He's a lucky man, even though I don't think he realizes just how lucky yet."

Her cheeks grew warm for the second time that day. "He appreciates everything I do. He's very good about telling me."

"When he starts to appreciate what you are, we'll talk again." Arthur smiled to lighten his words. "I'm going up to the house for a nap. Heidi's inspired me. Will I see you at dinner tonight?"

"Bridge afterward? I've been reading up on bidding, though I'll never be as sharp as Kevin."

"But much more fun to talk to." He lifted a hand in farewell before he vanished into a newly liberated grove of pines.

She gazed after him, in no hurry to resume her war with the poinsettias.

Matty could pretend that she didn't know exactly what Arthur had meant about Damon, but she tried to be honest with herself, as well as with others. Damon did appreciate everything she did for him. He was unfailingly grateful for her help with Heidi, for her patience with Nanny and Kevin, for the way she had subtly taken over a number of household chores so that Nanny could concentrate on nagging and cooking.

But most of the time Damon looked straight through her. Just as he'd done today.

Every night, in the quietest hours, Matty asked herself again and again if things would be different if she and Damon had shared a "real" wedding night. Perhaps then he would have been forced to view their marriage as something more than a legal convenience and her as something more than a housekeeper and baby-sitter.

Yet even when the answer came back "yes," she still couldn't regret her decision to wait before they made love. She needed to know Damon better. She needed to be in control of what was happening to her, what she was feeling and how much of those feelings she allowed Damon to see. She had thought that restraint might come with time.

Instead she fell more hopelessly in love with him every day.

She was still standing in the same spot when Kevin entered the pine grove that Arthur had exited minutes ago. She waited silently without smiling in welcome.

Since the day she'd rescued him from his Nassau crime spree, she and Kevin had existed under a truce. He didn't throw her belongings in the ocean, and she didn't remind him that she had risked her spotless reputation to save his Irish-Cuban hide. They had never talked about the way she had fed his pilfered wallets into a mailbox, then made an anonymous telephone call to the closest police station to alert them. But she thought her stock had probably risen a little in Kevin's eyes just because she had proved that she could be nearly as devious as he if the situation merited.

He stopped a good six feet away. "Damon told me to find you."

Since Kevin usually began their encounters with a disclaimer, she nodded. "And?"

"Arthur's here. Damon wanted you to know."

"I saw Arthur already. But thanks. I've already promised him a game of bridge after dinner. You'll play, won't you?" Kevin, who was just learning the game, was already nearly as good as Arthur, who had earned a fair number of masters' points over the years.

He tossed his head. "Maybe."

She knew by now that "maybe" meant "yes." "Well, I hope so. You're teaching me a thing or two."

"Why do you do that?"

As usual when she was with Kevin, she was at a loss to understand him. "Do what?"

"Say things like that."

"What? Things about bridge?"

"You're always trying to make me feel better."

"Well, it's the truth, Kevin. You're so bright it's a pleasure to play with you. I am learning—"

"You don't have to like me!"

She considered that for a moment. "Well, you know," she said honestly, "sometimes I really don't. You work pretty hard at being unlovable. But when you forget to try so hard, you're a good guy. Then I really do like you."

"You just want Damon to think you like me."

She was silent again, considering that, too. "No, I don't think so." She shook her head. "The thing is, it really wouldn't matter to Damon. He doesn't pay that much attention to what's going on around him. As long as you and I aren't staging fistfights right in front of him, he probably doesn't know what's going on between us."

"Then you can stop being nice."

She had a strong feeling that Kevin really didn't want her to stop being nice. In fact, she almost wondered if he was fishing for something a little stronger. "I don't think I can manage that," she said. "The thing is, most of the time you're darned easy to be nice to. I think we're working on a friendship here. Maybe I'm wrong, but that's what I think."

"I don't need friends."

"I sure do." She held up her hands, palms to the sky. "I love Inspiration. I really do. But sometimes, well, it seems awfully small. You know?"

She didn't expect an answer, but before she could go on, he gave a reluctant nod.

"I had good friends at home," she said. "And now I'd like to have good friends here. That's the only way to make the island seem bigger."

Kevin scuffed his bare foot against the Bermuda grass growing in pathetic, untended tufts in the sandy soil. His face was a study in disbelief. "Is that why you helped me? That time in Nassau?"

She wondered if there would always be a gap of weeks before they discussed the things that mattered. "I helped you because you needed help. The street's no place for kids. Not ever. But if it happened again today? Or tomorrow? I guess I'd help you because I like you, and I don't want to see you get hurt. Not because you're a kid, but because you're Kevin."

"Right." He rolled his eyes.

She rolled her eyes in response. "Right! And don't you forget it."

He snorted before he turned and disappeared back the way he had come.

Matty wondered why, on an island populated by less than half a dozen people, they all had to be so incredibly complicated.

Damon was an erratic bridge player. He had been told he was absolutely brilliant when his mind was on the game and absolutely horrible when it wasn't.

Considering how well Kevin and Arthur were doing on the first rubber, he suspected he was in the second category tonight.

"Three hearts." Matty looked at him, her face carefully blank.

No one would ever call Matty a sneaky bridge player. She didn't signal her intentions with so much as a lifted brow. He wondered how she was at poker.

He wondered if she had ever played strip poker.

Arthur cleared his throat. "Damon? I passed."

The vision of Matty taking off her clothing, one item at a time, wouldn't leave Damon's mind. "Six spades."

"Six?" Matty's voice emerged as a squeak.

"Trying to tell him something, Matty?" Arthur teased.

"It's a little late to tell him anything, don't you think?" Matty looked down at her hand, then back up at Damon.

"Double," Kevin said. He looked to Arthur as if for support.

"Good boy," Arthur said with a big smile. "Matty, it's to you."

Damon knew he'd had it. Kevin's "double" meant that he and Arthur had some important cards. Matty and Damon were probably not going to take enough tricks. In fact, Damon's cards would have told him the same thing. If he'd just been paying attention to them…

"Pass," Matty said. Arthur passed, too.

"Pass," Damon said, resigned to losing another hand.

"Well, I'm glad you're the one playing it, big boy," Matty told Damon, after Kevin led the ace of spades, now the highest card in the hand. Since she was the dummy for this round and wouldn't be playing, she laid down her cards so that Damon could play them, too. "Let's see you pull this one out of the hat."

Damon heard the challenge in her voice. Now that she wasn't bidding, she was signalling her feelings without restraint. He looked down at her hand, visible to everyone. "Lord…"

She folded her arms. "I opened with three hearts. Lots of hearts and virtually no points. A signal to you not to raise my bid. Right? Or are you playing a different convention than the rest of us?''

"Bridge brings out the worst in people, Kevin," Arthur said. "Watch and learn. Even someone as nice as Matty turns into a tiger at the bridge table."

"Watch and learn, Mattolina," Damon said.

"Learn what?" she asked sweetly. "Black magic?"

"There are a number of things you could learn from me, little woodlark." He raised a brow and stared her down. When the first telltale color began to rise in her cheeks, he looked down at his cards. Suddenly the game took on new meaning.

Since Kevin had taken the first trick, it was his turn to lead again. "Maybe I don't understand," Kevin said with a nasty gleam in his eye. "But if you lose even one more trick, you've lost the whole hand, Damon. Right?"

"Play," Damon said.

Kevin played the ace of clubs. The round progressed until it was Damon's turn, then he trumped Kevin's ace from his hand, winning the trick. Matty whistled. "Lucky for you, you were out of clubs, huh?"

"Watch and learn, Mattolina."

Damon took the next eight tricks, making liberal use of Matty's hearts. He had paid close attention to every card that had fallen so far. Now he calculated his chances of winning. With a less experienced opponent than Arthur, the odds were about even. But Arthur had an astounding memory. He, too, knew exactly which cards had been played.

"Gee, am I imagining things, or aren't you supposed to play another card?" Kevin said sarcastically. The sarcasm didn't fool Damon. The boy was having the time of his life. In another day and age he might have been a riverboat gambler.

Damon took his best chance.

Kevin cursed softly under his breath, and for once Damon didn't lecture him. The occasion almost warranted it. When the cards came around to Damon again, he had won that trick, too.

"Two to go," Matty said.

"Well, at least I won't have to teach you to count." Damon let his gaze linger on her lips. The tip of her tongue darted out to wet them nervously. He smiled, but not so that she could see. He made his final choice and laid down his next to last card. The play progressed to Arthur.

And Arthur played the wrong card.

For a moment Damon was elated. The game was his now. Arthur had made the wrong choice, and the game was Damon's.

Except that Arthur never made a wrong choice. Damon glanced at Arthur's face and saw guilt written all over it. Arthur had let him win. He would deny it until his dying day, but he had let Damon take the hand.

"I don't believe it. You're going to do it," Kevin said, when Damon played his card. "You're going to make your bid."

"A small slam. Doubled," Damon reminded him. "Add up those points in your head, genius."

"Damn."

"Mattolina?" Damon gave his partner, his wife, a wry smile. "Learn anything?"

She leaned forward. "Absolutely," she said in her most seductive voice.

Kevin's chair screeched against the wood floor. "Jeez, I'm out of here. I'm getting a Coke."

Arthur's chair made the same sound. "I'm opening a new bottle of Scotch."

Matty and Damon stared at each other until the others had left the room.

"And what did you learn?" Damon said.

"I learned that skill and intelligence can overcome the worst odds." She looked properly humbled, but for only the briefest moment. "Oh, and I forgot. I learned that men will stick together no matter what, even if one of them has to lose to do it."

He contained his smile again. "Now why would Arthur be willing to lose?"

"Because he wants you to teach me that lesson you promised?"

"Mattolina..." He shook his head. "You're so suspicious."

"I'm going to teach Nanny to play bridge and even out the odds here."

She looked as if she was going to rise, and before he knew what he was doing, he reached for her hand so that she couldn't. He didn't want her to go. "Maybe we men do stick together. But you're the one Arthur comes to see. He never came this often before."

She settled back into her chair, but he didn't drop her hand. "Arthur knows I like him."

"And that's all it takes? Because I've wondered how you do it. Everyone here is falling under your spell."

"Everyone?"

He realized that his heart was beating faster. He had worked hard since the night of their wedding to put Matty out of his thoughts. He had concentrated on his work, and when they were together, he had made certain there was no opportunity for intimacy. But more and more often he had found himself staring at her when she wasn't watching him. He knew the exact curves of her breasts and hips, the sleek length of her legs, the way her hair fell feather-soft against her neck when she turned her head. And even the most relentless self-control didn't extend to his dream life.

He dreamed of Matty nearly every night.

"Nanny tells me she'd be happy to watch Heidi one afternoon this week." Damon slipped his fingers between hers, and she didn't pull away.

"Oh? What for? Part of her campaign to make me relax?"

"Part of my campaign. I've wrapped up another round of experiments—" He shook his head at her expectant expression. "Nothing new and nothing good. But I need a break, too. How about going snorkeling with me tomorrow?"

"Snorkeling? Kevin told me there wasn't much to see off Inspiration."

"I wasn't talking about Inspiration. We'll take the boat, a picnic. I know a perfect place to go."

"Maybe Arthur and Kevin would like to go with us."

"I'm not inviting Arthur and Kevin. Just you."

She looked down at their hands. He wished he could hear her thoughts. He wished she would talk about her thoughts and feelings. But in too many ways Matty was still a stranger.

"I'd like that, Damon." Her gaze traveled back to his eyes.

"Good." He squeezed her hand and wished he were touching more of her.

The stomping of feet announced that Kevin was back. "You two lovebirds ready to get beaten once and for all? That last hand was nothing but luck." He belched in emphasis.

"My partner and I are going to take you for everything you've got," Damon said. "From this moment on, we are in perfect tune with each other."

Kevin cupped a hand behind his ear as if listening for something. "Is that what all that screeching's about?"

"Perfect tune," Matty said. "Watch and learn, Kevin. You might just come away with something."

Chapter Nine

"Nanny, that's enough food for an army."

"What you don't be eating, you feed to the fish. Feed it all, see if I care."

Matty examined the wicker hamper that Nanny had packed with sandwiches, fruit and leftover cake from last night's dinner. There was also a cooler with drinks, containers of potato salad, macaroni salad, tapioca pudding and cold fried chicken. "Well, if we get stranded like Gilligan, this will see us through to the next century."

"You living like Gilligan already. More people on his island than this one."

Matty lifted the hamper in one hand and the cooler in the other. If she'd been standing on sand instead of the kitchen floor, she would have sunk up to her knees. "Gilligan didn't have a cook like you. Thanks a million. We'll enjoy every bite."

"My babies coming today."

Matty had already started toward the door when Nanny spoke. She turned around and eyed the old woman. "Babies?"

"Grandbabies. Coming to visit."

"Really? And I'm going to miss seeing them?"

"They'll be here, you git back. Staying the night."

"Really? I'm so glad. I've wanted to meet them. Are you sure you'll have time to take care of Heidi, too? You're going to be awfully busy."

"Kitty's coming, too. Plenty of help here."

Matty contemplated this new turn of events. Although Nanny never discussed her family, Matty remembered the things Damon had told her. "I'm glad, Nanny. I know Kitty needs her mother."

"She needs me, she got a funny way of showing it, that girl."

"I bet she's just trying to impress you."

The wrinkles in Nanny's cheeks became deep chasms. "Impress me?"

"Sure. I think if you really love and respect your parents, you want to show them how well you've turned out, so they'll be proud of you. Does Kitty try to boss you around?"

Nanny glared her answer.

Matty nodded. "I'll bet she's just trying to show you that she's learned all the things you taught her. Like how to take care of people if they need you. Not that you need taking care of, of course."

"She boss me once too much."

"I'll bet if you tell her you're proud of her for everything she's ever done, she'll back off a little." Matty shrugged in disclaimer. "But what do I know?"

"You always taking care of people, too."

"I was born to be a nurse...or a doctor, I guess."

"You be good at either."

Matty's eyes widened. This was Nanny, and Nanny had just given her a compliment. "Ummm...thanks."

"You'll like my Kitty." Nanny spieled off the names of her grandchildren, six of them. "You'll like them, too."

"I know I will."

"Go on. Git out my kitchen. I gotta cook, since you taking everyt'ing in the cupboards with you."

Outside Matty started for the dock where Inspiration's skiff, the *Mink,* rocked slowly in the water. Damon was nowhere in sight. For a moment she wondered if he had forgotten their excursion, then she saw him coming from the east, a gym bag slung over one shoulder and a plastic gas can under his arm.

She waved and continued toward the dock. Since she'd gone to bed the night before, she had wondered exactly what had possessed Damon to suggest this trip. Guilt that he hadn't spent more time with her? A desire to get to know her better? Desire, period? She really didn't know, and now, as she had all morning, she told herself that it didn't matter. Whatever the reason, they were going to spend the day together.

On board the *Mink,* she tucked their lunch under the seat at the stern and a canvas bag with towels and sunblock under the one at the bow. By the time she'd finished, Damon joined her on board.

"I didn't see you at breakfast." Damon dropped the snorkeling equipment on the floor of the skiff and climbed over it to reach the outboard motor. He brushed Matty's arm as he passed but didn't seem to notice.

"I ate early." She had been up early, wondering about the day. Eating had given her something else to do.

"Did Nanny tell you her daughter and grandkids are coming?"

"She did. Did you arrange it?"

"More or less. Kitty's not quite as stubborn as her mother. She was the easy part."

"Not everyone would have bothered going to all that trouble."

"They need each other."

For a man who prided himself on not being swayed by emotion, Damon was surprisingly soft-hearted. "I'm glad it worked out," she said.

Damon didn't seem to be in the mood for conversation. He

busied himself preparing to cast off. When Matty asked what she could do to help, he shook his head. She took the bow seat and waited, but she didn't have to wait long. In minutes they were out on the water, leaving Inspiration behind.

The outboard motor was as quiet as one could be, but communication was still nearly impossible. Matty settled herself to enjoy the ride and apply sunblock to her legs. Damon hadn't told her how far they were going. In fact, he hadn't told her much at all. After their bridge game he had gone upstairs, and she hadn't seen him again.

But sometime during the long night, when she was supposed to be sleeping, she had heard him on the balcony they shared. He had sounded as if he were pacing. She had longed to go to him, but without knowing whether he would appreciate her company, she had decided it was best to leave him alone.

"Matty!"

She turned her head to see him. He pointed to the right. She could just see the outline of another island. She was surprised to find one so close to Inspiration.

"On a clear day you can see it from Inspiration if you know where to look," he shouted. "I'll show you sometime."

She nodded.

Over the next half hour the island grew larger as they sped toward it. When they were within hailing distance, Damon slowed and shouted to her again.

"I'm going to take her in. We'll set up camp and do some snorkeling off the beach. If we get tired of that, we'll take the boat out again. There are some other good places not far away."

He guided the *Mink* in slowly; then, yards from shore, he cut the engine and jumped into the water. "I'll pull it as close as I can. You stay put."

She busied herself taking off her T-shirt as Damon hauled the boat toward shore. When he'd gotten her in as close as he could, Matty was ready to slide into the knee-deep water.

"It's a sandy bottom here," Damon said, holding out his hands. "Let me help you."

She went into his arms as naturally as if she did it every day. "What's this cay called?" she asked.

He steadied her as she climbed into the water. "I don't even know its real name. We call it Shell Island. There's not much to it during a high tide. No one's ever lived here."

"It's so wild compared to Inspiration."

"It has its own kind of beauty. And Kevin has found some good shells."

"I'm glad you brought me."

He didn't release her, although she was standing in the water now. "We haven't spent much time together, have we?"

"You've been busy."

"You've been patient."

"I don't expect you to hover over me. I knew you'd be working hard when I agreed to this. You never misled me."

"Someday we're going to have a talk about what you'd like to see, not what you expect."

"I'll give it some thought."

He squeezed her shoulders. "Go pick out a place to spread the quilt, and I'll bring lunch. There's not much shade, but you should be able to find something."

If the Garden of Eden had been beachfront property, Matty thought, it would have looked much like this. As she waded in to shore, she examined the tiny island more closely. The sand was sugar white, almost iridescent in the late morning sun. Creeper and ground cover scrambled over the highest portion of the island, which was dotted by stark, sturdy trees that seemed to be sculpted of steel and granite. Wild trumpet vine covered one tree, softening its angles and adding a splash of orange to nature's more muted hues.

On the shore, she chose a spot where the shadows of several trees merged to form shade. The spot was close to the water, too, and the music of waves, of white-crowned doves in the trees overhead and gulls wheeling in the sapphire sky, was a lazy symphony.

She spread the quilt Damon had given her and sat down to wait for him. He hadn't followed her in. In fact, when she

shaded her eyes, she could see that he had climbed back on
board, probably to make certain they were securely anchored.
She lay back to stare up at the gulls, at the drifting filmy
clouds, at the austere patterns of nearly leafless branches form-
ing a canopy above her head. When the sun got too bright she
closed her eyes. And with the breeze rippling against her skin,
the sleep that had eluded her eluded her no more.

Damon didn't realize that Matty was sleeping until he was
nearly to the quilt. But when she didn't open her eyes at his
approach, he halted and watched the slow rise and fall of her
breasts. She looked even younger when she was sleeping,
younger and, if possible, more guileless. She was curled up
on her side, one arm outstretched, fingertips lightly buried in
the sand. A strand of hair lay across her cheek, lifting and
falling with the breeze. But Matty slept on.

He had seen her asleep before, of course. He had carried
her to her room on their first night together and undressed her
right down to her underclothes. She was wearing less than that
now. She was wearing the same two-piece bathing suit that
had so intrigued him on the eve of their wedding, and the top
of the suit had slid low over her breasts so that if he wanted—
and Lord, his self-control wasn't what it used to be—he could
move closer and view more than a hint of cleavage.

He wasn't going to do that, of course. He didn't want Matty
to wake up and find her husband staring down her suit.

Her husband.

Of course, if he really were her husband, she wouldn't mind
him staring at her. She might, in fact, be flattered or, even
better, intrigued. If he really were her husband, by now he
would have seen every part of her, seen it, touched it, tasted
it.

Damon didn't know when his libido had begun to assert
itself so vigorously. From the very beginning he had found
Matty attractive. But he had known other women who were
attractive, too, and some, like Gretchen, who were stunningly
beautiful. Never before, with any woman, had he found him-

self so immersed in every move, every gesture, every expression. He had never found himself hanging on words, searching for hidden meanings, listening for clues that would tell him what to do and say next.

Matty stirred and stretched one leg slowly over the other. Damon wondered if she was sleeping now because she was, as Nanny claimed, working too hard. Or was it because she, like him, tossed and turned at night, unable to find the deep, dreamless slumber that once had been hers.

He hadn't had a good night's sleep since the wedding. From the beginning, he had told Matty that the decision whether and when they would make love would rest with her. But the moment the words were uttered, they had become a test.

From the sky just above them a seagull cawed and another squawked a raucous reply. Matty opened her eyes and stared at Damon. She frowned, as if she wasn't sure where she was. His breath caught as her tongue darted out to wet her lips. She pushed herself upright and looked quickly around.

"You must be tired," Damon said.

"No, I'm fine."

"You were sleeping."

"I couldn't have been."

"Then you were doing a great imitation." Damon realized he was still gripping the picnic hamper and the cooler, gripping them as if his fingers would never uncurl again. He carefully set them on the edge of the blanket. He had intended to go back for the snorkeling equipment, then lie in the sun with Matty for a while before they went in the water. Now he knew what a bad idea that might be.

Or a particularly good one.

"Are you hungry yet?" she asked.

He debated answering that honestly. He shook his head rather than trust himself to speak.

"Then let's hit the water." Matty got to her feet. "I've always wanted to snorkel, but I've never had the chance. Does it take a long time to learn the fine points?"

He supposed his grin was as wicked as his thoughts. "Like

something else that comes to mind…snorkeling can be scary the first time, but if you let it, it can be wonderful. The fine points help, but they're icing on the cake.''

She understood exactly what he was referring to. More than the sun colored her cheeks. Before he'd gotten to know Matty, Damon hadn't known a single woman who blushed so conspicuously.

''We can start out beside the skiff,'' he said, taking pity on her. ''You can sit on the gunwale to put on your flippers.''

They waded back out to the skiff in silence. On the trip, he watched the way the bright sunlight warmed her skin and streaked her hair. Her coloring was delicate, not vivid or striking, but as soft and muted as pastel roses on porcelain, and every bit as appealing. Her body was neither voluptuous nor fashion-model sleek. There was nothing intimidating about Matty's curves. Her body had been made for a man to touch, to caress and possess and adore.

''I'm a strong swimmer. That should help.'' Matty rested her palms on the gunwale, and before Damon could help her, she hoisted herself up to the skiff. ''I should catch on pretty fast.''

Damon realized she was nervous. But he wasn't certain about what. He couldn't believe she was really apprehensive about learning to snorkel. More likely, and more intriguing, was the possibility that she was worried about something else.

And that something else was probably him.

He lifted himself into the boat and retrieved their equipment from the gym bag. ''The flippers aren't required.'' He held out a pair for her to try on. ''But they'll keep you from getting as tired. You'll get used to them fast.''

She took the flippers and sat on the gunwale with her feet over the side. ''Anything I should know about putting them on?''

Putting them on was the simplest thing in the world, but he wasn't going to tell her that. He saw his opportunity, and he wasn't ashamed to take advantage of it. ''Better let me do it. I have to make sure they fit.''

"Oh..."

He went back over the side. "Spread your legs."

Her eyebrows shot nearly to her hairline. "What?"

Sometimes a demonstration really was worth a thousand words. He came to rest in front of her. "This is the easiest way." He smoothed his hands between her thighs, slowly nudging them apart.

"Oh."

There was just enough room for him to fit between them now. He stood with his chest against the boat. Her inner thighs rubbed his shoulders and pulsated against him with every wave. The rhythm was very nearly his undoing. "Good," he said. "You look enticing from this angle, Mattolina."

"Here." She handed him a flipper.

He grinned another wicked grin. "Do you suppose Prince Charming kissed Cinderella once he was sure the glass slipper fit?"

"I suppose we'll never know."

"We could guess."

"Not until we're sure about the flippers."

"Ah. Details." He turned and faced away from her, enjoying the feel of her legs against him as he did.

He could see Matty's foot and reach it with one motion. But he took his time instead, sliding his hands along her leg, slowly learning the feel and texture and committing it to memory. "I wonder if Prince Charming did this?"

"I suspect Cinderella would have slapped his princely hands if he'd tried."

"But she wasn't married to him, was she?"

"Not at that point."

"I'm sure he tried it later. On a daily basis."

"Considering how long it's taking you to get to my foot, I wonder how the prince found time to run his kingdom."

"Maybe he didn't bother."

He took her heel in his hand and guided her toes into the flipper, pulling the flipper heel into place once her whole foot was inside. "Wiggle your foot, Mattolina."

She wiggled. Damon felt her calf muscles expand and con- tract against his arm. He closed his eyes as his body reacted in protest. "Does it feel secure?"

She wiggled again. "Yes. Perfectly."

He felt along the edge of her foot, pressing and probing, although there was very little he could tell. Either it felt right to her or it didn't. "Okay. Let's try the other one."

"I can do it, thanks."

"No, I insist. We can't have one coming off in the water."

"It's going to be tomorrow before we get in the water." She offered her bare foot, pointing her toe in the air. He took his time fitting that flipper, too. Then he turned and offered his arms. "Come on down and try them out."

She looked wary, but she let him take her by the waist and help her slide back in. He released her reluctantly once she was standing. "Let me get mine on, then I'll show you how to use your mask and snorkel."

He leaned against the boat and made quick work of his while she watched, eyes narrowed. "I could have done it that way," she said.

"Sure. But it was up to me to make the first time as good as I possibly could."

She lifted a brow in challenge. "You made it last forever. I'll give you that."

"Not a word about quality?"

"With nothing to compare it to?" She shrugged. "Not as good as the novels say, but then, what is?"

He laughed. "I could tell you."

"I'll just bet you'd like to."

She was only three feet away. So far she hadn't moved very far or fast. But he was experienced, and the flippers didn't stop him from catching up to her. He grasped her waist and turned her to face him. They were several feet apart, flipper to flipper. She waited silently.

"You're a good sport, Cinderella."

"You're all talk, Prince Charming."

"Really?" He pulled her closer. Her feet were firmly

planted, but the rest of her swayed toward him easily. "Get a little closer and you'll discover I'm not *all* talk."

"If I get that close, we're going to go under. Together."

"Just what I had in mind. Mattolina..." He leaned forward, and she closed her eyes. Her lips were as warm as the sunshine and as sweet as the air was salty. Her skin was like satin under his fingertips, and he blessed the designer who had left so much of her bare. He followed the length of her spine to the clasp that held the top of the suit together and played with it as he kissed her. He felt her gasp, just the tiniest, instinctive reaction to what his hands might do.

He backed away at last, forcing his hands apart. "Now I'll teach you something else."

Her breathing was unsteady. "Yes."

Damon didn't even want to consider what she might have just agreed to, because the moment he gave it too much thought, he might make a serious mistake. Their lovemaking was in Matty's hands. Only when he was absolutely sure that she was ready could he afford to push.

He went back to the boat and took his time assembling the snorkels and masks. When he was moderately under control and back in the water, he handed one to her.

He demonstrated how to clear the mask, then how to tighten it so no water leaked inside. "Let me fit this for you." He lifted the mask and set it on top of her head. Then he rested his elbows on her shoulders and framed her face with his forearms.

Her hair felt as soft as a tropical breeze. His palms glided over it as he slipped his fingers under the elastic band and gently pulled the mask down over her face. Her eyes were huge under the glass front, not wary, but watchful, as if she was prepared for almost anything. He rapped lightly on the glass with his knuckles, and she smiled, but her eyes never left his.

"Good fit. Now you put the snorkel between your teeth and cover it with your lips." He pulled his own mask down over his eyes and nose and showed her what he meant. Then he pushed it back up. "See?"

"Like this?" She did everything he'd said.

"You don't have to bite down so hard. Now try breathing." She squinted in concentration, and he wanted to kiss away the wrinkles in her brow. "Don't forget to breathe in and out through your mouth, not your nose. It will only take a little while before you get the hang of it."

She nodded, the wrinkles deepening.

He hooked a finger under the snorkel, brushing another finger over her lips as he did, them tugged the snorkel free. "Hey, don't make something difficult out of something that's the easiest thing in the world. Relax. Follow your instincts. This is all about pleasure, remember?" He bent and replaced the snorkel with his own lips, then reluctantly lifted his head. "Just let it flow, and do what comes naturally."

"You're incorrigible."

He grinned. "Let's go." He pulled his equipment back into place and beckoned for her to follow him a little farther out. Then he slid into the water until it was up to his shoulders and floated face down, waiting for her to join him. Once she did, he took her hand and began to kick gently. And he led her to an underwater world she had never seen before.

Matty stared up at the sky through amber-tinted sunglasses. Damon lay beside her, his leg brushing the entire length of hers. The quilt was small, and he wasn't. She couldn't be sure the touch was not an accident, although she had her suspicions.

They had snorkeled for nearly an hour, discovering a Technicolor world of fish and coral that she had only dreamed existed. Then, when she was too tired to kick once more, they had come back up to the beach to eat their fill of Nanny's lunch.

And now they were resting.

"Pretend we were marooned here," Damon said unexpectedly. "Just you and me, and no hope of anyone finding us for months and months."

She thought of Nanny's joke about "Gilligan's Island." "That pretty much describes our life, don't you think? Add a few people, and voilà. Inspiration Cay."

"Just pretend, Mattolina."

The vision was almost too enticing. "Um.... Okay. You and me. Alone on this island."

"Let's say you were afraid this might happen, so you packed one small suitcase. Besides necessities like clothes, a toothbrush, what did you put inside?"

"Tell me the point of this first."

Damon turned on his side. He was still lying against her, but he propped his head on his hand to see her better. "What do you think the point is?"

"To pass the time?"

"I'm not bored. Are you? I just want to get to know you better."

"Oh."

"What's in the suitcase?"

His face was wonderfully close to hers. If she propped herself at the same angle, her lips would be inches from his. She wondered what he would do if she were to move closer, to thread her fingers through his hair and pull him against her. Electricity had crackled in the air between them since the moment they had boarded the boat this morning. She knew, despite her inexperience, that all she had to do was make the first move and she and Damon would be married in every sense of the word.

She didn't move. Not an inch. "A medical kit," she said.

"Nothing practical. Assume we have everything we need."

"Vitamins?"

"Mat—to—li—na..."

"Okay. I'd pack photographs."

"Whose?"

"My father's. Heidi's, of course. Liza and Felicity. The big one of my college graduating class..."

"No men?"

"With you on the island? That would be asking for trouble, wouldn't it?"

"Why no men?"

She considered the limited men who had walked through her life. There were numerous reasons why she hadn't had time for socializing, but there was one she'd rarely admitted even to herself. None of the men she had dated so casually had even begun to measure up to this one.

"Because there hasn't been anyone important," she said. She didn't add "until now," although it would have been the truth.

"You can tell me if this embarrasses you." He reached out to draw his fingers across her lips. "But does that mean that you're…?"

"That's what it means." She caught his hand to still it. "No one was important enough to make love to." She could feel herself blushing, and she hated it. She tried to sound matter-of-fact enough to counteract such a noticeable reaction. "You would have found out eventually, I guess."

"You guess?" He brought her hand to his lips and began to kiss her fingertips, one by one. "And when is this eventually? Eventually some day in the future? Eventually this week? Eventually this afternoon?"

She was afraid her heart was in her eyes. She didn't know how to answer. She was still determined to keep her deepest feelings a secret. Right now Damon knew only that she wanted him. But what would happen when he found out how much and for how long? He was an honorable man. He would stay with her forever rather than hurt her. He would be chained to her side.

"This is your call." He placed her hand against his bare chest and held it there so she could feel his heart pounding. "Just know that for me, 'eventually' could mean right now. If you want it to."

She had known this time wasn't far away. And when would she be more ready? Each day she was with him she loved him more, not less. Her feelings for Damon weren't going to ebb into something more manageable. She could only hope that he wouldn't look beyond what she offered him, that he wouldn't look into her eyes and know that her heart would break if he ever stopped needing her in his life.

"Eventually could mean anything." She smoothed back a lock of hair that had fallen over his eyes. "I think enough time has passed for it to mean now."

"Mattolina."

She drew him down to her. It was as easy as she had hoped it would be. His lips against hers felt like a promise fulfilled, a familiar yet strangely new promise. Somewhere in the midst of the flood tide of desire rising inside her, she felt a quiet pool of serenity. Because this was right. This time was right. This man was right. For twenty-seven years she had waited for this moment.

Damon lifted his head and gazed down at her. "Tell me what you like. Tell me what you need." He framed her face as he spoke, sifting through her hair with his fingertips.

"I told you, I'm not exactly an old hand at this."

His smile was as hot and lazy as the sunshine. "Then we'll start with the basics. Tell me how you like to be kissed."

"By you."

"Not good enough. Do you like this?" He nibbled at her lips with his own, kissing her so lightly that she wanted to press against him for more.

"Or this?" This time he lingered, kissing her gently, but touching her lips with his tongue as the kiss deepened.

"Very nice," she said. "Very, very nice."

"We're not quite finished with the test."

"I was hoping you'd say that."

"How about this?" He lifted and tilted her head, his fingers warm and sure against her neck. Her lips opened against his, and for the first time he let her feel his hunger. The kiss began gently enough, as if he wanted to coax her to respond. But it deepened quickly, quickly enough to send her head spinning with dizzy, uncontrolled need.

"You taste like the ocean," he murmured. He kissed her

again, sinking lower against her. She swept her palms over his back. He was lean and hard, not heavily muscled, but fit, and wonderfully, powerfully masculine. Immersed in the spiraling reverie of his kiss, she still remembered how much she once had yearned to touch him this way, and her heart sang with joy.

The kiss went on and on until there was nothing but the kiss and the feel of his skin against her hands and the rippling of the breeze through his hair.

"Matty…" He groaned her name at last and rolled to his side, bringing her with him. She mourned the absence of his weight against her, the feel of his legs stretched along the length of hers. But she understood why he had so artfully changed their position when his hand moved to her midriff, then higher and higher still.

His palm settled against her breast as he kissed her again. Suddenly she couldn't think of anything except what his hand was doing. The world disappeared, and there was only his hand and its slow, sensuous movements. He rotated his palm against her breast. Through the bathing suit she could feel her nipple tighten in response. His fingertips grazed the bare skin above, grazed, only grazed. Softly, so gently, and still so wickedly seductive.

"How much do I want you?" he whispered. "Do you know, Mattolina?"

"Enough…"

"Oh, more than enough. Enough is for other people, not for us. Don't you want to know exactly?"

She knew he was waiting for her to make the next move. And she did want to make it. Because, despite all available evidence, she couldn't believe that this man, the man she had worshipped from afar so long ago, wanted her the way she wanted him.

"Exactly…" He breathed the word as she slid her hand down his side, slowly, as slowly as he had moved his hand to her breast. She reached his suit; then her palm curved over his narrow hip, crept lower. And then there was no doubt at all that "enough" was not nearly good enough. She could feel the heat of his arousal through the thin cotton. He was hot and huge and so incredibly hard, and for the first time she felt a flash of fear.

His hand jerked against her breast as she wrapped her fingers around him. She could hear his breath catch in his chest, then he kissed her, not the teasing, testing kisses of before, but with an explosion of passion that took her own breath away. She arched her back, offering herself more fully to him, but as the kiss grew more passionate still, the momentary fear she'd felt returned.

She pushed it away. This was new, so wonderfully new, and it was all right to be apprehensive. She hadn't expected things to move so quickly; she hadn't expected her own emotions to move so swiftly out of her grasp. But it was all right. All right.

His hand left her breast, and she felt bereft. She had already grown accustomed to the weight of it there, the glorious pressure. Before she could protest, she felt his fingers sliding under the fabric, sliding and nudging it away until skin lay against skin and the pleasure she'd felt before was nothing compared to this.

"Your breasts are so perfect," he whispered. "Exactly fitted to my hand. Can you feel how perfect, Mattolina?"

She could feel everything with such a heightened awareness that the air in her lungs felt like velvet, the quilt like the softest down. And Damon's hand, his long-fingered, beautiful hand against her skin, was like all the wonders of paradise.

He lifted her as he caressed her and slipped his arm under her, so that his free hand lay flat against her spine. Then he slid it higher and higher still until his fingers were hooked beneath the clasp. He twisted it once, and the top of the suit came apart. In even less time it lay beside them, no longer a barrier.

He lifted his head to look at her. "Perfect." His eyes smoldered with an emotion she had never seen there. "You're beautiful, Mattolina."

She felt beautiful. In that moment she felt perfect and beautiful and as desirable as he claimed she was. His gaze was as hot as the sun beating down on them. And she was warmed by it, to the very core of her.

He dipped his head to taste what he'd uncovered. She gasped, although she had known this would happen. Until that moment she had been so immersed in her own cascading pleasure that she had been able to force away the brief flashes of fear. Now, with the pleasure intensifying, the fear intensified, too.

An alarm sounded somewhere inside her. She had expected passion, but this was not what she had imagined. Soon there would be no time to pull herself away from the chasm opening up beneath her. No time to guard her own responses. She was frightened because this was new. She was more frightened because it was as old as the adolescent love she'd treasured so many years ago.

Damon loomed over her again and spread his hands at her waist. His eyes burned with something darker and much more dangerous than her girlish fantasies. He hooked his thumbs in the bottom of her suit and began to smooth it over her hips.

She could feel the fabric sliding away as fear began to overtake desire. She willed herself to find a place between the two, a distant place where she could be safe from both, where she could experience this first time in Damon's arms with pleasure and objectivity. But there was no such place, and fear was fast winning the battle. She felt her legs tensing, pressing together, as if that pitiful attempt could buy her much-needed time.

He stopped, the suit bottom low on her hips. He kissed her, his weight pressing her into the quilt, the hard breadth of his chest a counterpart to the softness of her breasts. She felt the fear recede under the more familiar pleasure. For a moment she believed she could find the balance she needed. Then, as her hips nestled against his and she felt the full impact of what was about to happen, she panicked. Damon wrapped his arms around her as she tried to move away. "Easy... Oh, easy, Mattolina."

She was breathing hard, her hips twisting against his. Damon responded by kissing her again. He grasped the fabric of her suit and tugged it down still farther. Too late she realized that he didn't understand. Caught up in his own response, he believed she was equally caught up in hers.

Panic blossomed. She edged her hands between them and placed her palms against his chest, sliding them higher, higher.

"Yes..." He arched his back to give her better access. "Perfect." His groan of pure pleasure was her undoing.

"No, Damon..." The panic was now as out of control as the passion had been, fed and nurtured by it and, in the end, destroying its very source. "No, Damon. I can't... Please..."

He stiffened and opened his eyes. He looked down at her, as if she was someone he'd never seen. Passion faded slowly into caution. His breathing changed, as if he was forcing himself to regulate it. He didn't say a word, and he didn't move away.

She pushed against his chest. "Please...I don't know... I'm—" She couldn't admit she was afraid. Tears filled her eyes, and she blinked them away.

He covered the hands that were pushing against him and rolled to his side.

"I'm sorry. I don't know what—" But, of course, she did know, and that made it all so much worse.

"We'll wait, Matty. We can wait." Damon clasped her hands in his. "It's all right."

He was not as calm as his words. His voice was a harsh rasp. The hands holding hers were damp and hot, and his face was flushed. Only his eyes were cool, as if he was already working to distance himself from her and from what had just happened.

"Damon, please, I'm sorry. I panicked, that's all. I don't want this to end."

"You do a pretty good imitation." He softened his words by lifting her hands to his lips and kissing them. "Let it go. I pushed you again. That's all we need to say about it."

How could she explain? How could she tell him that the

depth of her own response had terrified her? That she had looked inside herself for control and found nothing there to help her?

"If there's a next time," he said, dropping her hands, "it'll be your choice, not mine. I won't set up any more romantic encounters like this one. If and when you're ready, you'll have to find a way to let me know."

He turned away, as if giving her time and opportunity to cover herself. She couldn't let the day end this way. "I'm so sorry. I just—"

"Please." He didn't turn around. "There's nothing to apologize for. You've already given me a good shot at keeping my daughter. You don't have to give me anything else. Not ever."

Not ever. Matty wondered if he really meant that. They were married. He was a passionate man. Was Damon volunteering to live a celibate life, or was there more to what he'd said? Once again, he had reminded her she was a legal convenience, nothing more.

How could what had seemed so right turn out to be so wrong?

She fumbled with the clasp on her bathing suit until she was covered again. Damon stood and, without looking at her, gathered up the remains of their lunch and started toward the water, leaving her to fold the quilt and carry it back to the boat.

They made the trip back to Inspiration Cay in silence. The wind had come up in their hours on Shell Island, and the waves made the trip unsettling and unbearably long.

By the time they reached the cay, the skies were gray and rain was threatening. Matty sat quietly as Damon guided the skiff to the dock. She didn't even look at him until he spoke.

"Someone's here." He pointed to a familiar boat docked farther in. "That's Samuel's."

"Kitty and the grandchildren." They were the first words she'd uttered since leaving Shell Island. "Remember?"

"No. I made those arrangements myself. They were coming

from Staniel Cay, not George Town. I wonder who Samuel's brought with him?"

The answer stepped through the trees lining the path up to the house.

The answer was carrying their daughter.

"Gretchen." Damon breathed the word.

Matty stared at the extravagantly beautiful woman who had once shared Damon's bed, the woman who had given him a beloved child. For the first time since he had pulled away from her on Shell Island, Matty was glad that she and Damon hadn't made love.

Because now she knew exactly what she had to live up to. And she knew just how impossible it would be.

Chapter Ten

Damon knew how despicable he was. He had allowed Matty to think he had backed away from their lovemaking because her very natural hesitation had appeared to be a rejection.

Only *he* knew better.

"She's just such a little cutie." Gretchen, the picture of maternal devotion, sat in Inspiration's living room gazing down at Heidi, who was dozing fitfully in her arms. "Not a bit pretty, though, is she? I hope you're planning to have a plastic surgeon look at her ears when she's older, Damon. No one in my family has ears like this."

"There's nothing wrong with Heidi's ears. And I'm not going to put her through painful surgery just to meet some ridiculous standard of beauty."

"Just like a man. You don't know what it's like for a woman who doesn't have looks to trade on."

"And neither do you," he said pointedly.

She didn't, of course. Gretchen had been born beautiful. Her hair was an ash blond so pale as to be nearly silver. Her eyes

were the blue that poets wrote sonnets about, and her features
were a shade more earthy than elegant—just earthy enough to
capture the attention of every male she encountered. She had
the body of a sex goddess and enough available brain power
to make a success of anything she tried.

But Gretchen was better at living off men than anything
else she'd ever attempted.

"And what does Matty say about Heidi's ears?" Gretchen
looked up expectantly. Her eyes sparkled with humor.

"Matty doesn't say anything. She thinks Heidi is as beautiful as I do."

"She's not being honest." Gretchen winked. "And where
is the paragon, by the way? Did I scare her off?"

Matty had stayed on the dock just long enough to shake
Gretchen's hand and murmur words of greeting. She'd told
Gretchen where to find a bottle to give Heidi some water; then
she'd disappeared into the house.

"Matty doesn't scare easily," Damon said. "If she did, she
wouldn't be here. This situation is scary enough to turn a
lesser woman's hair gray."

"She seems nice. You've known her for years, you say?"

"We were in college together."

"Well, she's got the right credentials to fool the courts."

He didn't protest. He'd never had any doubts that Gretchen
would figure out the truth. She knew much more about him
than her parents ever would. Damon began to pace the room.
"Matty was born to be a mother."

Gretchen didn't take offense. "And I wasn't. We both know
it. It's a done deal, and I am who I am. Wish I could change,
but that's life." She looked down at their daughter. "But she's
a cute little monkey, isn't she? I'm glad I had her. This once
I did something right, didn't I?"

"You did."

"My parents don't think so, of course."

"Are they still planning to pursue custody now that I'm
married?" Damon had been hoping that the hearing, which
was scheduled for the end of the month, would be canceled

now. He was hoping that this was what Gretchen had come to tell him.

Gretchen gave a wry smile. "What do you think? Your lawyer's talked to my parents' lawyer. Do they seem like the kind of people who'll go down without a fight?"

"I'm going to win," he said.

"I'm behind you all the way, and that's going to count for a lot. And I've been thinking, Damon. I don't want to try for joint custody. It could cloud the issue. Neither my past nor my present is a mark in my favor, and that could affect a judge's decision about you, too. I want visiting rights, but that's all. I trust you. I know you'll let me see Heidi whenever I want to."

"Of course I will."

"So that's part of the reason I came."

"And the other part?"

"I'm checking out Matty. Just a precaution. Before I give up most of my legal rights."

Damon could understand Gretchen's hesitation. She wanted the best for their daughter, even if she couldn't provide it herself. But he had to warn her. "You do understand that Matty could see you as a threat. She may not be at her best—"

He was interrupted by a clatter of dishes, followed closely by the lady in question. "I brought you some of Nanny's appetizers. She and Kitty have been cooking up a storm this afternoon. I don't know how they do it with all those kids...." Matty, in a violet sundress, carried a tray heaped with delectable tidbits to the table beside Gretchen's chair. "I'll warn you, though, watch out for hot peppers and garlic. The air in that kitchen could clear the worst sinuses."

"Oooh... Doesn't this look good." Gretchen frowned at Heidi. "Now, how do I eat and hold her at the same time?"

Damon noted that Matty hadn't looked at him since she'd entered the room. "I'll take her up to bed," he said.

Gretchen kissed her daughter's hair, then lifted her into Damon's waiting arms. "Do we have something to go with the goodies?"

"I'll get you a drink," Matty said. "What'll it be?"

Damon wished he could stay and hear the conversation to follow. He didn't claim to understand women, or even people in general, but he did know that this meeting between Gretchen and Matty was going to settle a number of things.

He tried to catch Matty's eye, but she refused to look at him. He wanted to make some gesture of support and affection. But he had destroyed his chance for either when he had halted their lovemaking today. Before he could be close to Matty again, he would have to admit something so extraordinary, so incomprehensible, that it didn't even seem possible.

He hadn't just backed away from Matty because she resisted him. He'd backed away because he was afraid.

"Take your time upstairs, Damon." Matty still refused to look at him. "I'll entertain Gretchen for a while."

"Yes, take your time," Gretchen said. "Matty and I need to get to know each other."

Damon wanted to snatch Matty and run away with her. He had already put her through too much today. He knew that her sudden resistance on the beach had been brought about by his own carelessness. He should have moved slower, coaxed her into feeling safe and desired. He should have let her take the lead. Instead he had pushed her too hard and too fast, just the way he'd pushed her from the beginning. Not because he was a thoughtless lover or a selfish one. But because his legendary self-control had failed him. And the reason for that failure was both simple and terribly complicated. He had pushed so hard because he had wanted her so badly. Not because she was the most beautiful woman he'd ever seen, or the most dazzling.

Because she was Matty.

"Damon?" Matty finally looked at him when he didn't move away. She wasn't smiling.

If he ever wanted Matty to feel secure with him again, Damon knew he would have to admit that he had backed away from her because his own feelings had been so confusing, so new, that he hadn't known what to do with them. He had been frightened of what he was feeling, as frightened as she was.

And like the worst kind of coward, he had used her fears to put an end to his own.

"I'll be upstairs if you need me." Like the coward he was, he turned his back on her again and left the room.

"Well, so how do you like it here?" Gretchen asked. "A beautiful place, huh?"

"Spectacular." Matty handed Gretchen the glass of chardonnay she'd requested.

"It gives me the willies, though, after a day or two. It's so isolated. And absolutely nothing happens here."

Matty could tell Gretchen about more than a few things that were happening, none of them good. She managed a smile. "I had a high-stress job. The serenity appeals to me."

"Damon tells me you're a pediatric nurse? That's convenient."

Matty searched for rancor in Gretchen's voice and found none. "I guess it is."

"I can understand why Damon wanted you here. But why did you want to come? Was the job really so hard that you were willing to do anything to get away from it?"

"Anything?" Matty took a seat across from Gretchen, who had already dived into the appetizers and was blissfully sampling everything in sight.

"That's an exaggeration, of course. But this does seem like a pretty drastic solution to stress at work. So I'm guessing you had other reasons?"

Matty wondered how honest she needed to be. "My life seemed to be going nowhere fast. And I had very...fond memories of Damon."

"You were lovers in college?" Gretchen bit nonchalantly into a chicken wing.

"No. Friends." And hardly that.

"He's amazing in bed. I thought that might have been what brought you here."

Matty looked away. "I don't think I want to talk about Damon's sexual prowess."

"Our relationship was short-lived, Matty. We fell in and out of it without much thought. That was new for him, I think. Old story for me."

There was no rancor in her smile, either. "Damon's way too complex for someone like me. Somewhere between his heart and his brain, everything comes to a complete stop. He's all tied up inside. He's brilliant. He knows everything about everything, except who he is. Me, I'm all surface. What you see is what I am. No hidden depths." She selected a cheese-stuffed mushroom. "This is delicious. Don't you want something to eat?"

Matty was still trying to sort through the beginning of the conversation. "You really don't feel anything for him? You didn't even want to consider marriage?"

"Marriage? Not on your life." Gretchen shook her head. "I know myself. And I know what I'm good at and what I'm not. I've only made one mistake, and that was thinking I had what it takes to be a mother. But I've fixed that now. Heidi's where she ought to be."

"You didn't say what you feel for Damon."

"The utmost respect. He's the only truly decent man I've ever known. He probably doesn't see it this way, but I think of him as one of my best friends. I know if I ever get in trouble—and I won't, because I'm too smart, but if I did—I could count on Damon to help me. And I'd do whatever I could for him."

Matty tried to absorb all this. She had been prepared for a very different kind of woman. She hadn't been prepared to like Gretchen. She had expected to keep a wary distance.

"You seem like a decent sort yourself," Gretchen said. "Nanny's already warned me not to hurt you or I'll answer to her."

"Nanny said that?"

"She's a stitch, isn't she? And if she likes you, you must have passed some rigorous tests." Gretchen licked her fingers, one by one. "Yummm.... So tell me whatever you think I should know about you. And then we have to have a talk about Heidi's ears...."

Matty wondered how anyone could imply that life on Inspiration Cay was sedate. Not long ago she'd searched for projects to keep herself busy. But that was before Gretchen arrived, before Kitty and the grandchildren decided to stay on a while, before Arthur anchored the *Crown Sable* on the leeward side of the island for a prolonged visit.

"So then I told this guy he was whistling at the moon. But he didn't listen. Next thing I knew, he'd hired a moving van, bribed my landlord for a key and moved everything I owned into his house. A bi-i-g house it was, too. Took me a week to find everything and move it back out."

Gretchen was just finishing another of her stories. She had a million, and most of them were delightful, if amazingly shameless.

"I fixed him, though," she continued. "I moved his entire wardrobe with me and didn't leave a forwarding address. Overnight he went from Savile Row suits to Sears off the rack. By the time he caught up with me, he'd learned his lesson."

"You know I don't believe a word of this, don't you?" Matty said. They were strolling along the western beach. Heidi was sleeping in the gazebo not far away.

"I swear my life does sound like a fabrication, doesn't it?" Gretchen flashed her just-between-us-girls smile. "But if you move as fast as I do, Matty, these things happen."

"Why do you move that fast, Gretch?" Matty really wanted to know. Gretchen had been on Inspiration Cay for four days now. As impossible as it seemed, it had taken only the better part of one for them to become friends. But Matty still wasn't sure she understood her.

"I guess it's the way I was brought up. My childhood really was miserable. I know Damon's told you about my folks. Well, the best thing anyone can say about them is that they do their duty. But there was no love at home. Not a drop of it. And they told me every day and in every way that I didn't measure up.''

"What an awful way to grow up."

"Yes, well..." Gretchen shrugged. "Over and done with. But I decided back then that when I was finally able to get away from home, I'd have fun. I'd make up for everything, and I have. I know it's hard for you to understand, but I do have such a good time. Life's a ball, and I make sure it stays that way.''

Matty didn't understand, not completely. Gretchen had tossed everything out of her life that Matty wanted desperately in hers. But Gretchen didn't have a deceitful bone in her body.

Gretchen slipped her arm through Matty's. "Let's plan a party, shall we? Things are so quiet here.''

"A party?" Matty tried to imagine. The last party on the island had been a wedding reception. Hers. The thought gave her a familiar pang. She and Damon had been married now for weeks, and every day they grew further apart.

Matty wondered when she would stop reliving that awful moment on the beach when she had pushed Damon away. How could she have allowed him to think she didn't want him, no matter how overwhelming her emotions? In her inexperience, she had panicked. She had been so suffused with emotions, so deluged...

"So what do you think?" Gretchen continued. "Before Kitty and the kids go home. And I've got to get out of here sometime in the next couple of days myself.''

Matty tried to push her troubling thoughts away. "It's a great idea. What were you thinking?''

"I don't know. Let me give it some thought. But fun's what I do best. I'll make sure it's a real blowout.''

They parted at the gazebo. Gretchen and Arthur had a tennis date, and Matty had brought stationery so she could work on letters to her friends at home while Heidi finished her nap. But by the time Gretchen was out of sight Matty was thinking about Damon again.

In the four days since their afternoon on Shell Island, Damon had hardly spoken to her. She had avoided him, too. After all, what exactly could she say to him? I'm sorry I shoved you straight out of my life? I'm sorry I'm such a disaster as a woman? I'm sorry this is all so new to me?

She didn't know what to say. She didn't know how to put her feelings into words he would understand. Because if she was perfectly honest, she would also have to admit she loved him, and that was what scared her most of all.

She sat with pen poised over paper for a long time, but not as long as she'd expected. Heidi's nap was shorter than usual, and when she woke up, she was fussy.

Matty carried the baby back to the house and fed her a bottle on the front porch. Heidi took it all, but without her usual gusto. And afterwards she fussed some more.

"You doing somet'ing that baby don't like?" Nanny said, coming out to join them.

"I hope not. Where're Kitty and the gang?"

"Off swimming. Told 'em to go or I'd drown 'em myself."

"Sure you did." Matty decided to walk the length of the porch to quiet Heidi.

Kevin came from the back of the house and climbed the steps. "What's with the kid?"

Matty paused a moment. "I think she's teething. Want to try to quiet her?"

He held up his hands. "No chance."

Damon was the next to show up. He came from the direction of the lab, and if his expression was a mirror, his day hadn't been a good one. The other two drifted away immediately, and Matty was left to face him alone.

He climbed the porch, frowning. "What's the problem, Matty? Is she hungry?"

Matty was hot and tired. She was also heartily sick of the unacknowledged tension between them, and her words reflected it. "Of course that's the problem, Damon. I'm starving your daughter."

His frown deepened. "You don't have to bite my head off."

"And you don't have to ask silly questions."

"Let me take her for you."

"No!"

He leaned against a porch pillar and watched her pace. "Maybe this isn't about Heidi? Maybe you're angry about something else?"

"Like what?"

He hesitated. "I'm sorry about Gretchen coming. I would have warned you if I'd known, I—"

"In case you haven't noticed, Gretchen and I get along just fine. I like her."

"Is that so?"

"I said it was, didn't I?"

"Then what is it?"

Her anger evaporated as quickly as it had erupted. She was left feeling foolish. And lonely. Very, very lonely. "I'm just tired. And I hate to hear a baby cry."

"You've had more practice at it than anyone I know."

"Well, those babies weren't mine." She looked up, expecting, waiting, for him to remind her that this one wasn't either.

"No. I'm sure that makes a difference."

Heidi began to settle down. Her screams tapered into hiccups, and at last she was silent. Matty had expected Damon to leave, since she wouldn't let him help, but he was still there, watching her.

"I'm sorry, Mattolina."

She didn't know why Damon had used her real name, and she didn't want to make any guesses. She didn't look at him. "You don't have anything to be sorry about. I'm sorry. I'm just tired. I didn't mean to take it out on you."

"I wasn't talking about today." He pushed himself away from the pillar. And before she could find the courage to ask him for an explanation, he was gone.

Matty took forever to fall asleep that night. The air seemed particularly still and humid, the mattress seemed to have new lumps, and every time she closed her eyes, she wondered exactly what Damon had meant.

What was he sorry for? Sorry he'd tried to make love to her? Sorry he hadn't succeeded? Sorry he'd married her in the first place? The list went on and on, and each possibility seemed as likely as any other.

It was well past midnight before she finally succumbed. She'd heard Heidi crying once, but since the baby was still in the room attached to Damon's, he always got up with her at night. The crying had stopped quickly, and at last Matty fell asleep.

She was dreaming that she was back in Carrollton, pleading for her old job back, when she awoke with a start. For a moment she was so disoriented she didn't know where she was. She felt such a huge sense of loss that she could hardly breathe. Then she realized that she wasn't back in Minnesota. She was still on the island, but something was wrong.

She sat up, trying to pull her thoughts together. Somewhere not far away Heidi was screaming again. And the screaming seemed to be coming closer.

"Matty? Can I come in?"

Matty realized that Damon was just outside her room on the balcony they shared, and he was holding Heidi in his arms.

She felt for her robe but couldn't find it in the dark. She got up without it and went out to meet him. "What's going on?"

"She's burning up!"

Matty took the baby and knew immediately that he was right. "Yes, she's definitely hot."

"What could be wrong with her?"

"She's been so fussy today, I thought she might be cutting a tooth."

"Would she run such a high fever from a tooth?"

"Not likely." Matty realized that Damon was wearing a pair of boxer shorts and nothing else. And she was in the sheerest, coolest nightgown that she owned. "Look, let me grab my robe, then I'll take her temperature. Come on."

He waited; then he followed so closely that she could feel the heat of his body against her own. "She's on fire. How can she survive a temperature like this?"

"Children run higher temperatures than adults. Don't let your imagination run away with you."

"But she's so little."

She wasn't sure who to be the most concerned for, the baby in her arms or the man at her back. "She's little, but she's amazingly resilient," she said calmly. "The species has survived and flourished, remember?"

"Should I get Arthur? Should we try to get her to a doctor at George Town?"

"Not until I've checked her."

"This is my fault. I shouldn't be here. We should be somewhere closer to a hospital. Maybe the Otts are right."

"The Otts are selfish, miserable people who don't care a fig about this baby. So stop kicking yourself."

He fell silent, but Heidi filled the gap with angry shrieks.

In the baby's room Matty laid her on the changing table and took her temperature. Damon, who couldn't seem to watch, pulled on a pair of jeans.

She handed Heidi back to Damon when she'd finished. "Not quite 103 degrees. Not so bad."

"Not so bad? Her blood's boiling."

"Turn up the light, will you? I'm going to check a few things."

She busied herself laying out the medical kit she'd brought with her to the island. She was equipped to do nearly everything except major surgery. "First we'll check her ears. Hold her closer to the light, please." She checked to be sure the otoscope was properly charged.

"Is that going to hurt her?"

"Probably a bit. Come on, Daddy. We've got to do this." She peered in the baby's ear, trying to ignore her screams. "Now the other one."

She straightened when she'd finished a complete exam, including listening to the baby's chest with her stethoscope. "Notice how stuffy she sounds?"

"I don't think she's getting enough oxygen. What if she stops breathing?"

Matty tried not to smile. Damon had never seemed more appealing to her than he did at this moment. He adored this child, and he was falling apart with worry. His emotions were so involved that he couldn't step back and make a rational judgment.

His emotions were so involved that he couldn't step back and make a rational judgment.

She'd only seen him this way once before. When she'd pushed him away because *she* was overwhelmed with emotion. Could she have been so caught up in her own confusion, her own reactions, that she had missed his?

"What's going on, Matty?" Gretchen came to the door, clutching a satin robe.

"Damon, why's the kid screaming like that?" Kevin came up behind Gretchen and nudged her into the room so that he had a better view.

Matty waited for the rest of the household to show up. On cue, a tousled Nanny pushed Kevin to one side. "Somet'ing wrong with my baby?"

Matty held up her hands. Even Heidi quieted to dull whimpers in anticipation of the verdict.

"Heidi has a cold. And one of her ears is a little inflamed. I'm going to give her something to reduce the fever and start her on some antibiotics. End of story. Now everybody back to bed. She's going to be just fine."

"You're sure?" Gretchen said, with a yawn. "That's it?"

"I promise. That's it."

"Okay." Gretchen rounded up the others and herded them back down the hall. In her own way, Gretchen knew how to be helpful.

Damon and Matty were left alone.

"You're sure?" Damon said.

"Damon..." Matty shook her head. "Silly question, right?"

He nodded sheepishly. "I'm sorry."

"You're adorable." The words were out of her mouth before she'd even thought them.

He ran a hand through his hair. "I'm frazzled."

"That too."

"How'd she catch a cold?"

"One of the grandkids has been sniffling. Kitty asked me for some vitamin C yesterday."

"Maybe we should keep her away from other people's children until she's in college?"

She grinned. They were talking again. She was elated. "Silly. That's the worst thing you could do for her. She's going to get sick from time to time. That's life."

"I just felt so helpless. I don't know what I'd do..."

"I know."

He smiled at her. "I think we're going to be walking the floor tonight, medicine or no medicine."

"I know. Which shift do you want?"

"The one where you keep me company for a while."

Dawn was a long way off, but Matty felt the sun rising inside her again. "Do you remember that game we played on Shell Island?"

"Which one?"

She addressed the obvious. "Not the one that went awry, Damon. Not the one I feel so terribly sorry for. The other one. The one about the suitcase."

"I remember."

"You never told me what you would bring with you. Maybe you could tell me tonight."

"All right."

"Let's give Heidi her medicine, then let's walk a mile or two on the balcony."

He leaned forward. For a moment she didn't know why, then his lips brushed hers. "I have a feeling they'll be the first of many miles we walk with her."

"They won't be so long if we walk them together, will they?"

"No." He kissed her again, a light, casual kiss that set her heart racing. "I don't look forward to the miles, Mattolina, but I do look forward to the company."

Chapter Eleven

Damon was the child of older parents who had never expected to have children. He had been a change-of-life baby, and although his mother and father loved him, they hadn't accommodated well to having a child in their house. He'd been forbidden the messes, the noise, the distractions, of childhood. Instead he had been rewarded for quiet study, for good grades and academic honors. By the time he was twenty, his father was dead and his mother had remarried and moved to an Arizona retirement community, leaving him alone in Minnesota to continue his pursuit of the answers to life's questions.

These were things Matty hadn't known about Damon. Now, two days after their night on the balcony with Heidi, she knew these and more. For instance, she knew he would fill his island suitcase with books, but not the scientific tomes she had envisioned. He loved thrillers and poetry, biographies and classic Westerns.

And she knew that he played recordings of Mozart piano sonatas when he needed inspiration for his work and the Rolling Stones when he wanted to stop thinking altogether. She hadn't known that he loved Thai and Cambodian food, but now she'd filed that away. She knew a dozen little details that defined a different, more rounded Damon Quinn than the one she had loved.

She loved him more.

Of course, Damon knew more about her now, as well. She had shared memories of her father, stories about her tiniest patients, about her friends and their escapades together. She had confessed to her addiction to all things raspberry and to her abiding love affair with Robin Cook thrillers.

She hadn't confessed to the most important love affair of her life, though, the one that had begun so many years ago when Damon had hardly remembered her name. But she had told him she remembered exactly what he'd looked like in a particular blue sweater he used to wear to anatomy lab, and that had been enough of a revelation.

The day was a warm one, and Matty sat outside on a seaside bench with Heidi, thinking about how much things had changed in her life once again. She was so immersed in thought that she didn't even hear Gretchen's approach.

"Daydreaming, Mattykins?" Gretchen plunked down on the bench beside Matty and chucked Heidi under her chin. "Want me to take her for a while?"

"Sure." Heidi had just had a nap and a bottle, and she was at her best, which was the way Gretchen liked her. Matty handed the baby over. She wondered if there had ever been a situation quite like this one. She had been so afraid that she would feel competitive with Heidi's birth mother. Instead she was sad that Gretchen would never feel the bond with the little girl that Matty had already begun to develop. In her own way, Gretchen loved Heidi, but with the friendly distance of an older sister.

"I'm glad she recovered so quickly." Gretchen held Heidi in front of her and made a funny face. The baby beamed back at her.

"Me too. I like sleeping again."

"Matty, can I ask you something personal?"

"Probably not." But Matty knew that nothing she could say was going to stop Gretchen.

"Are you and Damon sleeping together?"

"Gretch, is sex the major thing you think about?"

"Doesn't everybody?"

"Don't you realize how strange this situation is to begin with? It's way too kinky to talk about my sex life, or lack of it, with the woman who had my husband's baby."

"You make it sound like a tabloid headline."

"No. It's a little too kinky, even for them."

"I'm just asking because I'm worried about you both."

Matty tried to take all this in. "What are you worried about?"

Gretchen made another funny face at her daughter. "I just want this to work out. You and Damon are perfect for each other. And he's going to fall hard for you, if you just give him the chance."

"Um… He'll have all the chances he needs. We're married, remember?"

"Sure you are. If you don't do something to screw it up."

"Are we doing marriage counseling here?"

"Just because I don't ever want to get married doesn't mean that I don't know what makes a great marriage."

"Let me guess. Sex. Great sex. Right?"

"You're on the right track. And love. And I know you've got plenty of that. How long have you been in love with him, Matty?"

Matty stiffened. "That's off-limits, too."

"Oh, don't worry. He doesn't know it, though the rest of us do. But Damon's oblivious. He's just about as sophisticated as the moppet here when it comes to his feelings."

"What are you trying to say?"

Gretchen made her final funny face, then she swung Heidi back into Matty's arms, tired already and ready to move on to something new. "I'm not *trying* to say it. I *am* saying it. Don't worry about giving yourself away with Damon. You don't have to work so hard at hiding what you feel, because he isn't going to figure it out, anyway. At least, not until he realizes he's falling in love with you. Then he'll begin to wonder what you're feeling. And then he'll finally get it."

"This is an extraordinary conversation."

"Yeah. Isn't it? Now…" Gretchen slapped Matty's knee. "Party plans."

Matty nearly sighed with relief. "Oh, good, a change of subject."

"We're going to have an old-fashioned picnic. Sort of an early Fourth of July. Volleyball, three-legged races, homemade ice cream, fireworks. Arthur's providing the bottle rockets and Roman candles. Nanny's going to do fried chicken. We're sending off for a watermelon."

"Darn, that's pretty down home for you. I thought it was going to be champagne, portobello mushrooms and artsy skin flicks."

Gretchen giggled. She sounded like a little girl. "No, family stuff. Good clean American fun."

"We're in the Bahamas."

"Close enough. Do you like my ideas?"

And because Matty couldn't help herself, she put her arm around Gretchen's shoulders and gave her a warm hug.

Matty had created a family. Damon watched the incongruous mix of people who either lived on Inspiration or were honored visitors. Matty had taken the most unlikely ingredients, mixed them up with a little Matty magic and created a family where before only lonely castaways had dwelled.

Ten feet away Gretchen screeched with laughter as Arthur and two of Nanny's grandsons crawled along the ground and rolled hard-boiled eggs toward a makeshift finish line. "Go, Arthur! Do it! Do it!" she screamed.

Kevin joined Damon at the sidelines to watch this extraordinary event. He folded his arms over his chest and shook his head.

"It's not every day you get to see a billionaire rolling an egg with his nose," Damon said.

"Jeez, I hope not."

"Don't get too smug. They've got you scheduled for the balloon toss."

"Yeah, but they put me with Kitty. She's sane."

"Watch out. She has Nanny's genes."

"There's no place to hide. That's the bad thing about islands."

Or the good thing. Damon thought that was part of the reason Matty had been such a success here. Everyone had been forced into contact with the sunshine that was Matty Stewart…Quinn. She was a healer, a nurturer, a ray of light in a world they'd all found dark and frightening at one time or another.

Kevin thrust his hands into his pockets. "I've gotta change into my bathing suit if I'm going to throw water balloons."

Damon waited for Kevin to roll his eyes or add a choice bit of profanity. He glanced at the boy and saw he was smiling. Damon stood perfectly still. He didn't remember ever seeing anything like a smile on Kevin's face.

"Will you look at Heidi?" Kevin shook his head. "What's that contraption on her head?"

"I think it's a pinwheel."

"Matty had better hold on tight or she'll catch the wind and fly away." Kevin strolled off, watching the end of the race as he went without even trying to hide his interest.

Matty joined Damon as the next event began. This one involved eggs again. Somebody had obviously pleaded with every hen in the Exumas to give a little extra for the celebration.

"What are they doing?" Damon asked.

"I have no idea. This is Gretchen's party."

Damon watched Kitty inch carefully toward one of her children with a spoon handle tucked under her gorgeous chin. A hundred intricate braids flopped in a hundred different directions, and the crepe paper ruffles around her waist and hips—

which owed more to the Bahamas Junkanoo Festival than to any American Independence Day celebration—shimmied with every move she made. The egg—and he was afraid this one wasn't cooked—was tucked into the bowl of the spoon.

"Gretchen is a sadist," he said.

"No. She's having a great time, though. If she wasn't a professional good-time girl, she could be a recreation director."

"You really like her, don't you?"

"I do." Matty balanced Heidi in front of her. "There's nothing mean or small about Gretch."

"Gretch?"

She smiled up at him. "Are you having fun?"

He had been. Somehow that fun seemed to have doubled in the last few moments. Ever since she and Heidi had come to stand beside him. "What is that thing on Heidi's head? Is it really a pinwheel?"

"We were told to dress up. Where's your costume?"

Matty herself was wearing striped suspenders with a white pleated skirt short enough to make Damon's heart beat faster. A bright red garter adorned one lovely leg, and a paper flower adorned the opposite ankle. Kitty had drawn a big pink heart on her right cheek and a blue star on her left. In addition to the lopsided pinwheel beanie, Heidi wore a ruffled sunsuit and booties that looked like smiling bumblebees.

Damon tugged his polo shirt out from his chest. "I'm fresh out of costumes."

"We'll have to do something about that. Here." Matty thrust Heidi into his arms.

"What are you doing?"

"Helping you get in the spirit." She bent over and began to smooth the garter down her thigh. "This will have to do until I can go back to the house and make you a bow tie."

Damon's mouth suddenly went dry. Matty bending over in a short skirt was one of the finest sights he'd ever seen. His fingers tingled as he watched her stroke the garter down her leg. He remembered all too well exactly how that leg had felt against his.

She tilted her head and gazed at him a moment. He might have thought she was studying his reaction, that she had provoked it, in fact, if this wasn't Matty in front of him. But Matty didn't play those kinds of tricks.

Did she?

Matty took her time. His gaze was glued to her leg. They were standing in the sun, and until that moment he hadn't realized just how hot it was outside. The garter was at her calf now, sliding slowly—much too slowly—toward her ankle.

"Liza gave me this on our wedding day." Matty's voice was as sweet, as flutelike, as always. So why did he imagine something new there, something designed to torture him? "I guess you never had the chance to see it, did you?" she continued. "I think you were supposed to take it off at the reception. But that's silly stuff, isn't it?"

Lord, he was about to volunteer to do it right that moment. Put it back on, Matty, some voice inside him shouted, and let's do this right!

"There." She slid it over her foot and held the garter in front of him. "Now put this on and join the merriment."

"I have my hands full." He stood clutching Heidi in his arms. She was beginning to whimper in protest.

"I'll take her." Matty reached for Heidi, but Damon refused to let go of her.

"No, she likes me holding her. She loves it."

"Really? She has a funny way of showing it."

He realized just how hard he was grasping the baby. He loosened his grip and began to jiggle her up and down. "She's happy with me. Extremely happy. You put the garter on."

She tilted her head in question. "Damon, I just had it on."

"No, put the garter on *my* leg."

She gazed down. He was wearing shorts and no shoes. There was a long expanse of bare leg to work with.

"You're sure?" She smiled, and like her voice, the smile was tinged with something new. "It could take some time."

"I've got plenty."

"Well, I guess any sacrifice is required to get you in the proper spirit."

There was nothing proper about his spirit. He was, in fact, having the most blatantly improper, unspiritual thoughts of his life.

"Lift your foot," she said. "Here, you can rest it on my leg." She knelt in front of him, a willing footstool.

The leg in question was nearly bare, but just in case, she hiked her skirt higher to give him more room. His mouth went dry as he rested the ball of his foot squarely in the middle of her thigh. She touched his toes lightly with her fingertip, one by one, then drew her finger higher, along the bones leading to his ankle.

Damon closed his eyes. He had never paid much attention to feet. He wondered why. They were remarkably sensitive. Her touch was feather-light, but the exquisite pleasure of it rendered him speechless until she cupped both sides of his foot and began to lift it.

He opened his eyes and saw that she was looking at him. "Poor Damon. Tired already? The day's barely begun."

He could swear her eyes were twinkling. "The sun's just bright."

"Really? I thought it was cloudier than usual." She held his foot aloft as she took the garter from the ground and stretched it around his toes, then inched it toward his instep. "There now, put your weight on the ball of your foot."

He leaned forward, freeing his heel and she slid the garter over it and up as far as his ankle. "We could leave it there."

"No."

"No? You think it will be more festive if it's higher?"

He would be more festive, that was for sure. The longer she kept her hands on him, the more festive he felt. "Definitely." Four syllables emerged like one. He cleared his throat. "Absolutely."

"You know, you really do have great legs, Damon. Tan and firm. I wonder why a man's hairy legs are so..."

"So what?"

"So..." She smiled up at him. "So acceptable."

"Acceptable?"

"Of course. You know, when they aren't acceptable on women. What did you think I was going to say?"

"I had no idea. I'm in the dark here."

"Are you?"

Matty never played games. Not this kind of teasing sexual game. But he was beginning to believe she'd been taking lessons. In fact, she guided the garter into place against his calf with the finesse and skill of an honor student.

"There..." She leaned back to look at her handiwork. "Higher, maybe?"

"No!" Damon set his foot firmly on the ground. The thought of those lovely capable hands moving farther up his leg was more than he could endure.

"Okay." She pushed herself to her feet and dusted off her hands. She looked down at his leg. "Nope. Not good enough. I know..." She lifted her foot and removed the flower adorning her ankle. Then she squatted in front of him and twisted it into the garter, one hand cupping his leg at mid-thigh to steady herself as she did. She lightly caressed the back of his leg as she stared at her handiwork. Then her eyes traveled higher, to the unmistakable evidence that he was feeling festive at last.

"Perfect," she said. "Absolutely the effect I wanted."

Kitty's oldest son was declared the day's best all-around athlete. At eight he had his mother's astonishing smile and his grandmother's alert eye for trouble. The combination made him unbeatable—particularly so when Kevin, whose adolescent strength and agility were formidable, developed a temporary limp during the final relay race and just couldn't seem to get ahead of the little boy no matter how hard he tried.

They ate their picnic dinner at tables on the beach where another of the children had been awarded a prize for the best sand castle. After dinner another took first in the pie-eating contest, and just before the fireworks, the youngest grand-daughter took first in the seagull naming. In fact, miraculously, all of Nanny's grandchildren went out to sleep on the *Crown Sable* that night with prizes clutched in their little hands.

Damon and Matty watched the dinghy heading out to the yacht long after Nanny and Kevin had gone inside for the evening. Gretchen was on board the dinghy, too. She had said a teary goodbye to everyone, particularly her daughter, but by the time she settled herself on the dinghy, she was talking animatedly with Arthur.

"They'll have a smooth sail to George Town tomorrow morning," Damon said, his arms folded across his chest. "Then on to Nassau. No storms on the horizon."

Matty watched the dinghy disappearing into the shadows. The *Crown Sable*'s lights were just visible on the horizon. "I'll miss them." She sighed. "Today was such fun, wasn't it?"

There would be more days like this one. Damon knew that now. Matty could move into a maximum security prison and in a week's time she would have serial killers organized into sewing circles and support groups. And somehow everyone would begin to care about everyone else.

Because Matty cared so much.

"I like Kitty." She waved once more, even though no one on the dinghy could possibly see them now. "And I think she and Nanny have made up, don't you? I caught them giggling together, telling stories about when Kitty was a little girl. And Kitty promised me she'll come back next month and bring her brothers. If Nanny's still here."

"Is Nanny leaving?"

"She told me yesterday that she needs glasses. And she wants to check on her house in George Town."

"She's going to see a doctor about her eyes?"

"Uh-huh. And a specialist about her allergies. I think that's why she's having trouble tasting things."

"What did you do to work that miracle?"

"I have no idea."

Damon did. Matty had listened to Nanny the way nobody else ever had. And she had accepted her, the way Matty accepted everyone.

"I guess that's it." Matty turned away from the water. "I hope they come back soon."

"Are you lonely here, Matty? Is that why you need them?"

She didn't turn back to him, but she didn't move away. "Of course not. I have Heidi. She's a pretty demanding companion."

"Is that all?"

"You know the permanent population as well as I do."

Damon rested his hands on her shoulders. "I don't want you to be lonely."

"Don't you? Not even after what happened on Shell Island?"

He was amazed at how swiftly the conversation had circled back to that afternoon on the beach. He gripped her shoulders a little harder. "That wasn't your fault. It was mine."

She was silent, as if she was gathering her courage. Then she turned. "No. It was mine. But you see, I felt so many things at once. I just—"

"Please let me take the responsibility. I pushed you too hard and too fast. But there's more." He placed a finger against her lips to silence her when she tried to speak. "I don't know how to say this. I don't even know what I was thinking exactly. But I was glad when you resisted. I wanted you so badly I was moving too fast, but I was still glad when you pushed me away."

She looked perplexed. He couldn't blame her. He felt the same way. He dropped his hand back to her shoulder. "Look, I don't know how to explain it any better. I just…" He shook his head. "Maybe I was afraid because it felt different. We're married. Maybe that's all. We're sharing the same life."

She nodded, as if she was encouraging him to say more. But he didn't know what else to say. Because as often as he had searched his thoughts, he couldn't seem to figure out his own reaction. "I could have made it better for you. Easier. I'm sorry."

"I don't need better or easier. I just need you."

His heart leaped in his chest. "I'm not pushing, Mattolina. I meant that part of what I said the other day. I pushed and look where it got us. I—"

This time she put her finger on *his* lips. "You're not listening. I need you. I don't need all the patience in the world. I may not have slept with a man before, but I'm not some little twit who doesn't know beans about what she wants and needs. I want you. In my bed or yours. Tonight, preferably. Unless that's too soon for you."

As he stared at her, she lifted an eyebrow in question. She had almost perfected the look. She was so very good at it that he wanted to applaud. There was only the tiniest tremor in her lower lip to offset the eyebrow. The tiniest nervous wiggle.

"Those are my choices?" He smiled at her, surprised he didn't scald her with the smile's heat. "My bed or yours? Tonight or some unnamed alternative?"

"I don't think I'm really giving you a choice other than tonight."

He kissed her, gathering her close and holding her against him as if she might change her mind. "My bed," he said, when both of them were gasping for breath. "My room. And right now."

She pulled away just far enough to see his face. "All right. But listen to me, Damon. If we share your bed tonight, it's not *just* for tonight. I won't be an afterthought, someone whose room you visit once a week. If we make love, we're making a marriage, too. Heidi needs a real mother."

He didn't know how it had swung back to Heidi when Heidi was the last thing in his thoughts at the moment. "Once a week?" He framed her face. "You badly underestimate what's happening here."

It was too dark to see if she was blushing, but he knew she would be. She could talk like a woman of the world, but there was still that trembling bottom lip. "Did you understand what I was saying?" she asked.

"Perfectly."

"And?"

"And I'll help you move your things into my room first, if that's what you want. Hell, I'll move your whole room into mine, furniture and all, if that's what it takes."

"Just my clothes. And I think it can wait."

"Good, because I don't want to."

"There's no reason why we should." She touched his cheek with her fingertips, drawing them slowly to his lips. "Shall I lead the way?"

He wished the house were closer. Even now, after everything he'd learned from their encounter on Shell Island, he knew his patience was nonexistent. He wanted to sweep her off her feet, carry her up the walkway and the stairs to his room. He remembered their first night together and the way she'd felt in his arms. Despite the circumstances, he had responded to her in a way that was foreign to him. Not just as a man to a woman, but as Damon to Matty. Even then, she had not been just a combination of warm flesh and tantalizing female curves. He had already begun to fall under her spell.

He kissed her fingertips, then he took her hand. "Lead the way."

They walked back to the house in silence. He didn't know what to say to her, and she didn't seem to need reassurances. She seemed to have resolved whatever had inhibited her before. He told himself that that could change, that no matter what took place between them now, he had to be understanding, somehow he had to summon patience and truly let her lead the way. All this while his body practically screamed its intention of sinking deeply into her and finding explosive, immediate satisfaction.

In the hallway outside his room, he stepped aside and dropped her hand, giving her a moment to back out. She stepped over his threshold. He followed her and closed the door behind them. Then he crossed the room and closed the door to Heidi's room, too.

Matty moved to stand beside the bed. "Definitely big enough for two." She looked up as he joined her there. "But then, I knew that, because I've been in here to get Heidi."

"And did you imagine yourself here with me? Because I've imagined it a thousand times."

"Have you?" She didn't sound quite as sure of herself suddenly. "Have you really?"

"Since the first night you came."

"I'm glad. That means a lot."

"Matty, tell me what to do. I'm afraid of scaring you again."

"I'm not scared. Unless…maybe a little that you'll be disappointed."

"That's the last thing that could happen."

She was still wearing her costume, though sometime late in the afternoon, after a particularly vicious water balloon fight, she'd washed away the last traces of Kitty's artwork. "I don't know, Damon. I may not be as enticing without these." She stretched out the striped suspenders. Then she let them slide down over her shoulders.

"I'll miss the skirt." He tried to say it nonchalantly. Instead he sounded the way he had when he'd been forced to endure her hands running up and down his leg. "I liked the view."

"Did you? I think this view will be better." She unfastened the button and zipper, and the skirt spread out at her feet like the petals of a daisy. Her panties were as scanty as his patience.

"I think it's your turn." She stepped closer and tucked her hands under his shirt. "I can help."

"And about all I can do right this second is stand here and let you."

She slid her hands up his chest as she lifted the shirt. He closed his eyes, and this time there was no sun to take the blame. "That feels so good," he said. "I don't know if you have any idea how good."

"As good as it feels when you touch me."

He took that as permission. He circled her waist with his hands and, just as she'd done, slid them higher, then higher still.

"I'm going to have trouble taking off your shirt...." Her breath caught as he reached her breasts. "Oh..."

"We seem to be at an impasse."

Her laugh was low and throaty, a laugh to drive a man wild. "How could an impasse feel this wonderful?"

He moved his hands reluctantly—and temporarily. "Take off my shirt, Mattolina. And then it will be your turn."

A lifetime seemed to pass before they were both undressed. Moonlight gave Matty's skin an opalescent glow, and the warm tropical breeze rippled through her hair. Damon rested his palms against her breasts as he kissed her. She sighed against his lips and moved her hips against his. Naked she felt exactly the way he had known she would. Right. Familiar, somehow, as if they had been lovers forever.

He wanted to be patient. He was determined to be. But his body betrayed him. Matty's inexperience was not the same as ignorance. She couldn't miss knowing exactly how much he wanted her. Her response was to touch him there, to move her hand slowly over him until he felt as if he were going to explode.

"I want you, too." She rose to kiss him again, languidly stretching her body along the length of his. "And I don't need as much patience as you seem to think I do." She moved away from him and walked to the bed to pull down the spread. She sat, then swung her legs so that she was reclining against the sheets.

He joined her, stretching out beside her. This new assertive woman was a joy, but he didn't believe everything she said. Her eyes were steady, gazing into his expectantly. But there was more than expectation. Somewhere deep inside her she was not as confident as she appeared. And suddenly it seemed like the most important thing in the world to make this good for her. Mattolina Stewart Quinn deserved every fine and wonderful thing he could ever give her.

"Lie back."

She did as he asked, gazing up at him still.

"Close your eyes."

Her eyelids drifted shut.

He began at her neck, massaging the slight incriminating tension there and in her shoulders, kissing her softly as he moved his hands lower, always lower. "You have no idea how perfect you are, do you? How womanly?"

She murmured something. He didn't catch the words, but he did understand the sentiment. She was entranced with his touch, her muscles turning warm and fluid under his caressing hands. He suspected it would take more than one night for Matty to believe the things he said, but she was responding anyway.

Again, as they had the first time, he marvelled at how exactly her breasts fitted his hands, how soft they were, how appealing. He took his time before he kissed them. His own needs grew hotter, stronger, and he steeled himself against them. She moved against his lips, but without pulling away, as she had before. She moved closer, arching her back and giving herself to him more fully. He lifted her, his hands meeting at the small of her back. One leg rested between hers until hers drifted apart to bring him closer.

She made a small sound of protest when his hand replaced his lips at her breast. He lifted his head and saw that her eyes were shining, not with tears, but with something far more joyous. His heart picked up speed at the expression in her eyes. For a moment he felt such a deep union with her that his breath caught. Sex was not new, but this mating of souls, this instant of total communication and understanding, was. He smiled at her, although a second passed before he realized he had.

"Mattolina..." He didn't know what else to say. He touched her hair, stroking it back from her face. He wanted to say more, but words failed him.

"Make love to me, Damon."

"I am."

She touched him as she had before, her palm cool in contrast to his heat. Her fingers wrapped around him, and he groaned.

There was so much more he wanted to do to her and with her. He had intended to do so much more.

She opened her legs farther still, and she guided him closer.

"We don't have to hurry..." His voice said otherwise.

"Oh... Yes... I think we do."

He grasped her hips to slow the pace, but she wrapped her legs around his. He hadn't expected that blatantly sexual invitation.

He moved on top of her. He was still determined to take this slow, to make this good and control his own needs. Then she lifted her hips, and he was lost. She was sleek and hot and tight around him, but she opened herself to him in a way that no one ever had before. Even though he was afraid he was hurting her, she gave no sign of it. She didn't look away, and she didn't close her eyes. She looked into his as he sank deeply into her.

And for the first time he really understood what it meant for two people to be as one.

Chapter Twelve

Matty looked down at her sleeping husband. She was used to the way that Damon slept now, although for the first week that she'd shared his bed, she had awakened every time he turned over or sprawled against her.

He was a cuddler. She never would have expected such a thing, but he was. He was a surprisingly physical man who liked to touch and be touched and needed no excuse whatsoever to take her to bed for another lesson in lovemaking—although he claimed she was a lightning-quick study who would soon outdistance her teacher.

Sometimes she still woke up at night with Damon's arms around her and wondered how she, plain, ordinary Matty Stewart, had ended up with a passionate, perplexing man like this one. But she had. Somehow she had. And if Damon's enthusiastic lovemaking was any clue, he wasn't one bit sorry about his part of the bargain.

"Matto...lina." Damon yawned her name and put his arm

around her waist to pull her back into bed beside him. "Where are you going so early?"

She resisted. Weakly. They were flying to Ohio this morning. Tomorrow was Heidi's custody hearing, and they wanted a day to settle in so they could be at their best. "I have to finish packing. We have a plane to catch. Remember?"

"Not for another couple of hours."

"But we have to get to Staniel Cay to catch it."

"We'll buy clothes in Cleveland if we have to. Come back to bed."

Matty wanted nothing more. She gave in with little reluctance. He pulled her against him, cupping her body in the curve of his. His hand settled on her breast. "Better..."

She sighed in anticipation. They had made love last night before falling asleep, but that only seemed to make this sweeter. Every time she went into his arms she felt like the luckiest woman in the world.

His hand crept lower, and her breath caught. "Every time, I plan to make this an event." His voice was morning-deep and even sexier than usual. "Maybe someday I'll have the patience to show you how wickedly seductive self-control can be."

"Promises..." She turned in his arms, and they were only a heartbeat away. "Besides, I like knowing I excite you."

He smiled a lazy wake-up smile. "Oh, I think you more than like it."

"Where do you get an idea like that?"

"The noises you make." He kissed her chin, her lips. "Right here..." He kissed her throat.

"I'm very proper. I don't make noises."

He laughed. "You are the least proper lady in the Bahamas, Mattolina. You're every man's fondest dream."

She glowed at the praise. Her reaction to him still embarrassed her sometimes. She was glad it didn't embarrass him.

"Let me tell you some of the new improper things we're about to do." He trailed his lips lower as he murmured the words against her skin. She made one of the noises in question, and he laughed a little. "Already, before I even tell you?"

She slid a leg over his and pressed her hips closer, just to give him a taste of his own medicine. But before he could do anything in return, a baby's wailing drifted down the hall.

"Maybe she'll go back to sleep." Damon didn't release Matty. In fact, he pulled her closer, as if her supple body might act as a sound barrier.

"Sure, and maybe Inspiration Cay attached itself to the continent of North America during the night."

"Does she know, do you suppose? Is this a baby instinct?"

"We were going to be late anyway."

"Damn. Tonight, then. When she's sound asleep again."

"She'll be in our hotel room," Matty warned.

"We'll set up her crib in the bathtub. Or the closet."

She kissed his nose. "We'll be back here in a couple of nights with the custody issue all settled. We'll tuck Heidi into her own little room, and then you can tell me all those improper things you have planned."

"That's a night I'll look forward to." He kissed her once for good measure, then let her sit up. "I'll get Heidi. You take your shower first."

Matty gathered her clothes as Damon left to get the baby. After their first night as lovers, he had moved Heidi into Matty's old room. She had been surprised and pleased. Heidi was still only seconds away, but somehow Damon's decision to move her had seemed like a sign. He was taking his relationship with Matty seriously and separating it from Matty's role in Heidi's life.

She thought back over the weeks that had passed since then, nearly perfect weeks that had given her a new outlook on life. Until she and Damon had become lovers she had believed that she could be content with their charade of a marriage. Damon and Heidi had needed her, and that had seemed like enough.

Now she knew better. She had been needed all her life; she knew exactly how that felt. But now she was wanted. Perhaps not quite in the way that would mean the most to her, but wanted nonetheless. Damon wanted *her,* not just a woman to share his bed, but Matty Stewart Quinn. Sometimes it seemed hard to believe. Sometimes she wondered if she was stretching the point. But then, in her darkest moments of doubt, Damon would smile at her, or touch her, or take her to bed.

Damon popped back into the room with Heidi, who was chewing her fist. "We'll meet you downstairs. It smells like Nanny's made homemade biscuits and hasn't burned them."

"I'll be there as soon as I've had my shower."

He smiled at her again, his eyes traveling the curves and contours he knew so well. "Maybe I could get someone to feed Heidi if I begged hard enough."

"Maybe we'd better just get ready to go."

"Your mommy's practical to the bone," he told the baby.

She could hear him continuing his conversation with Heidi as he went down the hallway. She took her shower and dressed in casual clothing before she joined them.

Heidi was almost finished with her bottle by the time Matty arrived. They were cuddled together in the kitchen, and Damon was munching a biscuit while Heidi completed her breakfast. He handed her over to Matty, dropped a kiss on both their heads, then went back upstairs to shower and dress.

Nanny bustled into the kitchen from the back of the house, followed closely by Kevin.

"You t'ink they gonna give you that baby for good, Matty Quinn?" As usual Nanny didn't ease her way into the conversation. She went straight to the heart of the matter that was uppermost in all their minds.

"I can't imagine why not." Matty draped Heidi over her shoulder. The baby really didn't need help to burp anymore, but Matty enjoyed the snuggling time. "Gretchen wants Damon to have her. He's a respectable married man with wonderful prospects for the future and a wife who just happens to be a pediatric nurse. The Otts are too old to raise a baby, and according to Damon's lawyer, the social worker who interviewed them was less than flattering in her report. He thinks the hearing tomorrow is nothing more than a formality."

"You come home, we have a party." Nanny nodded as if it was a done deal.

"Why don't you just leave her here while you're gone?" Kevin said. "We could watch her. Then, if something goes wrong, we could hide her."

"Hide her?"

"They can't take Heidi." His tone made it clear that he would do whatever it took to stop the authorities if given the opportunity.

Matty nodded. "We're going to do everything in our power to make sure of that, Kevin. But we have to give the law a chance to work. I know your experiences with the courts haven't been the best, but most of the time things work out the way they're supposed to."

Something simmered behind his eyes. "I know what it's like to lose people." He left the room.

Nanny snorted. "Kevin Garcia, he love that baby. Everybody love her except those people who say they want to raise her so bad."

"We'll take care of Heidi. We'll bring her home safe and sound." Matty held the baby tighter against her. In her heart she knew she and Damon were the best candidates to raise the little girl. She only hoped the judge would make the right decision, because despite the brave words she'd uttered to Kevin, she also knew that sometimes terrible mistakes were made.

The hotel room was comfortable, if plain, with a small dressing area that was perfect for a crib. By the time they'd made the boat trip to Staniel Cay and taken the three flights required to get them to Cleveland, the Quinns were exhausted. After check-in, Damon and Matty napped with Heidi tucked between them.

By dinner time they all felt better, although Damon was dreading the evening to come. He had agreed to take Heidi to visit the Otts that night. He had never met Gretchen's parents, and he wasn't pleased that he would have to. But he knew his duty. No matter what he had heard about them, the Otts were Heidi's grandparents.

"I know we have to do this." Matty presented her back to Damon so that he could zip her dress. He didn't know the names for the styles women wore, but this dress definitely captured his attention. It was the green of palm leaves, and it skimmed her hips in a way that made his imagination work overtime. It was a perfectly modest dress; she was a perfectly modest woman.

Until she climbed into his bed.

"You're smiling...." She faced him. "You're not worried about tonight?"

He sobered immediately. Matty in his bed was one thing. Dinner with the Otts was another. "I'm not worried, but I don't want to be there any more than you do."

"What kind of people plan a formal dinner for their first encounter with their baby granddaughter?"

"The Otts' kind of people. If nothing else, it shows how out of touch they are with what a baby needs."

"At least Gretchen will be there."

"I'm afraid that's not going to help much. Their animosity is so deep and mutual, it's only going to increase the tension."

"We'll make it through the evening." She flashed him an encouraging smile.

He wanted to kiss her in gratitude. Or in something else. He rarely needed an excuse. Matty was absolutely kissable. But when she was trying so hard to make him feel better, he realized more than at any other time what a lucky man he was.

She turned away, and he lost his chance. He made up for it half an hour later when he parked their rental car in front of the Otts' suburban Cleveland home. He pulled Matty close and kissed her quickly for good luck. From her car seat in the back, Heidi began to fuss.

"Take a deep breath and push down all the unkind things you want to say," Matty warned him. "And I'll do the same. If it's true they'll want nothing to do with Heidi if we get custody, then this may be the first and last time we ever have to encounter them.''

"Look at this house."

Matty turned her head to gaze at the house as he absorbed it, too. The house was an absolutely cheerless gray with tall, perfectly pruned junipers along the narrow front porch and white pines in a symmetrical triangle beside the road. Although the other yards in the neighborhood were newly planted with petunias and impatiens, the Otts' yard sported nothing but recently cut grass.

"They certainly aren't gardeners," Matty said.

Damon compared the house and landscape to Inspiration, with its vivid hues and effusive landscaping. "I guess we can't hold that against them."

"Gray shingles. Black shutters. No trim of any kind. But not a crack in their sidewalk or an oil stain on their driveway."

"That has to say something."

"It says no imagination."

"We don't know that."

She turned. "Okay. Think it says they have better things to do with their lives? That they're probably out saving the whales or feeding the homeless?"

He smiled despite himself. "I guess we have to go see for ourselves."

Heidi, in a bright red dress, was fussing louder by the time they arrived at the front door. She was still tired from the trip and having her nap schedule disturbed. Damon rang the doorbell as Matty jiggled the baby to quiet her.

The woman who opened the door looked nothing like Gretchen. She was tall and blond like her daughter, but her mouth was drawn into a frown that had rooted there over the years and carved deep unattractive lines into her face. She didn't smile as she held out her hand. "I'm Sylvia Ott. You must be Damon." Her gaze didn't even flick to Heidi.

"This is my wife, Matty." Damon dropped her hand and stepped back.

Mrs. Ott held out her hand to Matty, only then gazing down

at Heidi. "Yes, she's Gretchen's baby all right. She looks just like Gretchen did at that age, except for the coloring." The words didn't sound like a compliment.

Matty's eyes widened. "Heidi looks like Gretchen?"

Mrs. Ott made a rude sound of dismissal. "Did you expect her to look like someone else?"

Damon felt his temper flare, but Matty gave him a stern look. "No, I'm just surprised. I didn't see the resemblance."

Mrs. Ott repeated the same arrogant sound. "Well, we can only hope she doesn't resemble her mother in the ways that really matter."

Damon was already counting to ten, and they hadn't even set foot in the house. But he didn't need to say a thing in Gretchen's defense.

"Actually, I hope she resembles Gretchen in the ways that *do* matter," Matty said sweetly. "I hope she has her mother's sense of humor, her joy for living and her talent for finding the good in people." She paused. "But I guess there's no reason to hope that those things are hereditary, is there?"

Matty snapped a lacy cover over Heidi's diaper and pulled her matching blue dress into place. "You're going to look like your mommy, pumpkin." She tickled Heidi under her chin, and Heidi chortled with delight. "Just like your mama."

"I wouldn't have believed it if you hadn't demanded to see a baby photograph of Gretchen last night." Damon scowled at his tie in the mirror, then untied it and began again.

Matty imagined that Damon could tie a tie upside down and blindfolded. But this was his third go-round with this one, and that, more than anything else, signaled how nervous he was about the hearing that morning.

"Sylvia had one album of Gretchen's childhood. Just one. Two pictures on each page, each one centered exactly on its half of the paper. A page for each year."

"Maybe there were more photographs somewhere else."

"Do you honestly think so?" Matty hugged Heidi against her. She supposed she should be happy that the Otts had kept even one album of their daughter. And the resemblance to Heidi *was* amazing, right down to the ears. She and Damon were going to have to hire armed guards when Heidi became a teenager. They were going to have to live on Inspiration forever.

If Heidi was still theirs to raise.

"Matty, I can't tie this damned thing." Damon stripped off the tie again. "Can you do it for me?"

"You bet." She put Heidi in her infant seat and gave her a plastic key ring to rattle. She settled the tie under his collar again and restarted the process.

Damon held his chin high to give her more working room. "I just want to know why Gretchen wasn't there last night."

Matty wanted to know the same thing. Gretchen had never arrived, and Matty and Damon had been left to fend for themselves with Gretchen's parents. The evening had been the longest one of Matty's life. She and Damon had picked at tasteless food under the icy gaze of Mr. and Mrs. Ott and listened to their cold-blooded opinions of how Heidi's fussing should be handled. Both Otts had held the baby, but stiff-armed, as if too much contact was unhealthy for everyone concerned. Matty had no doubts now why Gretchen found it so hard to be a mother.

"Maybe she just couldn't face them," Matty said. "And who could blame her?"

"It's not unlike Gretchen to wiggle out of something unpleasant, but I would have expected her to phone and warn us. She knows where we're staying."

Matty made another loop. "I wish we could have gotten hold of her last night." Damon had tried the hotel where Gretchen was supposed to be staying, but she hadn't been registered. "If she doesn't show up at court this morning, that could make problems for us, couldn't it?"

"We have a stronger case for custody if Gretchen tells the court why she believes we're the best choice. Her opinion carries a lot of weight."

"She won't let us down." Matty finished the tie and slid

the knot into place under his collar. "She won't let Heidi down, either."

Matty told herself the same thing a half hour later when she, Damon and Heidi walked toward the big brick courthouse on Cleveland's east side. The hearing would be held in Juvenile Court, and if they were particularly fortunate, they would be out before noon.

Inside, the halls teemed with people. Heidi, who wasn't accustomed to being surrounded by crowds, began to whimper.

Matty followed Damon, who asked for directions. Outside the appropriate courtroom, she took a seat on a wooden bench beside a young woman not yet out of her teens who was holding a screaming toddler by one arm. The woman whacked the child on his behind to quiet him, and the noise level doubled.

Heidi, fascinated by the scene in front of her, forgot to whimper.

"I don't see Gretchen." Damon looked up and down the hallway. "Or my attorney."

Matty hadn't met Damon's attorney. So far the only professional she'd met was the social worker who had come to Inspiration ten days ago to interview them and examine the house. She'd spent a fair portion of the day in a bathing suit soaking up Inspiration's sun.

"They're probably here somewhere." Matty smiled at the screaming toddler, who screamed louder in protest. She winced as the child's mother jerked his arm and smacked his behind again.

"Come on, let's look for them." Damon gestured toward the end of the hallway.

She joined him, grateful to be far away from what she suspected was an all too typical example of the young mother's child-rearing techniques. "I hope we don't have to wait too long. Heidi's going to be a basket case."

"So am I."

She tucked her arm through his. "It's going to go well, Damon. It has to."

He covered her hand in the only reassurance he could give.

Gretchen did not materialize, but a man in a dark blue suit was waiting by the courtroom door after they made a tour of the hallway. "Mr. Quinn?"

Damon stopped in front of him. "Matty, this is Lawrence Clark, our attorney."

She liked the sound of that "our." She extended her hand as Lawrence, short and silver-haired, murmured greetings.

"Look," Lawrence said, "there's going to be a delay. The judge has asked for an attorney conference in his chambers. And he can't do it right away. I'm afraid you might have a long wait."

Matty didn't have to look at Damon to know he must be frowning.

"Why?" Damon had to speak loudly to be heard over the noise in the hall. "What's going on?"

"I don't know. I'll find out. Where's the child's mother?"

"Matty is the child's mother." Damon glanced at her. "The child's birth mother doesn't seem to be here."

"That's not going to help."

"If there's going to be a delay, that will give Gretchen a chance to arrive," Matty said. "I know she won't let us down."

But she did let them down. Noon came and went. Matty left Heidi sleeping on Damon's shoulder and went to find them sandwiches. When she returned, they ate in the hallway, still waiting for someone to tell them what was going on. The Otts hadn't appeared, either, and Lawrence didn't come back.

By three Matty was about to explode. She had seen more teenagers in handcuffs, more distraught families, more poor parenting skills, than she ever wanted to see again. The noise level had ballooned as the afternoon crept on, and Heidi, who hadn't gotten a long enough nap, was beyond comfort.

Lawrence finally appeared behind a uniformed policeman escorting a teenage girl who looked as if she'd been caught in the act of selling her voluptuous wares.

"He's ready for me. It won't be too long now."

"Do you have any idea what this is about?" Damon asked.

"No, but it can't be good news," Lawrence said bluntly. "Prepare yourself for the worst."

"Don't come out of those chambers and tell me I'm going to lose my daughter."

"I don't make the laws. I just do my damnedest to make them work."

"I don't like this." Matty watched Damon stroking Heidi's back. No matter how hard she screamed, he never got irritated with the baby. He was patience personified.

"That makes two of us." He kissed Heidi's head. "But something's wrong. Why aren't the Otts here? And what in the hell possessed Gretchen to abandon us this way?"

"Do you think she wants Heidi?"

"Unlikely."

Matty thought it was unlikely, too. Gretchen had shown absolutely no signs of changing her mind about her decision to give them custody. If anything, she had been prepared to give up even more of her legal rights.

Close to another hour passed before they were ushered into the courtroom. It was small and gloomy. A significant number of trees had been felled to provide the wealth of dark wood paneling. Matty and Damon were shown to a bench that resembled a cathedral pew. Heidi, exhausted from the strange and uncomfortable day, had fallen asleep in her father's arms once again.

They stood for the judge, then sat again once he was seated.

Lawrence joined them, leaning over to whisper, "Hold tight to your seat and don't lose your temper, no matter what happens."

The Otts still weren't present, which concerned Matty more than Lawrence's words. A middle-aged man in a more expensive suit than Lawrence's, who was introduced as the Otts' attorney, was asked to come forward once the basic formalities were past.

"Mr. Sawyer, who is representing the baby's maternal grandparents, has new information which affects this case. Mr. Sawyer, please make your statement for the record."

"Your honor, I have proof here, that the paternity of the baby named Heidi Louise Quinn by her mother, Gretchen Ott, is in question."

Matty saw Damon grip the edge of the bench.

The attorney continued. "I have two statements, one from a nurse at the hospital where the baby was born and another from an acquaintance of Miss Ott's, that Gretchen Ott told each of them that she was unsure which of two men had fathered her child and that she was going to choose the one who would make the best father to put on the baby's birth certificate."

Damon's jaw seemed welded from iron. He didn't speak, but Matty felt him grow rigid. Heidi slept on.

"When Miss Ott was confronted with this information by my clients, she admitted that it was true. She claims to be uncertain which man fathered the baby."

"Where is Miss Ott?" the judge asked.

"I don't know, your honor. She knows she was supposed to be here today. Perhaps she chose, under the circumstances, not to show her face."

"That's conjecture," the judge said. "Not fact."

"Yes, your honor."

"Mr. Quinn, did you have any knowledge of this?" the judge asked. "Did Miss Ott give you any reason to believe that the baby might not be yours?"

"No, your honor."

"Then this is the first you've heard of it?"

"Yes, your honor."

The judge addressed Matty. "Mrs. Quinn, I understand that you and Miss Ott have become friends. Is that correct?"

"Yes, your honor." Her voice was firmer than she'd expected.

"And did she ever mention this possibility to you?"

"No, your honor. She always spoke as if there was no question that Damon was Heidi's father."

"But there is a question," Mr. Sawyer said. "A rather large

question. One that will seriously affect the outcome of this hearing.''

The judge, an older man than the Otts' attorney, flashed him a warning with his eyes. ''Don't try to do my job for me, Mr. Sawyer. I'm perfectly capable of deciding what will seriously affect anything under my jurisdiction.''

''I apologize, your honor.''

''Mr. Quinn, do you have anything to say?''

Damon stood. ''Your honor, this is my child. Nothing that's been said here changes that one little bit. Whether she's mine genetically or not, she's mine in all the ways that matter. I love her. Matty loves her. We're her family, and we are the best and most qualified people to raise her.''

The judge clasped his hands in front of him. ''I appreciate your sentiment. It can't be easy to hear what you've heard today. I think you'll need some time to absorb it, to be certain you mean everything you've said. In the meantime, I'm going to order blood and DNA tests to be performed on you, Miss Ott and the child herself. The grandparents have rights in this case, particularly if you are not the biological father.''

''The grandparents don't love this child! They don't even know her. In their minds this isn't about love or who's most qualified, it's about—''

The judge leaned forward. ''I have to consider this carefully. When all the evidence is in and I've had time to reflect on this again, I'll make my decision. Then, and only then. I could ask you not to leave the country with this baby, Mr. Quinn. I could require that she be put in the temporary care of her grandparents to be sure you don't disappear with her. That's what they've asked me to do. Must I do it? Or can you follow my instructions on this and promise to bring her back for the final hearing?''

Seconds passed as Damon mastered his temper. ''I'll do whatever the court asks me to do, your honor.''

''Good, Mr. Quinn. See that you do.''

Lawrence stood and took Damon's arm before he could say another word. ''We're finished in here.''

The rest passed in a blur. Matty found herself out in the crowded hallway once more. Then, miraculously, they were outside in the sunshine.

Lawrence shook his head when they reached Matty and Damon's rental car. "Out of nowhere," he said. "I had no way of knowing any of this was in the works, Damon. Apparently the Otts hired a private investigator to get information on their own daughter so they could use it against her."

"They knew this last night and didn't say a word. Now we know why Gretchen didn't come today." Matty took Heidi, who was beginning to wake up. She was sure Damon's arms were numb. "She was probably so ashamed."

"What do you think our chances are of keeping her?" Damon folded his arms, as if he needed to be sure everything stayed locked deep inside him. "If the blood tests prove that Heidi can't be my biological child?"

"Then the judge will have to weigh everything again. But I'm afraid you and Matty will have no particular claim on Heidi except that she's been in your custody. Even if Gretchen still insists she wants you to raise her daughter, her word will carry less weight than it would have before. And the only blood relatives who want Heidi will be the Otts."

"Are you saying there's no chance at all?" Matty said. "If the tests don't prove Damon's the father, there's no chance we can keep Heidi?"

Lawrence looked as sad as an attorney in a four-hundred-dollar suit could look. "I'm saying you'd better get used to the possibility. Because if you don't, you're not going to be prepared for the worst. And the worst may very well happen."

Chapter Thirteen

Matty didn't need proof that Heidi was the only real link she and Damon shared. Damon had always been clear about that. He had married a mother for Heidi, not a woman. And although they had found physical satisfaction in each other's arms and a certain happiness in their daily lives, Heidi was still the bond that glued their marriage together.

Without Heidi there would be no marriage at all.

Matty stirred another teaspoon of sugar into her morning coffee. She had taken to sweetening it in the week since they had returned to Inspiration. She had also taken to adding milk. She wished life could be made sweeter and mellower with just a few simple additions.

"You stir that coffee enough, it suck you under."

Matty looked up to find Nanny glowering down at her. "I almost wish it would."

"No point in feeling sorry for yourself. No point a'tall."

"I know." Matty set her spoon on the saucer and picked

up her cup. "Maybe I need one of your magic potions today, Nanny. Some old-fashioned bush medicine."

"Some good Jamaican rum be just about fine."

Matty smiled. "I guess."

"I'm going picking this afternoon. Samuel's coming to take me. Lots of t'ings just right about now. You come, and I'll show you what's what."

The invitation didn't sound half-bad to Matty. Getting away from the island for an afternoon sounded promising. And over the weeks Nanny had been teaching her bits and pieces about local plants and what plant or combination was used for which ailment.

"I'd like to come," she said. "But Damon's going to be in the laboratory all day. I'll need to stay here with Heidi."

"Too bad. Samuel and me, we going to see some islands."

Kevin came to stand in the doorway. Since he had learned what had transpired at the hearing, he had grown even quieter. Matty was concerned about him.

She was concerned about all of them, but about Damon most of all.

"Where's Samuel taking you?" Kevin asked Nanny.

"Couple different places. Some t'ings grow one place, some another. Catch this one now, that one later. Gotta know just when and where. You coming, too?"

Kevin frowned. "You mean stuff grows one place, but not another?"

"Sometimes, sure. But some stuff grows everywhere, onliest not all of it as good in one place as in another."

"Why?" Kevin walked over to the counter and gestured to a row of glass jars filled with dried herbs. "You mean if you get something like parsley in one place it doesn't taste as good as parsley from another?"

"Sometimes."

"I remember when I was growing up my father always bought our summer vegetables from one particular farm outside of town," Matty said. "He always believed there was something in the soil that made them taste better. The owners were organic farmers, always enriching the land with manure or compost.''

Kevin lifted a jar and peered inside. "Just taste?"

"Just taste what?" Nanny said, taking the jar out of his hands and setting it back on the counter where it belonged.

"Is it just taste that's affected? You said the stuff you collect for tea wasn't as good in one place as in another. Were you talking about taste?"

"No. Some stuff grows one place, it's stronger. Works better.''

"How could that be?"

"Probably minerals in the soil," Matty said, when Nanny just shrugged. "I remember studying that in college. There's a county, in Texas, I think, where the soil has a high concentration of fluoride. The people who lived there ate their own farm products, wheat and other things, and they rarely had cavities. That was one of the discoveries that led to fluoridating water.''

"So where something is grown, how it's grown, can have an effect on what it contains?"

"I don't know how much and how often, but yes."

"Makes a difference," Nanny said. "No question."

"I'd like to come with you," Kevin said.

"Sure."

Matty was glad that Kevin was going to get away from Inspiration for a little while. He would be safe with Nanny. The old woman wouldn't let him get away with anything. Matty finished her coffee and left as Nanny told Kevin where to meet her and when.

Since Heidi was still sleeping, Matty didn't want to go far. She went back upstairs to the bedroom she shared with Damon and started the project she'd planned for the morning, cleaning the room and waxing the cypress floor. Keeping busy was the only way she could get through each day.

It was barely nine, but already Damon had been gone for hours. He'd gotten up just after dawn with Heidi, who really was cutting a tooth now, fed her breakfast and changed her, then put her back to bed. Matty knew all this because she'd heard everything. Damon had been very quiet, but there was little he did that she wasn't aware of.

She knew, for instance, that he wasn't sleeping well at night. She knew that sometimes, when he thought she was asleep, he paced the balcony, worrying about his daughter. She knew he was angry that Heidi might be taken away from him, and even that Gretchen hadn't told him the truth from the beginning. But she knew that, most of all, he was afraid.

Damon had tried not to let his feelings affect her. But nothing he could do could change the obvious. They were in danger of losing their daughter. Matty loved Heidi, too, and the little girl was in danger of being snatched away from her. She couldn't bear the thought of the baby growing up in the Otts' home without the love and understanding a child needed to flourish emotionally. Even if the court awarded Damon visiting rights—and even that much was in jeopardy—what would the Otts tell Heidi each time before Damon came to see her? This is the man who thought he was your father, Heidi, but he's no relation to you and what he thinks doesn't matter?

Damon had said very little since that afternoon in the parking lot by Juvenile Court. But Matty knew his feelings, and her own, as well. She was afraid for Heidi and for Heidi's father. But she was afraid for herself, too. She had found almost everything she'd dreamed about here on Inspiration with her new baby daughter and the man a younger Matty had silently adored. She had a child and a husband. She had Kevin and Nanny, Arthur and the others who made up their happy little extended family.

And the moment the court took Heidi away, everything would unravel.

Damon tried to pretend that things were going to be fine. The day he'd gotten word that the first and simplest blood test had confirmed the possibility that he could be Heidi's father, he had shared the news with quiet confidence. But Matty knew that even though he tried to be strong, he was still desperately worried. In the week since they had come home, silence had rooted between them, and the happiness they'd found in this room had disappeared.

The telephone rang just as she was about to start on the floors. Since the phone service to Inspiration was a complicated system of underwater cables and relays, it was erratic at best. Calls were a rarity and clear reception nearly unheard-of.

But they were waiting for a phone call that might change their future.

She lifted the receiver slowly, expecting the worst. Instead the voice at the other end was dearly familiar. "Matty? Is that you?"

Matty sat down on the bed. "Liza?" She could hear the other woman well, well enough to bring tears to her eyes. "What's going on?"

"I got your letter."

Matty hadn't wanted to share bad news with her friends, but she knew they would expect her to. She'd taken the coward's way out by putting it into a letter.

"Are you okay?"

"It's hard." Matty sat down on the bed. Now that she had someone to talk to, she hardly knew what to say. But Liza seemed to understand anyway.

"If Damon has to give up custody, what's that going to do to you, Matty?"

"I don't know. Damon married me because he needed a mother for Heidi."

"If that's the only way he thinks of you, maybe it would be better for you if the marriage ended anyway."

"That's not the only way he thinks of me." Matty heard her own words, said without so much as a pause. And she knew they were true.

"Then you still have a chance to make the marriage work," Liza said.

"I don't know. I just don't know." Matty felt the tears spill over. She wiped her eyes with the back of her hand.

"Don't tell me you're quitting. That you're not going to stay on and fight for him."

"I honestly don't know what to do."

"I'll tell you what. Show a little backbone," Liza said sternly. "This isn't like your job here at Carrollton, Matty. You've got to stop letting people walk all over you. Make some demands. Tell him what *you* need for a change."

Matty had expected sympathy. She didn't even know what to say to Liza's criticism.

"You think about it," Liza said. "It's about time for you to decide what you want out of life and make a stand." She changed the subject abruptly, recounting hospital rumors, then going on to tell Matty about Felicity's newest boyfriend.

Matty made rote responses, but Liza's words boomed in her head.

Liza finished her gossip report. "Oh, and, Matty, the other reason I called. There's a man in New York who's trying to get in touch with you. A…" She paused, as if she was looking for something. "Here it is, a Charles Cartwright. Does that sound familiar?"

"No."

"He says it's vital he get in touch with you, but I didn't want to give him your number. Do you want to call him instead?"

Matty wrote the number on a pad beside the telephone.

"And, Matty, please think about what I said. If you let Damon slip away without a fight, you'll always wonder if you could have done more."

"It may not even be a problem," Matty heard herself saying. "He may be Heidi's biological father. We just don't know."

"Who cares?" Liza said. "Maybe this is the right moment to discover whether you mean more to him as a woman than as a baby nurse. If you don't, do you want to stay with him anyway?"

"Damn it, Liza, you're the one who pushed me into coming here in the first place!"

There was a short silence. "No," Liza said at last. "You married Damon Quinn because you love him. Don't blame your greatest act of courage on someone else, Matty. For once you did something just because you wanted to."

Matty was still staring at the receiver moments after Liza had hung up. She didn't even hear Damon come into the room until he spoke.

"Who was that on the telephone?"

She put the receiver back in the cradle. "Liza."

"Is something wrong?"

"No, she…" She certainly didn't want to share the bulk of the phone call with Damon. She looked down at the number she'd scrawled on the pad. "A man in New York's been trying to get in touch with me."

"About what?"

"I don't know." She didn't want to talk to Damon. Not now. She picked up the telephone again as an excuse. "I guess I'll find out."

He went to the closet and began to rummage. She was stuck with completing the phone call, which took as long to put through as Damon's extended rummage through the closet.

She was surprised when a voice on the other end answered, "Cartwright Literary Agency." She gave her name and explained why she was calling, then she waited.

Damon left the room and returned again while she was on the telephone; then he left once more. She was still sitting there, receiver in hand, when he returned with a sleepy Heidi in his arms. But the phone call had ended.

"Bad news?" He frowned. "I'm sorry, I don't mean to pry."

"Do you remember my telling you about my father's book? He wrote a novel about a man raising a daughter."

Something passed over his face. Nothing as revealing as grief, but something very close. "I remember that he'd written a book."

"Well, his agent sent it out, and no publisher wanted it. They were looking for thrillers and science fiction. The agent died before my father did, and by then Daddy was too sick to think about sending it to anyone else. I have a copy, of course, but I never thought there might be others.''

"And?"

"The agency was sold to a man named Charles Cartwright. I remember now that I got a letter about it some time or other just before Daddy died. I guess Daddy's book was one of a million things he had to read and make a decision on, and when Charles didn't hear anything from him, he put it aside. But he finally got to it a couple of months ago, and he passed it on to an editor, just to get an opinion. She loves it, and she wants to publish it. She's sure it's going to do very, very well.''

Damon joined her on the bed. "This must be a huge surprise.''

"Charles says that the house is behind the book all the way, that it's perfect for today's publishing climate, and they're expecting it to make good money. He asked me if I still wanted to go to medical school....'' Her voice broke.

"Matty?"

She cleared her throat. "Charles found an old letter of Daddy's in his files. Daddy had written about how much I wanted to be a doctor and how much he hoped the book sold soon so that I wouldn't have to go into debt for the part he couldn't afford.''

She looked up, her eyes shining with tears. "I had the best father in the world, Damon. The very best.''

He sat without moving, and she realized exactly what she'd said. Her gaze dropped to Heidi, then back up to his face. And she knew that she and Damon were thinking the same thing.

Matty's father had meant the world to her. And very soon Heidi might not have a father at all.

Damon made a ritual of closing up his laboratory every evening. He was meticulous about details, following exactly the same routine every time so that he wouldn't worry through the night that he'd left something undone.

Tonight, even though he knew that he'd done nothing out of the ordinary an hour ago when he'd locked the doors, he found himself on the pathway to the boathouse to check everything one more time. He supposed he was using the lab as an excuse to get away. He was in between experiments again after another complete failure. He still had ideas to try, but he was beginning to believe that nothing was going to change. He was spending his most creative years chasing rainbows, and there was no pot of gold waiting at the end.

He wondered if that might not be the right analogy for the rest of his life, too. He had chased the dream of fatherhood, a dream he hadn't even known he had until Heidi entered his life, and quite possibly that rainbow was going to fade and disappear, as well. He couldn't face the fact that he might be losing his daughter. He tried to make himself look rationally at the possibility and plan for it, but there was nothing rational about the way he felt inside.

Then there was Matty. And he found her the hardest of all to think about.

As he neared the boathouse he was surprised to see a light burning inside. He never left a light on. The solar generator that supplied electricity to the boathouse was more than adequate, but he never pushed it to its limits. When he closed up the lab each day, he shut off everything he could to save energy for the times when he really needed it.

He unlocked the door to find Kevin sitting at the computer.

"What are you doing here?" Damon said.

Kevin looked up, his eyes bright in the dim light. "I'm checking something. I thought I'd check out some of your old records."

Damon had half expected the boy to admit he was using the computer to win some complex adventure game, or even that he was writing a program to shut down computer systems all over the world. Kevin was capable of nearly anything.

"What records?" Damon joined him at the desk, peering down at the monitor. "And why didn't you tell me?"

"Look at this." Kevin pointed at the screen. "Do you see that?"

Damon squinted as his eyes adjusted. He'd seen this particular page a million times. It was just one of nearly a thousand pages of meticulously kept notes he'd made the first time he'd run his experiment with plant-for-all. The first of the three times the experiment had succeeded.

"So?" He straightened, rubbing the back of his neck. "I can quote it chapter and verse. I can quote the whole damned—darned thing."

"You know, you're so careful, so particular, you make me crazy sometimes."

"When I was your age everything an adult did drove me crazy."

"Yeah, well, you're really getting to me now, because you know what? You never put anything in here about where you got the plant-for-all that you used on this experiment, or in any of them, for that matter."

"Of course I did." Damon bent over again and pointed to the screen. "You're looking right at it."

"Sure. It says Staniel Cay. I can see that. But where on the cay? Exactly where did you get it?"

Damon was intrigued by the question and tried to remember. "I didn't make note of it anywhere?"

"No. A pretty big error, wouldn't you say?"

Damon scanned the screen. "I've gotten it a number of places. I always choose the same size plants, at the same point in their growth cycle. I treat them exactly the same way. You know that because you've gone with me to collect. We've collected it right here."

"We've never collected it on Staniel Cay. Not together."

Damon tried to think. "I remember being on Staniel with Nanny the first time I picked the plant. She was the one who showed me what it looked like and where to find it. We weren't far from the airport."

"We were there today. She showed me the place and told

me that's where you'd gotten it. At least, I hope it's the same place."

"What's this about, Kevin?" Damon asked the question, but he was already beginning to form his own opinion.

"Plants absorb different nutrients from the ground they grow in. Matty and Nanny were explaining that to me today. Wheat can pick up fluoride from the soil and a whole county can be free of cavities."

Damon was already nodding, way ahead of Kevin now. "And you think that where the plant-for-all was growing might have made the difference? That if I used samples from other places, that even if the plant was the same size, the same color, at the same stage in its growth cycle—"

"Couldn't that be true?"

"But I've put every plant, including the original, through exactly the same rigid tests. They always come out within the same parameters."

"Yeah, but what if you aren't testing it for the right things? What if you didn't know exactly what to look for and skipped over something? I mean, in that place in Texas, they probably grew wheat for years without understanding about fluoride and stuff. They just knew they didn't have cavities."

"It can't be that simple."

"You keep saying you're missing something simple. The experiment worked, and then it didn't."

"Let me see something." Damon replaced Kevin at the computer and opened another page. "Look," he pointed to a line. "This is one of the experiments that failed. And I got the plant-for-all from Staniel Cay for this one, too. That's why I never considered that this might be a problem. Later I used some from other places, but for the fourth experiment I—"

"But where on the cay? You don't specify it. Don't you get it? The same island could have different kinds of soil. There could be more rain, less rain, different rocks leaching different minerals. I don't know, but something."

Damon tried to think back. He had gathered the plant-for-all from a field near the airport. But hadn't he gone back later and found it somewhere else because the field was being used for something? There had been tents. A festival in progress...

He just didn't know. "This is good thinking, Kevin. Whether it turns out to be right or not, it's a good idea. I think we should move on it. We'll go over to the cay tomorrow and collect in different places. And we'll start a new trial."

"I already collected today. Exactly the way you and I collected before. And I labeled everything according to where on the island I got it. Nanny's pissed...upset with me for ruining her day. I made her take me to every source she knew about."

Damon tried to push down hope. He had experienced this surge of excitement before, and when the experiments failed once again, the disappointment had been deeper. His mind flashed forward anyway. If Kevin was right—and wouldn't it be wonderful if Kevin, who needed tangible successes in his life, had provided the key?—then Damon's life would change enormously. He could take the proof of his success back to his university adviser, explain what had happened and finish his degree out from under the black cloud that hung over his professional reputation. Doors would surely open again, opportunities that had been snatched away would be his, and he could begin to contribute in a significant way to the body of cancer research.

His little family—including Kevin, of course—would move back to the United States. Matty could pursue her career or even a medical degree. Kevin could be persuaded to begin college, and Heidi would have all the opportunities a child deserved. They would visit Inspiration and Nanny whenever...

And suddenly the whole happy fantasy fell apart.

"You're angry with me, aren't you?" Kevin said.

"Of course not."

"You look angry."

"Not about this."

"What then?"

Damon didn't know how angry he was until his fist slammed into the desk. "You could be right. We both know it's a long shot, but you could be right. And what if you are?

Success is what I've been living for, and you know what? Even if we're successful here, it's not going to change a thing. I could still lose Heidi.''

And Matty. He didn't want to think the words, but his heart wouldn't be denied.

Kevin exited his program and turned off the computer. "You can run, go somewhere else where they can't find you."

"I've thought about it. But that's no life for a child. Pick up, move on. Pick up and move on again, always looking over our shoulders. And besides, I promised the judge."

"You and Matty can have a baby."

"Babies aren't replaceable, Kevin. People aren't replaceable. Do you think if you disappeared from my life I'd just go out and find another rotten teenager to take your place? Do you think anybody ever could?"

Kevin got slowly to his feet and faced Damon. "Yeah, I thought you probably could replace me, as a matter of fact. Just like Matty probably thinks any old wife will do. You don't know sh—" He swallowed. "You don't know nothing about telling people whether they mean something to you or not."

Damon stared at the boy. "What are you trying to say?"

"I'm not trying. I'm saying it loud and clear. You wearing earplugs or something?"

"You mean you've never figured out that I care about you? What did you think all this was about?" Damon waved his hand angrily to encompass the room. "You think I brought you here as slave labor? I look at you, Kevin, and I see myself at your age. Angry, confused, not sure anyone anywhere even knows you're alive. Oh, my circumstances were different, but the feelings were the same."

"So you felt the same way. So what? You brought me here because you felt sorry for me? That's supposed to be better?"

"I brought you here because I cared what happened to you. And now you're like a son to me."

"Right! I'm a son to you the same way Matty's a wife."

"What does that mean?"

"You figure it out. You're the genius." Kevin tried to move past him, but Damon put his hand on the boy's arm to stop him.

"Kevin, what do you mean?" His voice had lost its angry edge.

"You like having us here. We make your life easier. We feel like a real family, one you don't have to do any work to keep together. But when things get shaken up a little, you'll forget about us. If Heidi goes, it's a matter of time before I disappear, too. You'll get busy with your work and forget I exist. Matty's probably already looking for a job somewhere because she knows her chance at a real marriage is over."

Damon was stunned. He couldn't address Kevin's comments about Matty. They were far too personal. But he could address the others. "What are you talking about? I want you with me. Even when you're in college, I expect you to come home and spend holidays with me."

"College?"

"Of course. I'm going to help you find a good one. We'll find a way we can afford it."

"You never said a thing about college."

"Apparently I haven't said a thing about a lot of issues that matter. But I was afraid I'd scare you off."

"I'll tell you about scared. Scared is when you're out on the streets by yourself and nobody gives a damn!"

"I give a damn." Damon put his arm around Kevin's shoulders. "More than a damn. I couldn't care more if you *were* my son, Kevin. Don't you dare desert me now. I might lose Heidi. I can't lose you, too."

Kevin stood tense under the embrace, but he didn't pull away. "For a smart guy, you're pretty stupid sometimes."

"Apparently." Damon squeezed Kevin's shoulders hard before he dropped his arm. "I'm glad you're not. Now, since we're already here, let's get the lab set up for tomorrow. You want to?"

"Yeah. I guess."

"You go ahead. I'll be there in a minute."

Damon watched the boy shuffle off toward the lab. He was awash in a sea of feelings. He wondered how close he had been to losing Kevin as well as Heidi. He had been blind to so many things. He had taken Gretchen's word that Heidi was his. He had assumed that Kevin knew how much he cared about him, even though he had never told him as much.

And Matty? What assumptions had he made about her? What secrets lay between them that could alter their relationship forever? He had married a woman to give his child a mother. Now he might very well lose the child, but did he have to lose the woman, too? Would Matty consider staying with him and trying to grow a marriage on different ground?

A lump formed in his throat. How odd it was that Kevin might have discovered the key to achieving success in the laboratory at last. Damon had never wanted anything more than he had wanted that.

And now it seemed like the least important thing in his life.

Chapter Fourteen

Matty knew that her future was being decided by two laboratories in two very different places. Somewhere in Ohio her husband's DNA was undergoing the most careful, scientific scrutiny to determine whether the daughter they both adored could grow up in their home, cherished and accepted. And here on Inspiration, Damon was undertaking yet another set of trials of plant-for-all, this time using the plant samples that Kevin had gathered with Nanny on Staniel Cay. If the experiments succeeded, his professional future would be assured and their days on Inspiration would end.

Matty had never expected to feel so helpless, so trapped by events she had no control over. At first she'd felt only sorrow that she might lose Heidi and almost certainly Damon, too. But now the sorrow had changed into something more bitter, something wholly different from anything she had ever experienced.

When her father died, she had felt helpless, too. But illness and death were natural occurrences that she understood and reluctantly accepted. But now she couldn't accept that everything and everyone she'd come to love might very well slip from her grasp. And there was nothing she could do about it.

"Will you remember this?" Matty asked Heidi one morning several weeks after the trip to Ohio. "I know you won't remember with words, but will you remember being held this way? And hugged and kissed and cuddled?"

Heidi beamed up at her from Matty's bed, one new baby tooth just beginning to show at her gumline. She batted at Matty's face, and Matty ducked lower so that Heidi could grab her hair. "You'll remember, won't you?" Matty had to believe she would, even if the memory was so deep inside her that it was nothing more than a feeling that once someone had loved her.

"She'll remember," Damon said from the doorway. "No one ever forgets what it's like to be loved."

"I didn't know you were in the house." Matty straightened to face him. "I thought you were down at the boathouse."

"I came to get you."

Icy fingers clutched at her heart. "I heard the telephone ring...."

"That was Arthur. He's on his way from George Town. He'll be here in a couple of hours."

She remembered now that Arthur was expected. She imagined he might be visiting to cheer them up, but she was afraid the contrast with his last visit would be marked.

She didn't want to look at Damon. She had begun trying to avoid him as much as possible. Their lovemaking had tapered off to nothing, and he seemed as uncomfortable in her presence as she did in his. Instead she looked down at Heidi, waving her hand playfully just out of the baby's reach. "What do you need me for?"

"I didn't say I needed you. I said I came to get you. Will you bring Heidi down and leave her with Nanny? I've got something to show you."

She realized she was mentally inventing excuses not to be

alone with him. She also realized how childish that was. "Give me a minute."

"Take your time. I'll be in the kitchen."

She changed Heidi's diaper and collected some toys. In the kitchen she handed Heidi over to Nanny, who skillfully tucked the baby into her infant seat and set it in a safe place where Heidi could follow Nanny with her eyes.

"She need somet'ing bigger than this chair before long," Nanny said. "She be too big for it soon."

Matty wished she could spend the next twenty years watching Heidi outgrow one thing right after another.

Damon was waiting in the doorway. Outside, the morning was bright and already growing humid as the sun rose higher in the sky. "It's going to be a good day for a swim." She walked beside him down the path, but not too closely. "I think I'll take Heidi when we get back, before it gets too hot. She loves the water."

"I took her last night. The tide made a shallow pool down by the gazebo."

That seemed as indicative of the gap between them as anything could. Before the trip to Ohio they would have taken Heidi swimming together. But they hadn't spent time together as a family since the day they realized they probably wouldn't be a family much longer.

As if he'd read her thoughts, Damon spoke. "Let's take the boat out in a little while. We can spend the afternoon on the water."

"Heidi's really not old enough to be out in the skiff." She'd thought that Damon felt strongly about that, too. In fact, they had hired Samuel to take them to Staniel Cay in his larger, safer powerboat the day they'd flown to Ohio.

"I know, but Arthur's on his way. I'll have him bring Kevin and Heidi. Nanny, too, if she'll come. They can meet us at Shell Island."

"Shell Island?" Memories of another afternoon on the island colored her voice.

"We need to get away. Or at least I do. Maybe you don't?"

She heard the challenge and squared her shoulders. "It's a nice day to be out on the water."

"Good. It's settled, then. We'll make an occasion out of it. Like we did before—" He paused.

"Before everything changed," she finished for him.

"Not everything. But too many things."

She wanted an explanation, but she didn't want to ask for one. "Where are we going right now?"

"To the boathouse."

They finished the trip in silence.

The boathouse was cool inside, and the air was almost clammy against her skin. She walked with Damon to the laboratory door and waited as he unlocked it and ushered her inside.

"This place never changes," she said. "You need a new decorator."

"Oh, something's changed, all right."

She realized she'd been repressing hope. She'd gotten much too good at that lately; it was beginning to feel natural. "Do you mean what I think you do?"

"Come here and look at this." He led her to the microscopes along the far wall. "Check this out."

She closed one eye and put the other against the eyepiece. She recognized...nothing. She straightened. "Maybe you'd better just tell me."

He was grinning now, his face boyish and his eyes sparkling. "We ran six different trials with plant-for-all from six different locations. This one is from a field near the airport at Staniel Cay."

"And?"

"And it stopped the cells from mutating."

"It worked? The way it did the first time?"

"And the second and third."

"You're sure?"

"The results are primitive, to say the least. We'll have to run it over and over again with more sophisticated equipment, then start the business of trying to figure out why it works with plants from this particular area and doesn't work with those from others. It's possible the other plants have a weaker concentration of whatever it is, and the reaction they cause isn't as measurable without—"

He stopped himself and grinned again. "But the experiment worked, Matty. I wasn't imagining it. And it can be replicated. Now, at the very least, I can prove I wasn't trying to fool anybody."

And down the road somewhere, people, millions of them, perhaps, might have Damon Quinn to thank for longer, healthier lives.

"Matty?" He touched her cheek, rubbing his knuckles along her cheekbone. "You're crying...."

"I'm sorry. It's just so wonderful." She threw her arms around his waist and hugged him with a spontaneity that had been missing from their relationship for weeks. "I'm just so glad for you."

He wrapped his arms around her and held her close enough to squeeze the breath from her lungs.

For a moment she fell victim to hope. Surely this was more than a victory hug. Perhaps Damon had shared his success this way because she meant more to him than he'd ever admitted.

She lifted her head to see his expression, perhaps even to kiss him, and found him looking past her. She turned to find Kevin in the doorway looking sheepish.

"I..." Kevin shrugged.

"What is it?" Damon dropped his arms, and Matty moved away, the moment gone.

"I filled the gas tank and the gas can, like you asked. The *Mink*'s ready to go."

"Thanks."

"We'll bring Heidi when Arthur gets here. Nanny says she'll come, too."

"Good."

"Nanny packed a lunch."

"Okay. Thanks."

Kevin shook his head, as if the sight of the two of them

together was more than his sixteen-year-old sensibilities could bear. Then he left.

"How did Kevin know we were going out in the boat when you just suggested it to me a few minutes ago?" she said.

"I needed to celebrate. I was counting on your wanting to come with me. But I guess I shouldn't take you for granted, should I?"

She could understand why he had. She had never given him a reason not to. "Maybe not." She lifted her chin. "I actually do have a mind of my own, and a life."

"I know that."

"I'll go change and meet you at the skiff."

"Okay. I'll close down here. Matty…" He reached out to hold her back for a moment. "You're the first person who knows about this, except for Kevin."

She didn't dare hope that meant anything. "Thank you. I'm glad." Then she left before either of them could say anything more.

Damon didn't know exactly why he'd brought Matty to Shell Island. In their short relationship, this had been the scene of their worst moment as a couple. But perhaps that was the reason he'd wanted to come back. He wasn't good at accepting failure. He pushed and he prodded until he got the results he wanted. A less tenacious man would have given up the plant-for-all research years ago. But he had been determined.

He was determined now, as well. The problem was that he didn't know what he was determined to do. His emotions were in chaos. He might very well lose his daughter, and, by rights, he ought to be preparing himself to lose his wife. She had married him in exchange for something he couldn't give her anymore. He had needed her desperately, and he had shamelessly used that need to persuade her to marry him.

Did he have the right to ask anything else of her?

"I don't remember a day as hot as this one." Matty finished smoothing sunscreen over her arms and held the bottle out to him. Damon had just dropped anchor about fifteen feet from shore.

She was wearing a different suit today, one that was cut high at the legs and—unfortunately—high at the neck, too. He supposed he should be glad there was less of her exposed. This trip to the island wasn't about sex—although, given the chance, certain parts of his body might have argued the point.

"I've gotten everything but my back. Will you get it for me?" He ignored the sunscreen and turned in his seat to present his back to her.

He could feel her hesitation. For a moment the boat didn't rock; then it swayed from side to side, and he felt her coming toward him. He closed his eyes as her hand began to slide over his flesh.

"When do you think the others will join us?" Her tone was light, somewhere between friendly and polite.

"Before too long. We'll have time to do some snorkeling, maybe lie out on the beach for a while." And talk, if he could think of the right things to say.

"I'm surprised you wanted to leave the lab."

The lab seemed very far away; her hands were all he could think about. "I don't know how many more days we'll have like this."

Her hands stilled. "No, I guess not."

"All done?"

"Uh-huh."

He turned. "Would you like to go right in? We could have lunch first."

"No, let's snorkel. Who knows when I'll have the chance again?"

He didn't want to scour the depths of the ocean, he wanted to scour Matty's depths. He wanted to find out what she was feeling, thinking, dreaming about. He wanted to know if he had the right to ask her for anything else after everything she'd already done for him.

He bent over and pulled the equipment bag out from under the seat. "Do you need any help getting this on?"

"Not this time." She smiled politely.

She was right about the sun; it blazed down on his head and shoulders in the hottest display of the season. But the warmth was only skin deep. This wasn't going well, and he didn't know how to make it go better. The distance between them seemed to be growing.

She rooted in the bag and took out the same fins and mask that she'd used last time. "Meet you in the water."

He watched her swing her legs over the side and pull on the fins; then she was up to her waist in the gently rolling waves.

They snorkeled side by side, but without touching, for close to an hour. He led her farther out this time, to a section of the reef where the coral was particularly lovely. When they were both growing tired, he signaled for them to swim to shore. At the boat they stood and rested, their masks on top of their heads.

"That was spectacular." For a moment she seemed to forget all their problems and favored him with one of her radiant smiles. "I've never seen anything so beautiful."

She was vulnerable, the walls were down. He opened his mouth to speak and didn't know what to say.

The moment passed. "Shall we get the lunch?" she asked. "The others will be joining us soon, and I'm starved."

"You go on in. I'll get everything."

"I'll take the quilt."

He lifted himself into the boat and took off his snorkeling equipment. Matty handed hers over the side, and he exchanged it for the same quilt they'd used before.

He gave her a head start, watching her wade through the waves, her hips swaying back and forth seductively, until she was on the beach. He would have some uninterrupted time to talk to her now, but he was still as unsure of himself and his right to speak as a boy on his first date. He realized he was staring at her.

As if she realized the same thing, she turned, shading her eyes with a hand. Then she pointed behind him. He turned and looked up to see that while they had lost themselves in the underwater world, the world above them had changed. On the eastern horizon a storm was brewing.

He grabbed their lunch and slid back into the water to join her on the beach.

"Do you think we ought to head back?" she asked when he was still ten feet away.

He was torn between what he ought to do and what he wanted.

She saw his hesitation. "I'm sure the others aren't going to come if there's a storm."

"The *Crown Sable*'s a yacht, Matty. It could survive a hurricane."

"I don't care. I know them. They won't bring Heidi out if the water's rough."

"You're right." He ran his fingers through his hair. "I don't want to go back. I thought we could talk...."

"We can talk on Inspiration."

They could, but it would be harder. Here she was a captive audience. He could talk until he got it right. If he ever did.

She stared past him to the sky. "Damon, I really don't like this. I think we'd better go while we still can."

He knew she was right. Caribbean thunderstorms could be vicious, and they had no shelter to protect them. Completely frustrated, he turned and started back into the waves. The storm was miles away, but already the waves seemed higher, reflecting what was to come. He turned his head. "Come on. Do you need a hand?"

"No, I'm fine."

He trudged back to the *Mink* and dropped the picnic basket over the side before he scrambled on board. He held out his hand for the quilt when she reached the boat, then held it out again to help her up.

"I hope you don't think I'm being silly," she said, reaching for a towel.

"No, you're probably right. It's just that—"

"Just what, Damon?" She frowned. "What did you want

to talk about? About how you want to end this gracefully? That you hope I'll be a good sport about it? Well, I will, so please don't worry. I'm nothing if not a good sport. You can count on me. You should know that by now.''

He frowned, too. "What are you talking about?"

"I know why you brought me here. You want to prepare me for what's coming. If you lose custody of Heidi, you want me out of your life. You've got plans for your future, and you don't need a wife anymore.''

"That's not—"

She waved him into silence. "Please don't worry. I've got plans, too. I've been too unsure of myself to follow my own dreams, but not anymore. I have the grades and experience to get into medical school, and now it looks like money won't be a problem, either. With what I'll get from my father's book and the sale of the house in Carrollton, I can go to med school and graduate without a mountain of debt. And that's what I'm going to do.''

"Med school?"

"That's right.''

"That's what you want?"

"That's what I want.''

Seconds passed. He didn't know how to respond. This wasn't something he could examine at his leisure under a high-powered microscope. He wished he could take apart everything she'd just said and put it back together a thousand different ways until he understood it completely.

She pointed at the sky. Was he imagining that her hand was unsteady? "Look, we can finish this later. I'd really like to get back before the storm hits.''

He moved past her and settled himself in the back of the boat to refill the gas tank. With unnecessary force he jerked the gas can out from under the seat where Kevin had wedged it for the trip.

The can was empty.

Damon unscrewed the cap, just to be sure, shaking it from side to side with his ear against the rim.

"What's wrong?" Matty leaned closer.

"There's been a mutiny."

"What?"

Damon turned the gas can on end to demonstrate. Not so much as a drop spilled out. "Kevin was supposed to fill this."

"And you didn't double-check?"

"You were standing right there when he told me he'd filled it. When I got into the boat the can was under the seat, and I didn't give it a second thought. He's usually conscientious."

"He's conscientious when it suits him. He conscientiously threw my suitcases into the ocean, remember?"

"I thought he'd outgrown that."

She gave him a look that was answer enough. "How are we going to get back?"

"I don't have any magic tricks up my sleeve. We have enough gas left in the tank to get us into trouble and that's all. We won't make it back to Inspiration. We'll have to stay here until they come for us."

"What about the storm?"

He was almost glad to have something to think about besides their relationship and the bomb Matty had just dropped. "How strong are you?"

"Why?"

"Can we pull the boat up to shore and turn it over for shelter? I can't do it alone, but if you help…"

"I'll do whatever it takes."

Nearly three-quarters of an hour had passed by the time they crawled under their makeshift shelter. The rain had begun before they'd completed the preparations, but it intensified as they settled themselves under the boat.

Damon had stripped off the outboard motor and covered it with canvas. Together they had pulled the boat up to the shore and wedged it between two low sand mounds. The mounds weren't as high or stable as real dunes, but they served as walls, and between Matty and Damon they had scooped up enough sand over a second tarpaulin behind the boat to serve as protection in that direction.

Matty had spread the quilt beneath the boat, and they dried off as best they could before they settled themselves on top of it.

Thunder rolled, moving closer by the minute. "Good thing the *Mink* is fiberglass. I'd hate to be under here if it was aluminum." Damon put his hands under his head and stared morosely up at their new accommodations. The ceiling was so low that they couldn't sit up all the way, and the only light came from the end near their feet, which was propped up on the stump of a fallen palm. Worst of all, it was getting hotter by the moment.

"Good thing we're not claustrophobic." Matty turned to her side and rested her head on a seat cushion.

They lay quietly and listened to rain falling on the boat above them.

"Are you hungry?" Matty asked. "We never ate."

"Not really."

She fell silent again. "Why did he do it?" she asked at last. "Why did Kevin tell us he filled the gas can when he didn't?"

"Because he wanted to be sure we talked. He, of all people, knows how hard it is…for me."

"Is it?"

He rolled to his side so he was facing her. He couldn't see her clearly, but it didn't matter, because he knew her every feature, every curve of her cheek and chin, the way her hair spilled over her throat when she lay on her side.

Kevin had given him this chance, and Damon knew he had to use it. But he still felt himself floundering in a sea of feelings. He struggled to put them into words. "We've been going on the assumption that I'm not Heidi's birth father and that she's going to be taken away from us. But even if the tests don't come out in my favor, there's still a chance we'll be given custody."

"Is that what you're worried about? You know if that's the case I'll stay with you long enough to be sure you keep Heidi."

"And then?"

She was silent for so long that he didn't think she was going to answer. When she spoke, it was so quietly that he had to strain to hear her over the rain. "I can't do it anymore, Damon. I can't pretend indefinitely that we're a family when we're not. It's all been a fantasy, and two weeks ago reality came crashing in."

"If it was just a fantasy, it was a pretty wonderful fantasy."

"Don't you see? The minute you realized you might not be able to keep Heidi, everything changed. You married me to be her mother. Without Heidi on the scene, you don't need me anymore. And even if you keep Heidi, I can't pick up where we left off and play house again. I deserve more. I deserve a man who loves me and children who can believe in that love and count on it. I can't believe I was ever willing to settle for less."

He could hardly breathe. Even though the boat was inches above him, he felt as if something was crushing his chest. "Why did you, then?"

"You really don't know, do you? Gretchen told me you didn't. She said I shouldn't even worry about trying to hide it from you. And she was right."

"What was she right about?"

"Can't you see what's smack-dab in front of you? Don't you know why I couldn't make love to you when we were on Shell Island the last time? Not because I *didn't* want you. Because I was afraid if we made love you'd see how much I *did*."

"Matty, you're not making sense."

"Really?" She propped herself up so she was looking directly into his eyes. "Then try this. I love you. I guess I always have. All those years ago it was an adolescent crush. But after I came here, after I lived with you, it turned into the real thing. Only it's not the real thing, is it? Because the real thing is mutual."

"You love me?"

"You know what? I'm not ashamed of it anymore. That's why I'm telling you. And I'm not sorry I came and gave this a try. Liza told me not to blame anyone else, and she was right. For the first time in my life I went after something I really wanted, against all the odds. And even if I didn't win—''

"But you did. You won, Matty." The storm was directly overhead now, fiercely pelting the boat above them. Their voices had risen to compensate, and now he had to shout his words. It was so dark that he could hardly even see her face, but he found her with his hands and pulled her down until she was lying across his chest.

He threaded his fingers into her hair to keep her there. "Matty… Mattolina, you won, and you don't even know it because I've been afraid to tell you."

She tried to protest, and he brought her face to his and kissed her. He wrapped an arm around her to hold her tighter and silenced her momentarily, but only momentarily.

"Damon, I—"

He slung a leg over hers and rolled to his side, nudging her even closer as his lips took hers again. And when she stopped resisting and kissed him back hungrily, he lifted his head just far enough to speak.

"I love you, too. This hasn't been about Heidi for a long, long time."

"You don't have to pretend—"

He kissed her again, a passionate, sexy kiss that promised everything. "You're right." He kissed her nose, her chin, her forehead. He couldn't seem to kiss her enough. "I don't have to pretend. What would be the point when I don't have to?"

"But you've never said a word!"

"It takes me a while to get things. I'm sorry. I was coasting along, soaking up all the wonderful things about having you in my life, and I wasn't even thinking about exactly what you meant to me. But that day at the courthouse, when I realized I might lose you if I lost Heidi, it all came into focus."

"Then why haven't you said anything? That was weeks ago."

"Because all I've done since you came to Inspiration is

push and push to get my way! I knew that you realized how frightened I am of losing Heidi. I was afraid you'd agree to stay with me even if you didn't really want to anymore. You can't say no to anyone who needs you. I've known that right from the beginning, and I've used it shamelessly."

"I like being needed. But what *I* need is to be wanted. Really wanted. Not because of the things I can do for you, but because of who I am."

"Oh, I want you. Make no mistake about that. No matter what happens with Heidi or my research or med school. Stay with me because we love each other. Help me make this work."

"Damon..." This time *she* kissed *him*. Water was seeping in through their makeshift shelter now, but it didn't matter. He hardly felt the water, but he felt her touching him in places that had yearned for her in the last miserable, lonely weeks. There was so much that was unsettled, but not this. Never this again.

They made short work of each other's clothes, pulling and tugging, then running their hands greedily over each other when the clothes were gone. They kissed and tasted and absorbed each other in every possible way. And at last, when their patience ran out—too soon, as always—they came together as explosively as the thunder shaking the heavens above them.

Hours later they were waiting on the rain-washed beach when the *Crown Sable* appeared on the horizon.

"Looks like we're going to be rescued." Damon stood with his arm around Matty's waist and pointed.

She was almost sorry to see the yacht. She and Damon had used this time together well. She wished they'd had days—weeks, even—before life intruded again. But they would have the rest of their years together now, and there would be other moments like the ones spent here, moments when they could pour out their hearts to each other and find solace in each other's arms.

Damon loved her, too.

"I wonder if Kevin's on board," Damon said.

"I imagine he's been frantic. I'm sure he wasn't counting on the storm. He's probably afraid we washed out to sea."

"A little guilt's good for his soul."

"He's part of the deal, you know." Matty looked up at the man who was her husband now in all the ways that really mattered. Her heart was so full of love that she wondered how it could beat. "I'm planning to make some demands on you from now on, and Kevin's the first. If I stay, he stays, too."

"Of course he stays. No matter what happens with Heidi, we'll still be a family. Wherever we go, he goes along."

"And we have to visit Nanny and Arthur as often as we can. No matter where we are."

"I've learned a thing or two about priorities."

Matty rested her head against his shoulder, content just to stand beside him and wait.

The yacht grew larger and larger until it stopped in deep water off the shore. They could see people moving along the deck and the dinghy being lowered. But it wasn't until the dinghy was halfway to shore that Matty squinted and leaned forward to try to catch a better look. "Damon, I think that's Gretchen and Kevin."

She felt his tension. He had every reason to be angry with Heidi's mother, but her heart sank. Reality was intruding on the little paradise they'd made for themselves. Maybe their future together was assured, but their daughter's future was still very much in jeopardy.

"Please, give her a chance before you say anything," Matty said.

"A chance to do what? What can she say?"

"Let's find out. Please?"

He squeezed her waist in answer, but his jaw was set. She hoped Gretchen could talk fast.

The dinghy came nearly to shore. Gretchen and Kevin got out, and Kevin towed the boat toward the beach, but slowly, as if he was afraid he might actually reach it.

Gretchen, dressed in lemon yellow rompers, waded on ahead of him. She stopped just a few feet from Damon and Matty.

"I'm so sorry." She didn't avert her eyes, but they filled with tears.

For a moment Matty felt the sun go under another cloud. She was certain that Gretchen had come to tell them that the tests had proven that Damon couldn't be Heidi's father.

"Why did you do it?" Damon said. "Why did you lie to me?"

"I don't think it's a lie, Damon. I think you are Heidi's father. There's just the slightest chance you might not be. The other man was a one-night mistake, and I couldn't track him down to tell him about Heidi even if I'd wanted to."

"Then you still don't know anything from the blood tests?" Matty said.

"No. But it doesn't have to matter."

"Of course it matters!" Damon paused and made an obvious attempt to lower his voice. "Your parents will probably get custody if that slightest little chance just happens to be a bull's-eye. You can't make this go away because it's not fun, Gretchen. Life's just chock-full of consequences."

"I know. But sometimes they can be changed."

"What are you talking about?" Damon demanded.

"My parents have withdrawn their bid for custody. They've written a letter explaining that they don't feel they have the right personal qualities to raise another child. They've asked that you and Matty be allowed to keep Heidi, even if the tests prove you're not her father."

"I don't believe it."

Matty drew in a sharp breath. "Why would they do something like that?"

"Let's just say they had a change of heart," Gretchen said.

Matty could feel Damon winding up to spring. "Let's not," she said. "Let's just hear the truth. Okay?"

"Well, I'm not overly proud of it."

"I don't care," Matty said. "Tell us anyway."

"On the morning we were supposed to go to dinner together at their house, I found out that my father had hired a private investigator and gotten those statements. I knew I had to do something—"

"You did. You disappeared and left us to find out by ourselves," Damon said.

"I'm sorry, but I knew I had to do something and do it fast. For Heidi's sake and for yours. Both of you. And I had a hunch. So that afternoon I flew back to the little town where I grew up. Until I was about thirteen, my father owned his own business there. Then we left. Just like that. I always wondered if something had happened."

"And?"

"It took me a week to find out what I needed. I discovered that all those years ago my father got into some serious legal trouble with his business and was facing arrest. Rather than defend himself, he pulled up his tent stakes and stole away in the night. The charges were never formally dropped, although apparently no one pursued him."

The rest was clear to Matty. "You went back to Ohio and confronted your parents?"

"I met with them yesterday, and I told them what I knew and what I would do about it if they didn't withdraw their bid for custody. They decided that perhaps they didn't want the responsibility of a baby after all."

"I'm sorry," Matty said. And she was. Despite the absence of love in the Ott household, the Otts were still Gretchen's parents.

"I'm sorry, too. The whole thing was too close to blackmail to make me feel good about it. But maybe in the long run it won't be too bad. I got to say a few things I've needed to say for years. They'll think twice before they criticize me now. If nothing else, maybe we can call a truce." She stepped closer. "What about Heidi? Will you still take her? If she's yours—"

"As far as I'm concerned, that's never been an issue." Damon's arm tightened around Matty's waist.

"And it won't matter if the tests say she's not?"

"I don't care about the tests. I'm going to ask the judge to seal the results. My name is on Heidi's birth certificate. She's ours." He looked down at Matty.

"Thank you." Gretchen sniffed, and her eyes filled with tears. "I don't know what else to say."

Kevin had secured the boat now, and he couldn't avoid them any longer. He slouched up the beach toward them, and his face clouded over when he realized that Gretchen—and now Matty, too—was crying.

"Ah, jeez, I guess I blew it good, huh?"

"Come here," Damon said.

The boy stopped an arm's length away, but Damon hauled him into a hug. Gretchen and Matty fell into each other's arms, and suddenly the four of them were embracing.

Matty searched for Damon through tear-fogged eyes and found he was searching for her, too. She smiled her most radiant smile.

He found his way through the maze of bodies and took her into his arms.

Epilogue

Heidi, enveloped in a pumpkin-colored life jacket, ran to the side of Samuel's boat and pointed out to sea. "Where's our island?"

"It's out there somewhere, munchkin." Damon lifted her to his lap, as much to cuddle with her as to keep her safe. Cuddling time with a five-year-old was a rarity, and he took advantage of it whenever he could.

Matty joined them on the seat and shaded her eyes with her hand as she searched for the first glimpse of the cay. "Remember the first time we made this trip in Samuel's boat?"

"You're not going to swoon again, are you, Mattolina?"

"That sounds much too old-fashioned for a busy pediatrician."

"Dr. Quinn, medicine woman." He leaned forward and kissed her nose. Heidi giggled.

Matty smiled at their daughter. Heidi's dark pigtails flopped in the breeze, and her blue eyes shone with excitement. She was a lively kindergartner now, with a quick mind and a quicker laugh. She looked more and more like Gretchen every day, but Matty sometimes caught glimpses of Damon in Heidi's profile. For that matter, she caught glimpses of herself in the little girl's smile.

"You're sure Nanny's going to be there, waiting for us?" Matty said.

"Kitty promised that the whole Rolle family will be waiting for us. And Kevin's flying in from Boston tomorrow to meet Arthur at Staniel Cay and sail over."

Matty knew that Gretchen was also expected in the next few days. Gretchen and Heidi were good friends, and although they didn't see each other often, they always enjoyed the time they did spend together.

"We needed this," Matty said. "The whole family."

Damon grinned. "Try explaining that to someone outside the charmed circle."

"It doesn't matter. We know what family is."

"And maybe, before too long, the family will be larger?"

She wondered why Damon could still make her blush. She had survived medical school and her hospital residency without so much as heightened color. She was known for her level head and calm presence.

Except when it came to Damon.

"Expanding the family is top priority," she promised.

Expanding the family was part of the reason they were coming back to Inspiration Cay. Damon's research with plant-for-all had opened doors into one of the most prestigious research laboratories in the country. He was Dr. Damon Quinn now, and he headed his own division at a facility in Maryland. He was sought after as a consultant, and he was often a featured speaker at scientific gatherings. His work kept him busy, but not so busy that he couldn't make time for his family—and not so busy that he couldn't make time, now that Matty was about to join a local practice of pediatricians, to increase that family's size.

They wanted two more children, and, sentimentally, they wanted to create that first new life on Inspiration Cay. They were practical, logical people who understood priorities. Because of that, they would always make time for sentiment, for romance and for each other.

"Is Uncle Kevin going to bring me something?" Heidi asked.

"Undoubtedly. He always does," Damon said. Kevin, a six-foot, dark-eyed heartthrob, was finishing his last year at Harvard and considering offers at several top graduate schools. Matty knew that, as always on Kevin's frequent visits, Damon would spend part of the time trying to persuade him to consider going into the "family business." Matty thought that one day soon Kevin might just agree.

"The cay just ahead," Samuel shouted. "Follow that fluffy white cloud to the sea, Heidi girl, and look left."

Heidi stood at the side, and Damon and Matty joined her. Inspiration Cay came into view, exactly where Samuel had said it would be. "Our island," Heidi said.

Damon reached for Matty's hand. She grasped it tightly, resting her arm on Heidi's shoulder. "Our island."

She turned to Damon and saw he was smiling at her. They leaned over their daughter's head and sealed the perfect moment with a kiss.

* * * * *

New York Times bestselling author

LINDA LAEL MILLER

Two separate worlds, denied by destiny.

THERE AND NOW

Elizabeth McCartney returns to her centuries-old family home
in search of refuge—never dreaming escape would lie over a
threshold. She is taken back one hundred years into the past and
into the bedroom of the very handsome Dr. Jonathan Fortner,
who demands an explanation from his T-shirt-clad "guest."

But Elizabeth has no *reasonable* explanation to offer.

Available in July 1997 at your favorite retail outlet.

Bestselling author

JOAN JOHNSTON

continues her wildly popular miniseries with an
all-new, longer-length novel

The Virgin Groom

HAWK'S WAY

One minute, Mac Macready was a living legend in
Texas—every kid's idol, every man's envy, every
woman's fantasy. The next, his fiancée dumped him,
his career was hanging in the balance and his future
was looking mighty uncertain. Then there was the
matter of his scandalous secret, which didn't stand a
chance of staying a secret. So would he succumb to
Jewel Whitelaw's shocking proposal—or take cold
showers for the rest of the long, hot summer…?

Available August 1997
wherever Silhouette books are sold.

Silhouette ®

Share in the joy of yuletide romance with brand-new
stories by two of the genre's most beloved writers

DIANA PALMER

and

JOAN JOHNSTON

in

LONE STAR
CHRISTMAS

Diana Palmer and Joan Johnston share their favorite
Christmas anecdotes and personal stories in this
special hardbound edition.

Diana Palmer delivers an irresistible spin-off of her
LONG, TALL TEXANS series and Joan Johnston crafts an
unforgettable new chapter to HAWK'S WAY in this wonderful
keepsake edition celebrating the holiday season. So
perfect for gift giving, you'll want one for yourself...and
one to give to a special friend!

Available in November at your favorite retail outlet!

Only from

Silhouette®